The Breath of Juno

The Breath of Juno

• A Novel by •
Beverly Olevin

Elk Horn Press

This book is a work of fiction. Names, characters, places and incidents are either products of the author's imagination or are used fictitiously. Any resemblance to actual events or locales or persons, living or dead, is entirely coincidental.

The Breath of Juno
Copyright © 1996 by Beverly Olevin

All rights reserved, including the right of reproduction in whole or in part in any form.

Published by Elk Horn Press
7269 Creeks Bend Court
West Bloomfield, Michigan 48322

Library of Congress Catalog Card Number: 95-90741

ISBN: 0-9647894-1-8

First Printing
Manufactured in the United States of America

Cover illustration "Night Flight" © 1996 Wendy Thon

DEDICATION

For my sister Marsha,
my mother Merriam,
and my grandmother Elsie.
They live in my memory,
three generations
flowing through time.

The Breath of Juno

PART I

Messenger of the sky
Circle my dreams
Teach me how to fly

ALONE, THE CHILD MOVED THROUGH the tall wheat grass, her unblinking eyes staring straight ahead as if she were in a trance. At her back the full moon was cresting over the ancient mountain ridge, casting her small frame in a long shadow.

Awake but not aware, she moved toward the open expanse of the meadow, toward the bank of the dark river that snaked through the valley. Indifferent to the cold night air that penetrated her flannel sleeping gown and to the sharp thistles that attacked her bare feet, she broke into a run as if the moon itself were chasing her. There was no wind, but still her long blond hair flew after her like a graceful train of lace.

Her eyes, the rich blue of the north, remained glassy and unfocused as she ran to the river's edge. An old wooden rowboat was tied to a post in the muddy shallows. She released the coiled rope that held it safely to the shore, then waded out into the icy waters, leading the boat like an obedient dog. Once the boat had cleared the bottom, she slid into its belly.

As her father had promised, she had learned to navigate the wide river in this tiny craft on her eighth birthday, less than a year ago. In his deep Welsh voice he had tenderly warned her, "Listen to me, Mary Alice, never are you allowed out on the river alone." His words of caution were erased from her memory as she struggled to lift the heavy oars that lay beneath her feet and lock them each in place.

It was the longest day of the year, the summer solstice, and without knowing why, she belonged to this night. It had called her from her bed and beckoned her to the shore, it had demanded that her thin arms thrust the oars into the black water over and over, pushing against the current until she was carried into the middle of the river. Her will had disappeared and was replaced by the urgent need of the night.

Once at the river's middle, the tiny boat lay still in the quiet night. The child looked up at the moon, now high in the sky. Her breathing quickened. A wind suddenly whipped the water beneath the boat, transforming the flat surface of the river into churning waves. The violent jerking of the boat released the child from her obedient trance. Her heart pounded against her chest as she realized where she was and what danger surrounded her.

But as she fought to keep the boat afloat, a pressure built inside her lungs. Her head fell back as she gasped for air. Above her a giant hawk swooped down, its wings barely missing her as the boat overturned in the swirling water. She felt her breath, her very life, being pulled from her body even before she was tossed, as lightly as a feather, into the dark river.

Coughing, straining for breath as the water filled her lungs, she desperately reached for the surface. The nightgown twisted around her body, pulling her down. Her long blond hair trailed after her as she sunk deep into the blackness.

• 1 •

1983: San Francisco

In the summer of 1983, a young child with brilliant red hair and haunting green eyes sat perfectly still between two nuns. She was a tiny doll held in place by black-robed bookends.

Sara Morgan was the head case worker on the day the nuns came to the San Francisco Department of Social Services with the child. The intake officer had given Sara a brief note when he ushered the nuns into her office.

> Abandoned female child. No name. Determined to be at least three years old. Dropped off by nuns from Saint Andrews. Claimed the convent could no longer care for her. No explanation given as to how the child came to them. Refused to say how long she had lived at the convent. Requested that she be placed in a foster home and that all attempts be made to keep her whereabouts secret.

The nuns were from a conservative order that required their sisters wear traditional habits. Perspiration dampened the white fabric that crossed their foreheads as they sat before Sara in their black robes.

"There is no need for all this paper work," the smaller of the two nuns said. "We are simply asking you to place this girl in a good and caring home."

Sara removed her glasses and rubbed her tired eyes. Thin lines trailed out from the corners, giving her a gentle softness. "How did she come into your care? Was she brought to you by her mother?"

The nuns looked at one another, but both remained silent.

"Ladies," Sara said, not knowing how else to address the nuns. She wasn't comfortable calling them *sisters*. "It is against the law to abandon a child. I need to know how she came to Saint Andrews."

"I'm sorry," the second nun spoke. "We are unable to tell you anything more."

"A police report will have to be filed." A tone of accusation crept into Sara's voice. She suspected that the girl had been born to one of the nuns in the convent and that they had kept the secret for as long as they could. "There will be an investigation."

While the three women spoke, the child sat motionless, staring at the ceiling.

Then the nuns stood in unison, moving towards the door. The child made no attempt to follow them.

"Just a minute," Sara tried to stop them. "You can't just leave. I have more questions to ask you."

"Take care of her, and please don't let this get into the newspapers," the small nun said as she hurried out the door. The other nun followed quickly behind her.

Sara rushed after them, angry at their abrupt departure, but they were already gone. She turned back to the girl who sat frozen in her chair and managed to smile warmly despite her frustration. "Can you tell me your name, honey?"

The child didn't move. Sara got up from behind the desk and sat down next to her, but the girl's gaze remained fixed on the ceiling. A vacant, distant look possessed the deep green eyes, frightening Sara. The child seemed so utterly alone. Although Sara had been a social worker for twenty years, she had never felt so strangely drawn to a child.

She appeared to be in excellent physical health. So many of the children she saw were born of mothers on drugs or alcohol; thin, sickly, unwanted kids tossed into an overloaded system that could offer them little real hope. It was a surprise to see a child with full cheeks and rosy skin. She had clearly been well-cared for as a baby.

Sara took the girl by the hand and led her to the intake playroom. She offered her a stuffed teddy bear to play with, but the youngster didn't respond to the toy or to anything else in the room. Although she appeared healthy, the vacuous look in her eyes worried Sara. She had seen that look before—in autistic children, children who simply could not relate to people, who could not feel emotion or be touched by love.

There were no well-run places for unwanted children. If a temporary foster home could not be found immediately, they would be put in a state-run institution, which in most cases amounted to nothing more than a holding tank. Only a handful of good people would be willing to open their homes to an autistic child even if for only a short time. Then there were marginal foster homes where the caretakers' only incentive was the money the state paid them.

While the child sat motionless in the playroom, Sara went through all her listings, trying to locate a temporary way station. She called one telephone number after another, but was unable to locate anyone who could take the child that day. She filled out all the proper documents, recording the girl under the name "E. Andrews." The nuns had refused to give her the child's name—not even a first name could she carry with her from the first three years of her life.

But the nuns had come from the convent of Saint Andrews, so Sara gave her the name of their order. Since she had no first name, Sara simply used the letter "E." Perhaps, she thought, for Eve, since she was alone on earth and might never know her parentage.

SARA HAD LIVED alone since her husband, Brad, had died a year earlier. Every day for twenty-seven years, since they had married, she had considered herself one of the lucky ones who had found the right match. In all those years they never ran out of things to talk or laugh about. The subject of children came up every few years but they had always decided that their life was complete with just the two of them. Secretly, Sara had feared that a child might disturb the forces that held their love together in such perfect harmony. As a social worker, she had seen hundreds of marriages go sour when children were added to the mix. In the early years of her marriage she had worried that she was committing a sin of selfishness by not wanting children—that one day she would have to pay for all the happiness she had found in the sole company of one man. They had married in 1956 when no one considered a couple a true family until children were born.

The heart attack had come out of nowhere. One day he was alive and full of plans, and the next day he was gone, taking all her joy with him. But she never regretted their decision not to have children, not even when she lay in bed late at night listening to the silence with the weight of the empty space next to her, pulling at her heart. A child would have held her to this world. Without Brad, she wanted no obligations to tie her to a lonely future.

She was fifty-three years old in 1983 when the nuns brought the red-haired child into her office, but she thought herself an old woman who now only lived through the routine of her days to arrive at the quiet nights when the memories could play through her senses like a perfect concerto. Pain came into her office every day in the form of abused and unwanted children. People's lives were mostly made up of pain, she thought. So although she missed Brad desperately, she felt that she had been blessed with more than her share of happiness. The future was a shadow, a dark space without laughter or love, but the past was locked inside her, waiting to be relived whenever it pleased her.

Several times in the past year she had thought of becoming a foster parent herself. The idea of having a child in her home for a limited amount of time, perhaps a year, intrigued her. For all her years of working with children and families, she had no real knowledge of what it was like to wake up with a child in the house. The thought usually passed quickly—a child would take up space, emotional space. It would deserve to be given attention, affection, and maybe even love. The attention and affection she thought she could manage, but love was out of the question. That was all promised and given years ago. Her allotment was already spent in this lifetime. There was nothing left to give to a child. And even if she had considered it seriously, there was a conflict of interest with her work. The state did not think it appropriate for their social workers to be earning money as foster parents when it was their job to determine the credentials and suitability of homes.

WHEN SARA LOOKED up from her work she realized it was six o'clock. There were two places she could take the child for the night, but once she was in her car with the silent little girl she found herself driving across the Bay Bridge towards her home in Berkeley. No one could object to her taking this child home for at least the night. The child followed her, as if in a trance, into her small wood frame house.

The Breath of Juno

Sara cooked some macaroni she was glad to find in the cupboard, and was relieved when the child simply ate the food and then went silently to bed.

The next morning Sara called the convent to find someone who could explain how the girl had come to them. She was astonished when no one would help her. It was as if they knew nothing about the child's existence.

Sara lost her patience.

"And you call yourselves people of God! Whichever one of you brought this child onto this earth, you're responsible for her, and you can't just throw her away like a broken old rosary! If you don't tell me something about how this child has lived for the last three years, I will have to talk with the police to be sure that they are following up on this investigation."

There was a long silence. Then a voice said, "Wait. I'll get the Mother Superior."

Sara waited for ten long minutes, twisting the cord and growing angrier with each minute. Finally she heard soft whispers in the background as if several woman were deciding what to do about the phone call. Then a deep authoritative voice came on the line.

"I am Sister Mary Katherine, the Mother Superior at Saint Andrews. How may I help you?"

"You can tell me who this child is in my home who doesn't speak or seem to see me." She realized that she sounded harsh and demanding, so she took the edge from her voice. "Has she always been this way? Do you know what has caused her silence?"

"I'm sorry, I wish I could help you," the Mother Superior said with compassion.

"How can I find a good home for this child when I don't know anything about her? At least tell me her name. What have you called her for the last three years?"

"I understand how you feel, but you must trust me," said the Mother Superior. "The child came to us under special circumstances. Her safety, her very life, depends on our secrecy here at the convent. I cannot answer any of your questions. The police have already talked with us this morning. I don't think they will be able to find out anything more."

"You don't understand. I work with foster children all the time. I can't place this child unless I have some background on her. I need medical records, date of birth, family history of disease. What if she gets sick? Surely you won't deny me the most basic information."

"There is nothing more I can tell you." Her voice softened. Sadly, almost if she was giving a blessing, she whispered, "I wish you well. She is in God's hands now." And with that, the Mother Superior hung up the phone.

The forbidding tone in her voice drained the anger from Sara's body. There was something mysterious about this child—something that could not be probed further.

She had to find the child a home. But this was 1983 and San Francisco was a city living with an unspoken fear. A strange new disease was creeping into the streets. No one understood where it came from or how to stop it. As more and more people became sick and died, rumors gripped the city. Some said it was a plague sent from God. Extreme groups thought it was the beginning of Armageddon, the final plague that would wipe out the whole human race by the end of the millennium. No one knew how the disease was spread so they began closing themselves off from strangers—anyone who might carry the illness that was hidden within them. Who could she find that would open their home to a child who was withdrawn and unnatural—a child who might carry a disease inside her?

Finding the child a home became Sara's obsession. She called all the churches in the Bay area, trying to locate a family who would take the child, even if only for a short while. The days rolled into weeks, and still she couldn't find the right place for her.

At first the girl was distant and responded to neither sound, color, nor affection. Every day Sara took the child to work with her. It was an easy responsibility. She never caused any problems, never cried, never laughed, and never played. She sat quietly in the day room as Sara worked and went home with her at night.

It was on a Friday evening in their third week together that everything changed. Sara was reading the child a story just as she did every night. The tiny collection of children's books was growing rapidly. Sara found that she loved reading the tales out loud. Each was a wonderful enchantment, taking her back to her own childhood, into distant worlds with magical creatures. Even though the child seemed to pay no attention, Sara believed that she was listening.

The Breath of Juno

She was just finishing a Native American tale about how Father Sun and Mother Moon had created the world.

"Then Mother Moon, whose voice was the wind in the trees, came down to sit upon the earth and breathed life into all the animals they had created. The fox, the lizard, the owl, the wolf, the bear all took her magic gift and disappeared into the night."

When the story ended the child looked up at her. Their eyes met. At first Sara thought it was nothing more than accidental eye contact. But in that brief moment something had dramatically changed in the child's appearance. It was as if the switch that connected her to the outside world had been turned back on again. The intense green eyes came sharply into focus. For Sara, it was a major breakthrough. She took the child in her arms and held her. To her amazement, the child hugged her back. Sara had no idea what it was about the story that had caused the sudden change in the child's behavior, but she was grateful for it.

Tears rolled down her cheeks as the little hands went around her neck. She took the child's face in her hands and said, "Eve. I christen you Eve. And as long as you are with me, that's what your name will be."

"Eve," the child said the word clearly.

"That's right!" Sara was shocked. "Eve—you are my Eve. I knew you could talk. You've just been keeping it a secret from me, haven't you?"

The child looked into her eyes, and said, "I can talk. But only to you."

The child's words were so clear and articulate it startled Sara. It was almost as though she were listening to the voice of an adult. For just a moment, the child seemed like an alien, come to life on this planet fully grown, in the body of a three-year old.

Before this thought could plant itself deeply in Sara's mind, Eve hugged her and said, "Bad people and good people. You're good. I know you're good." And with these simple words, the child seemed to summarize and validate all of Sara's life. Good.

She felt good. The child had split people into two categories, and she had fallen on the side of good.

"Mommy told me . . . ."

"What did your Mommy tell you? Who is your Mommy?"

The child pulled back from the questions. Sara gently touched the frightened face.

"Sweetheart, help me. Tell me, who is your Mommy? What is your name? Can you tell me your name, honey?"

"No!"

"Just your name," Sara whispered. "It will be our secret. What does your Mommy call you? I need to know your name."

"Can't. Can't say."

"Why not? Why can't you say your name?"

"It's bad. The bad people will hurt me."

"They'll hurt you if I know your name?"

"Yes." The child was close to tears.

"You know it, don't you?"

"Yes."

"You can tell me. Just me."

"Mommy said no! Never. Not ever!"

"Was your Mommy a nun in the convent? Can you tell me about living at the convent?"

The child put her hands against Sara's chest and pushed her away. Sobs came from her quivering body.

Sara saw that it was pointless to continue pressing the child. What could possibly have happened to her, she wondered.

This was more than an abandoned child; there was something sinister in her past that caused her to close up this way. What fate had thrown this child into her path? What was she supposed to do with her?

Touching Eve's red hair, she wondered what secrets were hidden in the child's mind. What had happened in those first three years of her life to leave her so silent and distant?

Her mother, whoever she was, had given her away with clues and messages. She had told the child not to tell anyone her name or anything about herself. She had burned it into the tiny head of this three-year old so completely that the child's past was probably lost forever.

Why would a mother do such a thing, unless she felt that the child's very life was in danger? And wasn't that what the nuns had said? That she was in the hands of God? Well, Sara thought, she's in my hands now, and I'm going to protect her as best I can.

* * *

The Breath of Juno

IT WAS THE BEGINNING of a powerful bond that developed between them. Still aloof and quiet with others, Eve slowly opened up to Sara. It was as if she were a lone wolf cub who could only be comfortable with the familiar smell and touch of her mother.

After another month had passed, Eve's behavior began to appear more normal to the outside world, but there remained dark spots that worried Sara. Every night the child woke up screaming, terrified and shaking from dreams that haunted her. It was to be expected, Sara told herself, from a child abandoned without any sense of security, perhaps even without a memory of love.

And yet there was something strange about these night wakenings, but nothing specific she could really put her hands on. Still it was there: a difference in the eyes, in the way the child held her head, the way her body swayed with her arms stretched straight out at her sides. If Sara had believed in such things, she would have thought something was taking possession of the child's body every night, pulling her young mind far away from the safety of the bedroom. But in the morning the child would always be herself again, warm, increasingly gregarious, and curious about everything.

Sara petitioned the social welfare services to find a loophole in the foster parent agreement so she could keep the child herself. But her supervisors were vehemently opposed to the idea.

"You're a single woman now, a widow, living alone, working full-time. You can't care for this child—surely you know that. She needs to be in a two-parent home. Keep trying to place her. It's the best thing for her."

For almost twenty years, Sara had uttered those very words to other people with confidence and even with a touch of arrogant superiority. "It's the best thing for her." As if she actually could see into the future and predict with certainty what the best thing might be. The words seemed ridiculous now that they weren't coming from her mouth. Who could possibly know the best thing for anybody? Was sending a child off to live with a family that wanted the state's support money more than they wanted the child the best thing? Was moving children from one family to another the best thing? This was not a world that offered the best thing. Was Brad's dying at only fifty-eight the best thing? There was no such thing as best. Things just happened, she decided. We make choices with no promises as to whether these choices are right or wrong.

The weeks stretched into months. The child's paperwork sat on a corner of her desk unprocessed, unfiled. In the middle of the day Sara would stare at the door with the odd feeling that it might burst open, revealing a desperate weeping mother looking for her three year-old child.

ONE SATURDAY AFTERNOON late in September, Sara took Eve grocery shopping. Riding in the cart was always fun for Eve, so Sara was shocked when the child suddenly stood and began screaming. Her little arms shot up to protect her face as if someone was about to hit her. A small crowd gathered as Sara tried to calm the child, but she was beyond quieting.

"Looks like she's seen a ghost," said a girl with black nail polish and rings on every finger.

"It must be some kind of seizure," another onlooker volunteered. "Maybe we should call a doctor."

Sara shielded the child from the crowd, continually talking to her in a soft reassuring voice. But she too was alarmed by the child's eyes. They looked right through all the confusion and focused on thin air. She was seeing something, something not there, something in another time—a memory that terrified her.

"Look at me, Eve. Look at me! I'm here right in front of you." Sara grabbed the child's face and forced Eve to look into her eyes. With a jerk Eve was back, recognizing Sara and reaching for her. Sara picked the child up into her arms and held her, telling the crowd, "Everything is alright. She's just fine. Please give us a little room." The drama was over, so the crowd went back to their shopping.

Left alone in the aisle hugging the girl, Sara was aware of a wonderful excitement building inside her. The strangest feeling of happiness came over her. It seemed an inappropriate emotion to be having when a moment ago she had been so frightened. At first she didn't understand the feeling, but then she realized there was no need to understand it, only to welcome it into her heart. The compassion she had felt for the child for so long had transformed itself into love. Without any conscious awareness she had fallen in love, and the feeling was as familiar and comfortable as any she had ever known. The elation was the same as when she had realized for the first time that she was in love with Brad. Somehow this child had broken through her determination to keep love as a sacred memory. Whatever was to happen, she knew she had found love again.

"You O.K. now?" she asked.

The child nodded.

"Something scared you. Can you tell me what it was?"

"Don't know."

"What did you see that made you scream?"

"Can we get some ice cream?"

"Anything you want, honey."

They finished their shopping, and wheeled their basket up to the checkout counter. Just as Sara finished placing her groceries on the counter, a tall man with a broad frame moved into line behind them.

The whole incident from moments before repeated itself. Eve jumped up, pointed at the man, flailed her arms in the air and began screaming.

The man backed off, confused by the girl's reaction to him. The gathering crowd made him feel like he had just been accused of abusing the child.

"I didn't touch her!" he said. "I didn't do anything! What? Why is she screaming?"

Sara looked closely at the child's eyes to see where her gaze was landing. It was not on the man's face, but on the long black coat he was wearing.

"Excuse me," Sara said quickly to the man. "Could you remove your coat?"

He did so obediently.

Sara took the coat from him and put it around her own shoulders. Eve's gaze then refocused on her and the screaming continued. It was not the man who had frightened her, but the long, black coat.

Sara went through the same quieting ritual she had done only fifteen minutes earlier. As soon as the coat was out of sight, it was easy to distract the child and bring her back to the present.

As they drove home in silence, Sara tried to imagine how this could be relevant. But what could she do? Go to the police and say, "She has a fear of long black coats. Trace everyone who has bought one in the last three years." They would laugh at her. What was it that triggered this reaction on this day?

Getting any information out of Eve was impossible. She wouldn't talk about the screaming episodes. It was as though she had forgotten them the minute they were over. Sara decided she would call the department psychologist first thing Monday morning to see if she could arrange to be seen. Perhaps the therapist could help her remember if a traumatic event had frightened her, or if she had been abused. Sara would also meet with her supervisor tomorrow to see how she could begin an adoption procedure. This child's fate was somehow entangled with her own.

Words like "fate" and "destiny" had never been in Sara's vocabulary. Yet when she thought about it, she believed that meeting Brad had been a divine act of fate. Similarly, once she had given her heart to the child, nothing else mattered. For whatever reason, it was her mission to protect this child, and she was committed to doing just that.

Sara arrived at work Monday morning with her plan of action outlined. She was greeted by her supervisor, Carol, and Wayne Reese, the department head.

"Good morning," Wayne said nervously, adjusting his wire-rim glasses with their thick lenses that magnified his eyes to what Sara thought were grotesquely large proportions. "Could I see you in my office?"

Sara obediently followed Wayne and Carol to the corner room, a cubicle really with no windows, stuffed with file cabinets and Salvation Army-style furniture. Once Wayne had positioned himself behind his cluttered desk, Carol and Sara took their stations in the armless wooden chairs that faced him.

"Good news for you, Sara." A happy little smile tried to form itself across his long, usually expressionless face. "We have finally found a suitable home for the child who's living with you."

"What? That's my case!" Sara was furious. She had known that a discussion about Eve was coming but she had never expected this. "I'm in charge of finding her a home!"

"Yes," Wayne said, placing the child's file in the center of his desk. "But you've been dragging your feet on that for over four months now, so we had to take action. There's a family up in Rosehill. It's a little town just north of Sacramento. They're a stable family with three children of their own and two foster children." He offered Sara the sheet with the family's profile but she made no move to take it. "They have a large house out in the country, even a couple of horses. It's ideal. She can be with other children close to her age, in a real family. It's time to get her away from the city and whatever memories she has of her past. We can't . . . ."

Carol jumped in. "Sara, I know you've grown attached to this girl. But it's really inappropriate for her to stay with you. This is the best thing for her. They have a good record with other foster children. There is even a possibility that this could be a long-term home for the girl. You wouldn't deny her that opportunity, would you?"

Sara wanted to shout at them, demanding that they stay out of her life, that the child was not their concern anymore. But she knew that an emotional reaction would get her nowhere, so she decided to argue her case as professionally as she could.

"I know you think this sounds like a good move for the child, but she is in a very delicate state. She has bonded with me, and breaking that bond at this point could do her irrevocable harm. You see how much progress she's made in the last three months; she couldn't even talk when she first came in, and now she is almost as open as any normal child."

"Yes, you've done wonders with her, and we congratulate you for that," Wayne said, moving the file to the basket marked *completed*. "But still—a real home. A full family is what she needs, not a single parent."

"I don't want to give her up," Sara said, appealing to Carol. "She's part of my life now."

Before Carol could respond, Wayne stood, indicating the conversation had come to a close.

"Surely you can see that your attitude is based on your needs rather than the child's."

Carol turned to Sara, taking her hand. "She's filled a place in your life since Brad died. But you can't expect her to be everything for you. She's just a child. Give her a chance to live a normal life."

"She has nightmares," Sara said, refusing to move, "terrifying nightmares. She wakes up screaming every night. I'm always there for her. She trusts me. How can I possibly tell her that she's going to move to some stranger's home and start all over again?"

"That's the very point," Wayne said. "Once she has other children around her, lots of activities, a normal life, the dreams will go away and probably even her memory of you at this age. You know that most children can barely remember their life before the age of three. Perhaps it's best if this child is encouraged to forget the first three years of her life."

"I won't give her up," Sara said defiantly. "I can't."

"I'm sorry, Sara, but this is simply not your decision." Carol was empathetic but stern. "The arrangements have already been made. She is to be delivered to the foster family this weekend."

Once Sara realized she had lost, she fought for what she could still retain. "I'd like to know the name of the family and their address. I'd want to keep in touch with her."

"I don't think that's a good idea," Wayne said, glad to have the difficult meeting over. "In fact, given the circumstances of this child's arrival here and the recommendations from St. Andrew's convent, we believe that sealing the file here is most appropriate. We'll send it on to Sacramento and it will be filed and reviewed by a social worker there."

"I can't have any contact with her?"

"It's in her best interest," Carol said, supporting Wayne.

"Her best interest! How can we presume to know what her best interest is?"

"We can't," Carol said sadly. "We're not gods. We just follow the rules and do what seems to make the most sense. You have to agree—this is a more reasonable alternative."

ALONE ONCE AGAIN, lying on the left side of her bed, feeling Brad's absence, Sara felt more hollow than she ever had. The child had come into her life in a moment and had left just as quickly. In the end, she'd agreed to let them take all the toys and clothes she had purchased for her, so nothing would remain to remind her of Eve. At the last minute, she decided to keep one small thing, a bracelet. It was probably of no significance, but she felt a strange sensation as she put it in the bottom of her jewelry box, as if she had stolen an important piece of the child's past.

Although she had promised herself she would be stoic, she cried when the final moment came. Eve put her arms around Sara's neck and said, "Don't cry. I'll find you. I'll come back."

The Breath of Juno

As she walked the child out to the car that would carry her up to the Central Valley of California, Sara held tightly to the small hand. Letting go was the hardest thing she had ever done. The light had come back to her life for such a short time and now it was turned off again. All the rest would be in darkness.

• 2 •

1993: Highland, California

THE GIRL, NOW THIRTEEN, KNELT IN THE garden, breaking the darkness with the tiny beam of her flashlight. At three in the morning she was pulling weeds from between the sweet peas. Her thin body shivered in the chilly night air.

The dreams were devouring her nights. Tonight, when the terror had pressed against her small chest, she'd awakened choking on the scream that wanted to explode from her lungs. She lay awake trying to remember the dream that haunted her nightly, leaving her body covered in a cold sweat. But only the thinnest image penetrated her conscious mind.

When sleep threatened to seduce her again, she had gotten out of bed, quietly climbed down the stairs and slid out the back door to the safety of the garden. Now she pushed her fingers into the soil, damp with dew, being careful that the entire root of the weed was dislodged so that nothing remained to steal the nutrients from the flowers. The night was still and moonless. The lights of the city were too distant to wash away the deep black of the sky. It calmed her to sit inside the fenced yard. She loved the smell of the earth at night.

She sat quietly for so long that a pale green Luna moth found her finger tangled around a vine. It startled her. Didn't it know that she was not plant but animal? That she didn't belong in its domain? It rested on her finger for what seemed like several minutes, its fragile wings iridescent in the darkness.

It was thrilling . . . the moth.

* * *

The Breath of Juno

THE PERFECT SILENCE was broken by heavy footsteps on the cracked planks of the old back porch. A short fat woman in a white nightgown waddled down the stairs and crossed the grass. The girl watched her foster mother, thinking that she looked like the overfed goose that lived on Lord's Pond. It no longer migrated with the flock because its wings didn't have the power to pull its great bulk off the ground. She wanted to laugh as the goose woman came towards her, but she didn't because she also wanted to cry.

"Child, what are you doing out here in the middle of the night? You'll catch your death!"

"My death," the girl snapped, angry that the goose mother had destroyed the quiet of the night. "Is it here in this old yard? Hiding behind a bush? Will it run away if I see it?"

"It's just a silly thing that people say, honey. I didn't mean to scare you."

"Everything you say is silly. Why don't you talk like a regular person?" The child watched to see if her sarcastic remarks had caused any visible pain. But the woman laughed as if she had heard a delightful joke.

"Lord knows, I'm about as regular a person as you'll meet, so maybe this is how they talk." Cruel words bounced right off this woman who wanted so much to be her mother.

"Come on inside. I'll make you a cup of cocoa. That'll put you right back to sleep. I promise."

The woman stretched her arm out to the child sitting in the dirt at three in the morning. The girl wanted to refuse the open hand, but before she could stop herself her own hand reached up to the goose mother, and she allowed herself to be led back to the house. A scent of cinnamon rose from the woman's skin and floated in the night air. The girl knew that she was not of this woman, not in flesh or in spirit—that they lived in different worlds. This woman's home could never be more than a temporary stop, but at least for tonight the scent was sweet and the woman's hand was warm.

IT HAD BEEN THREE months since May 8, 1993 when the case worker had brought the girl out to the Wilkes' home in Highland, California, a poor suburb of San Bernardino. In spite of the dry desert heat the girl had worn a baggy wool sweater that she clutched around her tiny frame as if she could disappear in its folds. Her striking red hair hung in loose curls around her face, in sharp contrast to the bright green eyes that seemed to be staring at the air.

"Emily, this is Mr. and Mrs. Wilkes," the social worker had said, pushing the girl forward. "Can you say hello to them?"

Of course she could say hello. She wasn't retarded or autistic or crazy or any of the other things they said was wrong with her at all the other homes and clinics. And most of all, she wasn't Emily. Emily was the name her last foster family had given her.

She looked at the tall skinny house and the two short round people standing in front of it. This was going to be another disaster, she thought, as the Wilkes closed ranks and herded her into the house.

"Emily," Bud said, reaching for the two small beat-up suitcases the girl carried, "let me take your things upstairs. I'll show you your new bedroom."

She wanted to tell this rotund man not to call her Emily, that she had left Emily behind, but she said nothing. People had called her whatever they wanted for so long that it didn't really make any difference. And anyway, she didn't have anything to replace it with. Bud Wilkes climbed up the narrow stairs, but instead of following him she lagged behind so that she could hear the social worker talking about her.

"The records identify her as E. Andrews," the social worker explained. "There isn't an exact birth date for her, just a year, 1980. I think she's been in the system ever since she was a baby. I don't know why she wasn't put up for adoption. She's gone from one foster family to another. We warned you that she won't be an easy child. Her behavior is erratic. There are the blackouts and then there is the ongoing issue of her nightmares."

"We'll take good care of her," she heard Dora say. "She's Emily Wilkes now."

"The state requires that you continue to use the child's surname, Andrews. Without that it would be impossible to keep track of her."

"As far as I can see from the sloppy files the office showed us, the state can't keep track of nothing anyway. She's our girl now." Dora raised her voice. "Oh, I know we didn't adopt her, that she's not legally ours. But it seems to me that it's a lot more important for a thirteen year-old girl to have a first name than worrying about a last name. Besides when she goes to school everything will be new to her. They sit those classes alphabetically. If we put down 'Andrews' they'll stick her right in front and she'll freeze up like an early squash. 'Wilkes' puts her at the back of the room where she can stay quiet until she gets to know a few people." Dora's words floated up the stairs with the hot stuffy air.

An early squash. The girl snickered at the expression, then climbed the stairs to the attic bedroom where Bud was waiting for her with the two small suitcases that contained everything she owned. But she didn't intend to unpack them completely—this didn't look like a place she would be staying for long.

Now, three months later, they still remained unpacked.

ON SUNDAY MORNING she woke to the sound of Bud mowing the back lawn. She pulled on baggy jeans with slits cut through the denim just below the knees, and a black tee shirt. When she came down to the large old-fashioned kitchen, breakfast was already on the round table in the alcove. The pink tablecloth was covered with yellow daisies created by hours of needlepoint. The three of them sat down; pancakes floating in hot, sweet-smelling syrup lay on plates before them. Dora and Bud ate with delight while she sponged the sticky syrup off her pancakes with a napkin. She could never have imagined on that Sunday morning that years later, when she was half a world away, she would remember the rich aromas and try to picture herself in the safety of this kitchen.

They ate in silence. She knew the Wilkes were disappointed in her. She hadn't lived up to their expectations of the perfect young daughter. Watching Dora eat, she wondered how long it would be before they gave her up—not that she cared if they did. Living with Dora and Bud was like living on one of the old fifties television reruns she watched late at night after they had gone to bed. When she was afraid to sleep, she would sneak down and watch the *Donna Reed Show* and *Make Room for Daddy* on odd cable channels at three and four in the morning. They were television families from forty years ago. She was fascinated by the children in these shows who had simple little problems that were quickly fixed by a few words from a wise parent. The worst thing that could happen to these children was getting caught cheating on a spelling test or being disciplined for leaving their room a mess. The parents never yelled at one another, no one got divorced, no one was ever lonely or scared. That was what Dora and Bud wanted from her.

Everything was so perfect in those television shows just like this kitchen. She looked at the counter. Nothing was ever out of place. The canisters with more daisies painted on them were lined up according to size—six of them, each one smaller than the one before—like little ducks following the mother canister. Flour, sugar, salt, rice, oats, raisins.

Bud broke the silence by telling Dora about a new weed killer that had just come on the market. They talked to one another like the television parents. It was as if they didn't live in the real world but were stuck in a time warp.

Every Sunday since she had been in their home, Dora had pleaded with her to join them at their Pentecostal church. She had refused, boldly declaring that she didn't believe in God. Her last foster family had never made her go to church. They were atheists. She enjoyed saying the word, atheist. She wanted to shock them, to prove that the fantasy family they wanted had died a long time ago.

The first time she said *atheist* in front of Dora, she thought the woman would go crazy. She kept swatting her head as though somebody had unleashed a hive of bees to swarm around her. Then she prayed out loud, asking for the strength to bring the child back to the word of God.

Now, Dora finished her breakfast and smiled at her. "The choir is going to sing 'Amazing Grace' today." She leaned forward, imploring her, "Won't you please come with us? It's a beautiful hymn."

The girl was disgusted by Dora's begging tone. She wanted to push her to the point of anger. "I don't want to listen to that shit."

"Don't use those words in this house, young lady," Bud snapped.

Dora cringed when the girl said such things. The words offended her and her God. But more deeply, they frightened her. Not so much the words but the way the girl spoke them. It wasn't just bitterness and anger in her voice but something beyond that. It was as if the words came from a dark place inside the child that love could never touch.

"I'll say whatever I want," the girl said defiantly.

Dora drew in her full lips until they were pursed and angry. "If the devil has burrowed its way into your soul, it is my duty to force it out." These were the first harsh words she had spoken to the girl since she had arrived. "You are coming to church with us. If you want to live under this roof you will respect our ways. After you're done with your breakfast, you'll go up and change clothes so that you look decent in the house of our Lord."

The sudden outburst of anger from her goose mother didn't frighten the girl. Rather it pleased her to see the face, always posed in gentle calm, turn harsh and red. They are all like that, she thought, wearing their sweet polite masks to cover up what they really feel. She decided to reward Dora for her show of anger. "I'll wear the blue dress you got for me. Would that be all right?" she said sweetly, as she got up from the table and carried her plate to the sink.

Her sudden change of attitude confused Dora and Bud. They stared at one another in surprise.

THE CHURCH OF THE Holy Spirit was not an impressive sight. It looked more like a converted grocery store than a place of worship. It sat at the end of a block of retail stores in the old part of downtown Highland. A white cross and a sign announcing the week's sermon were all that identified it as a church. The sign in six-inch letters read, "Losing the Way." The Wilkes proudly entered with their new daughter by their side. There was a crowd of people already gathered. When Dora and Bud began chatting with friends, the girl slid away to sit on a wooden pew in the last row. A bell rang, indicating that the service was about to begin. People hurried to take seats. The Wilkes saw her at the back and quickly moved up the aisle to sit with her.

The room was silent. A preacher in a black robe entered, walked slowly to a raised platform at the front of the hall. He climbed onto the makeshift pulpit and placed his written sermon on the lectern in front of him. From the back of the hall, he appeared ten feet tall in his long robe. When he spoke he extended his arms out to the small congregation.

"Welcome to the House of God." His deep voice filled the room. "Today we will talk of our eternal struggle against our base instincts, our darker selves. It is a timeless battle that we each fight alone. And I must tell you we are losing that battle." He clenched his right hand into a fist, then pointed his index finger at the congregation. The girl sat frozen, staring at him. The finger seemed to be aimed straight at her. Her jaw began to tremble. There was something frightening and familiar about him.

"We are allowing evil to grow all around us." His eyes darted around searching their faces. When he singled someone out, his gaze rested on that person until each in turn lowered their heads in shame.

"The clouds are gathering, blackening our skies, blinding us from the light of God. The signs have all been shown to us. Do you know your Bible?" His voice reached a crescendo.

"First, Plague! A terrible disease is spreading across the land . . . it is to be the final plague. Then, Flood! The great rivers that run through the middle of our land are screaming with our pain. We saw them push out over their banks and cover the land, drowning us with their tears. And still we don't hear their cries. These great floods were sent to show us that the darkness is upon us."

She watched the words come from his mouth, filling the hall. In spite of her fear, she felt strangely drawn to him. The passion in his voice pulled her in as it caressed something hidden within her.

"Wind!" He said the word as though its very sound could lift his body. "The mighty hurricanes that destroy our homes and tear apart our lives have been sent to let us know that time is running out. The signs are everywhere. Look within yourselves. Can you feel it rising inside you? Can you feel yourself being carried into the great darkness?"

The meaning of his words escaped her, but the emotion simmered within her. As he spoke she felt the cotton fabric of the thin summer dress clinging to her chest. Secretly she put the fingers of her left hand on her neck. They were ice cold against her bare skin. Slowly she ran them down her chest until she could feel the small breast that had just begun to develop. It barely filled her palm when she held it. To her surprise the nipple hardened with her touch. A flush came to her skin. Embarrassed, she glanced quickly at Dora, relieved that the woman was transfixed by the sermon.

As the preacher continued, she felt as if she was being transported to a world that was ancient yet familiar. Her fingers grew cold, then numb. The sensation traveled up her arms, crept into her chest and throat. It was happening again! Not here, she begged silently. Whenever she felt the numbness, she knew the hallucinations were about to take over her body, but there was nothing she could do to stop them from coming.

The windowless hall suddenly filled with streaks of bright sunlight. Her breath came in short gasps. She bowed her head to hide her distress from Dora. The gray cement floor beneath her turned to dark stone. Her breathing became more labored. When she looked up she saw that the dingy church had been transformed into a grand cathedral with glorious stained glass windows and soaring arches. Where was she? Her hands rose to her breasts. They were full and heavy under a red linen. Who was she? Her temples throbbed as she struggled to push away the hallucination.

The vision lasted only a few moments and then the cathedral vanished and she was back, sitting next to Dora, feeling exhausted and confused. When the sermon was over, the choir sang and the aroma of incense filled the old building.

Then everyone was getting up, moving towards the aisle. Dora was reaching down for her arm, guiding her through the crowd and out the door, helping her into their pale blue station wagon.

Had Dora noticed anything? How could she not have seen! Maybe it had all happened too fast. Blackouts. That's what the last psychiatrist had called them. Brief periods of memory loss. But her memory was not lost. She remembered everything that she had seen. It hadn't happened for almost a year. She had hoped that whatever it was, it was over—it would never happen again.

She sat in the back seat of the car, knees pulled up to her chest. She wanted to tell someone it had happened again, but there was no one to tell, no one who could help her. There was only loneliness and despair.

"You're so quiet back there." Dora turned to talk to her. "You haven't said a word since the service ended. Now tell me, aren't you glad you came? That was so uplifting?"

"Uplifting! How can you think that was uplifting?" She remembered some of the preacher's words. "He said we were cursed with plagues and evil. You think that's a good thing? It was terrible. I hated it. I'm never coming here again."

"That's not what he said at all, child." Dora was her usual calm self. She was not about to get angry again and let the dark side of herself take over. Not after that sermon. The rest of the way home she explained what the preacher had meant, but the girl heard none of it.

FLOATING, WARM AIR blowing gently over her flesh . . . the night breathing in and out all around her body . . . the sky's breath becoming thousands of soft hands touching her thighs . . . her stomach . . . her face . . . holding her up as she hovers weightless looking down at the white clouds beneath her . . . flying, her arms extended, curving gracefully . . . cupping the breeze.

Below, figures moving, reaching for her, calling to her . . . needing her.

Losing balance, spinning . . . the hands no longer holding her . . . grabbing at her skin, tearing into her flesh. Clutching at the emptiness with her fingers . . . nothing to hold on to . . . falling . . . the ground coming up towards her . . . struggling to see through eyes blinded by the infinite darkness of the night . . . plunging towards the ground.

A shrill cry stabs her ear drums . . . her own scream breaking free, piercing the night.

The scream jerked her body awake. Covered in sweat, she fought to bring back the dream. She remembered the sensation of flying. It had been both wonderful and terrifying. Sitting up in bed, she squeezed her eyes closed and allowed the lightness to fill her. For a brief second she could feel herself high above the earth. She remembered the fear of falling, but the real terror was hidden from her. She needed to see who was calling to her from below. Remembering was a breath away. Each night she could feel them getting closer, and tonight they were begging to smash through to her waking consciousness. The dream lived like an alien world within her all of her life. Now the creatures within that world were demanding that she come to them.

Her concentration was broken by the sudden entrance of her foster mother.

"It's all right, child, you're just having another one of your dreams. I'm here now to take care of you." The large woman sat on the narrow bed causing the mattress to sag downward. The girl's body rolled towards Dora's open arms. The words of reassurance and the gentle pats on her head and back were more of an annoyance than a comfort. They distracted her from her purpose. Remembering what happened in the dream was crucial.

"I must remember all of my dream. Why can't I remember?" she said in frustration. "It slips away from me even when it knows I am calling it back."

"Child, whatever it is that haunts you at night, it is better left to the darkness. Don't try to remember. Let it go. It's nothing. You will outgrow these dreams, I promise."

Dora's eyes strained against sleepiness to open their fleshy lids. The girl looked away from the warm brown eyes to avoid the intense love coming at her like a hot summer wind. It was love without reason. How can this woman love me, she thought. She doesn't know anything about me. What good is her love? This woman who wants me to forget my dreams.

"You can't promise!" the girl said, pushing Dora away. "Who gives you the power to promise anything? You can't stop my dreams—they'll keep coming. They don't give a damn about your promises!"

Dora continued patting her, trying to comfort the girl, not letting the harsh words interfere with the unwavering love she felt for her.

But the girl didn't want the comfort this woman gave. She wanted to wound her until she reacted, until she became angry and cried out, until Dora's pain reflected her own.

"Every night you promise me that the dreams won't come again, that I'll outgrow them, but it never happens. How can I believe your promises when you sleep through the night and never wake up from a dream. Do you ever have dreams? Or is your mind as empty at night as it is during the day?"

Dora was a sponge, sucking in all the girl's anger, becoming larger and larger with it, never bursting, always able to absorb more. This morning at church she had allowed the child to get to her, to make her angry. It wasn't going to happen again. She swallowed the anger in her great bulk, and held it away from the child. Tears came but not anger.

The girl didn't cry and Dora's tears only infuriated her more. Crying was a waste of time. This woman only interfered, pulling her back into the present, pulling her away from her memories and her past. She needed to remember, to bring back the dreams, to understand why they were sent to her every night. Even though she was afraid to remember, she knew they held clues to help her make sense of her waking world. If she understood the dreams, maybe the hallucinations would stop. In some way she knew the two were connected.

Through all the foster homes, the institutions and the clinics, the only thing that remained with her was her dreams. They haunted and frightened her but they were also the only link to the past she might ever have.

· 3 ·

THE GIRL WALKED TO THE WINDOW of her third floor bedroom and parted the lace curtains. It might be high enough, she thought, as she looked down at the stony ground beneath her. She placed her small hands on the window sill, picturing the moment as it might happen. She would push up the heavy frame, swing her long legs over the edge, and then she would allow her body to tumble forward, flying through the air. Her head would hit first and the dreams would stop forever.

She pulled herself away from the window and, barefoot, crept down the stairs. They were talking about her. She knew they were sitting at the kitchen table talking about her. They all talked about her late at night when they thought she was asleep. This was her fourth month with Dora and Bud Wilkes. Until now she had been indifferent to their kitchen discussions. They were just another in a long line of foster parents who meant nothing to her. But things were changing fast. The night terror was getting worse. Each night she woke, grabbing for the vivid dream that dissolved before she could clearly see it. She would rather jump from her bedroom window than be sent away once again to another house of strangers. She crouched on the first floor landing and listened to them talk about her.

"We are *not* taking her to a psychiatrist!" Dora was vehement. "I don't care what the social worker thinks! They just mess with your head and make everything worse!"

"I don't see why you're so against this!" Bud stood his ground. "After all, the state would pay for this. It's not like it's money out of our pockets."

"We're not talking about money here! We're talking about that child's mind!" Dora was surprised to hear the anger in her voice. She hated to have any cross words with her husband, especially now that the child had made them a real family.

"It's up to you," Bud said. "She's yours. It was your idea in the first place. You're the one who's getting out of bed every night and running upstairs to her when she's having those dreams."

The conversation made Dora uncomfortable. She was sorry she had ever told Bud about the dreams, but it had gotten to the point where she couldn't handle the secret alone.

"I don't believe in psychiatrists," Dora said.

"It's not a religion. You're not supposed to believe in them. Just think of him like any other medical doctor."

"But that's just it. It is like a religion! Or opposite to one. They get inside your mind and start you thinking about things in ways that God never intended. Why, that child's already walking around telling people that she's an atheist. Now where do you think she got those ideas from? One of your psychiatrists, no doubt."

"Whatever you want is all right with me," he said giving in to Dora. "Is she asleep yet?"

"Yes. She went to bed about ten." Dora looked at the kitchen clock. It was eleven fifteen. "She usually wakes up around two or three in the morning. If only she could sleep through one night."

When the girl heard Dora get up and move around in the kitchen, she sneaked back upstairs to her bedroom. People had talked about her and planned her future for as long as she could remember, so she had learned to listen to the things that were said behind her back—that way sudden changes came as less of a surprise. Once they assumed she was asleep, they whispered to one another about how strange and difficult she was. The next day, the next week, or the next month they would summon their courage to sweetly tell her that she might be happier somewhere else. Knowing what they were going to say in advance gave her the upper hand. She could react without emotion, turn away from them with indifference, never give them the satisfaction of seeing her tears or her pain.

The walls of the attic bedroom felt like they were closing in on her. She approached the window carefully as if it were a dangerous animal that was stalking her. The moon was just cresting over the mountains. In the quiet hours before sleep forced itself upon her, she could find peace in her loneliness. The struggle to appear normal consumed all her energy during the day, but for a short time at night she could let down her guard and breathe in the silence. But once sleep had her in its control, the dreams came screaming through her. The night was both her enemy and her only true friend.

She sat down on the bed and began to examine her body, running the tips of her fingers lightly down her arm. The soft blond hair stood up, tingling at her touch. Ever since the hallucination in the church, checking her body had become a nightly ritual. She wanted to believe that if she was careful enough, it wouldn't happen again. She had to learn to control it or they would put her away forever.

The worst time had been three summers ago when she was ten years old. It had happened so suddenly. She was at a park, sitting on the wet, freshly cut grass, watching the other children play soccer, when her fingers grew cold, then numb. The eucalyptus trees that lined the park began to blur as waves of heat distorted her vision. Before her eyes, they withered and shrank to stumps with protrusions that grew grotesquely from their sides like arms reaching up to the sky. Needles popped through their skin. The grass beneath her shriveled and disappeared, leaving hot sand in its place. It had taken her a moment to realize that she was sitting in a desert, surrounded by cactus. She had raised her hands to shield her face from the burning sun, but it was not her face! The nose was too long, the eyes set too close together. Then she felt a terrible burning around her neck as if something was choking the breath from her body. Disoriented and frightened, she had looked directly into the blazing sun. Then she fainted.

That was all she had remembered when she woke up in the Camarillo Psychiatric Center three days later. It had taken her months to trust herself again, to believe that she still existed, that she wouldn't dissolve and drift into empty space, leaving her body in someone else's care.

Now that it had happened again in the church, she forced herself nightly to remember everything she had seen and heard . . . to bring it all back with her to her own body.

They all thought she was crazy. That's why they put her in that terrible hospital. She remembered hearing the words they whispered when they discussed her behavior: multiple personalities, schizophrenia, disassociation. But they were guesses. Nobody knew what was really wrong with her, so during the day they gave her drugs that made her feel confused and empty. At night they gave her more pills to make her sleep without dreams so that she wouldn't wake up screaming. When they had finally let her out of the hospital, she was determined that they would never send her back. For over a year she had checked every night to be sure she was still whole and alone.

And now it was happening again. When she was sure that she still lived alone inside her body, she pulled back the quilt and crawled into bed. They were going to send her to another doctor. Oh, Dora was refusing tonight. But before long she would give in and then eventually they would send her away. She told herself that the Wilkes were stupid people, that she wouldn't miss them. But her eyes stung with tears when she thought of starting over once again. The aroma of a baking peach cobbler traveled with the warm kitchen air up through the house to fill the attic with its sweetness. The tears that she wouldn't let Dora see fell from her eyes and rolled down her cheeks. She laid a feather pillow across her chest, then folded her arms across the pillow as if shielding herself from attack. Curling her fingers so that her hands were small fists, she spoke out loud her own private prayer of defiance for the first time.

"Come to me. I can't fight you anymore. You can frighten me all you want. Take me, but in return I'll bring you back with me into the daylight, and I'll remember everything you have shown me!"

She held her heavy eyelids open as long as she could. Then sleep came to her, stilling her thoughts, quieting her body.

A DARK SHAPE hung over her. Her arms and legs were paralyzed, refusing to respond when she willed them to move. Directly above her was a giant bird of prey, its wings extended across the width of the room, its talons reaching down towards her flesh. Her body rose up from the bed and moved towards the black slanted eyes and the sharp beak. Terror raged through her blood as her body was pulled inside the vast body of the bird.

A twisting agony ran through her arms as the bones within them stretched until they were long and slender. Her breast curved and closed in, sucking the air from her lungs. Her skin disappeared and was replaced by layers of thick feathers. A pain shot through her chest as she felt her heart pound more rapidly, threatening to explode as it pumped blood into the powerful wings. Her small face was contorted, pushed forward into the hard pointed beak. When the pain lessened, she was amazed to discover that she could see through the eyes of the great bird. The heavy wings bent as it took flight and the earth fell away beneath her. She was a prisoner with no will of her own, trapped within the creature. The talons pulled up close to her body as she sailed through the clouds. From miles up her sharp eyes spotted a squirrel on the ground. It raced from the black shadow the bird cast under the full moon.

Then the right wing dipped, causing her to swoop swiftly downward, leaving her dizzy and nauseous. Circling just above the tree line in a dense forest she could see movement below—human figures in the darkness. A line of women dressed in white robes moved silently between the trees, each carrying a candle despite the moon that hung low in the sky. The tiny candle flames shimmered, making the chain of women look like a white river reflecting the moon's light on its surface as it flowed peacefully under a canopy of ancient oak and cypress trees.

She flew above, following the river of women to a small glade where they were gathering. The night's silence was broken by the gentle sound of humming—not a melody, but a soft chant that pulled the white robes together in a circle. The candles were placed one at a time in the center as the chant grew stronger.

The clouds parted, revealing the full moon creeping low near to the earth, hugging the horizon. It sailed so low that it appeared to touch the earth, and in that moment it was transformed into an unearthly vision that was half human, half hawk. A woman's face, but a silver beak extending from her forehead, black brilliant eyes, and skin the color of rich red earth after a rain; the human-shaped body covered with gray, black, and white feathers. Her arm extended slowly, like a wing unfolding. The hand reached out with the palm upward. Instead of fingers, five sharp talons beckoned the girl to approach. She went to the woman and perched on the outstretched arm. To her amazement, the marvelous vision spoke to her.

"Child, come from the Aeron. Your name shall be your shield. Follow the Aeron. It will take you home."

The winged arm retreated. Then the bird woman was slowly transformed into a great globe of soft white light, ascending upward, and became the moon hanging in the sky.

The women in the circle continued to chant.

A baby not more than a few hours old was brought to lie among the flickering lights. All eyes turned to the sky. They looked to her as she hovered just above the trees, her wings moving just enough to keep her suspended as if by a string from heaven. Then the white robes closed in on the infant.

Diving towards the earth, towards the infant, with her sharp beak and extended claws, her cry echoed the screams of the baby.

Tearing through the sky, the hawk's shrill call pierced the night.

THE SCREAM STUCK in her throat, choking her. It took all her energy to push the scream out until it thundered in her ears. The piercing sound that came from her own body woke her. She sat up in bed soaking wet, remembering the pieces of the dream. Images came back, vivid images! Flying inside the body of a hawk—a ribbon of women dressed in white.

"I'm here! It's all right, child, I'm here!" Dora rushed into the room.

"Don't touch me!" the girl shouted, pushing her away. "Don't touch me."

The wild look in the girl's eyes frightened Dora. The words of the preacher rang in her ears: "Look for the evil that lives inside even the most innocent among us. It is carrying us into the great darkness."

Dora pulled back from the child and sat in the rocking chair across the room. "How can I help you to remember? What should I do," she said, almost to herself. "When I hear you scream in the middle of the night, I can't imagine what can be causing you so much pain. I want to help you remember."

"Give me some paper and a pencil," the girl demanded.

Dora jumped to her feet and brought a notepad and a pen from the desk under the window. For a moment the page lay blank in front of the girl. Slowly she lowered the pen to the paper and, with her eyes closed, she began to draw a crude picture of what looked like a wing with long serrated tips. At first Dora couldn't make out the sketch, but as the girl continued to move her hand, the image emerged. It was some kind of bird—a raven or eagle. Then the girl scrawled a word in the middle of the page.

The Breath of Juno

The letters came so automatically that the girl hardly felt her hand form them. When she opened her eyes, the word AERON lay before her. She had seen it, as well as heard it, in her dream. She got out of bed and went to the open window to look out at the moon, now high in the sky.

"Aeron," she whispered the word into the night, "what does it mean? Why did she give it to me?" She spoke to herself, forgetting Dora was in the room.

Then it hit her. "It's my name! It was given to me by the hawk woman." The moonlight cast the girl's thin body in a long shadow that ran the length of the bedroom. She stood still, staring into the night.

The girl's strange words and behavior terrified Dora, so she broke the silence, trying to sound as if odd events like this happened every day.

"Aeron," Dora repeated the name. "Well, that's just fine. Did that come to you from your dream? It's a lovely name, especially since you found it yourself. Everyone ought to get to pick out their own name. It sticks with you your whole life, so it should be something that's yours. And it's just in time, too. School will be starting next week. Bud and I have been filling out the papers . . . ."

Dora rambled on, but Aeron ignored her.

"Come on now, that's enough of those dreams for one night." Carefully Dora approached the girl. "Let me help you change nightgowns. This one's all wet. We'll get you dry and then you can get back to sleep."

Aeron allowed Dora to remove the soggy nightgown and replace it with a fresh one. A quiet filled her as Dora tucked her back into bed. Sleep returned.

Dora sat in the rocking chair until the child was deeply asleep. The small face that had looked so tormented a few moments before was now peaceful and still. Maybe she was wrong about the psychiatrist. Somebody had to help this child to sleep through the night. Tomorrow she would call the number that the social worker had given her.

FOR THE THIRD time, Dora checked the address on the business card against the number on the house. "Dr. Lee Edwards, Psychiatrist. This is where he is all right. It sure doesn't look like a doctor's office."

She had expected something different—a clinic, a hospital. But instead they found themselves at an old but freshly painted Victorian house. The light blue walls were accented by the rich maroon color that framed all the windows. A giant oak tree dominated the front yard, some of its heavy branches so large that they looked like trunks of their own tree. A well cared-for rose garden spread out behind a white picket fence.

The child, who now called herself Aeron, didn't respond. She was guarded—she'd been to so many therapists over the years. They had talked to her endlessly, then given her more drugs. None of them had made the hallucinations or the dreams go away.

The porch was a wide veranda with old wicker chairs lined up facing west so that the inhabitants of the house could watch the sunset behind the hills. It spoke of earlier times when people sat together at night, talking quietly of small things. Now when the sun disappeared, people retreated into the private spaces inside their houses and tried to believe that the walls of wood and plaster could keep out the dangers of the night. But the late news glowing from their televisions pulled that night world into their sanctuaries, reminding them that the rising tide of violence was never far away from their door.

A sign tacked above the doorbell read: "Please come in. Do not ring the bell."

The screen door opened onto an old-fashioned parlor. It was now a patient waiting room with magazines and books sitting about on end tables. A coffee urn was set on a side board with a small plate of sugar cookies. Dora helped herself to three cookies and a cup of coffee. "Mmm. Honey, do you want one of these? They're delicious." She offered the plate to the girl.

"My name is Aeron, not honey," she said pushing away the plate.

"Don't talk to me like that," Dora said firmly. She was through tolerating the girl's rudeness. "I'll call you Aeron when you start treating me with some respect."

Aeron took a cookie from the plate and ignored Dora. They sat and waited in silence.

Ten minutes later, Dr. Lee Edwards walked through the door: a striking woman in her early thirties, dressed in khaki pants and a casual cardigan sweater. She greeted them. Her long brown hair was pulled back, tied loosely at the nape of her neck. She wore no makeup.

"You're a woman!" Dora blurted out.

"Yes, it does look that way," Lee said. "Don't be flustered. A lot of people make that mistake. It's part of having a first name like mine. You must be Dora Wilkes. And this is . . . Aeron? Is that right?"

Aeron was startled. All of her psychiatrists had been men, old men, in suits and ties.

"Okay, Aeron, would you like to come in and talk with me for a while? Dora, help yourself. There's some coffee and some . . . . " She turned around and noticed that all the cookies were gone. "Ah, well, I can get some more of those."

"Oh no," Dora said, embarrassed. "I guess I didn't have much lunch. I'll just wait out here. I'm fine . . . I'll be fine. You've got good magazines. I'll just be reading them. Go ahead."

"At the first meeting, I think it's important that the child and I spend some time alone. I'll call you in a little while, all right?"

Lee opened the door to her office and invited Aeron in. The room was full of comfortable chairs and beautiful pictures. There was a desk, but Lee didn't sit behind it. Instead she sat on the sofa, inviting Aeron to join her.

All the previous therapists had begun these sessions by slowly paging through Aeron's thick and confusing file. Lee had nothing in her hands—no paper, no pencil, no tape recorder. She just talked.

"So—I guess you've been through an awful lot of these meetings, and every time you meet a new therapist, they probably start out by asking you a whole lot of questions, right?"

"Yeah."

"Well, I'm not going to do that. Why don't we just start talking? Maybe we'll get to be friends."

Aeron wanted to say, "I doubt it," but she didn't bother.

"So, what would you like to talk about?"

"I don't know."

"I think it's only fair to tell you that your foster mother, Mrs. Wilkes, filled me in on the dream you had a few nights ago, and she told me about your naming yourself Aeron. You don't have to explain any of that if you don't want to, but we can always talk about your dreams if you like."

"I don't remember my dreams. You all ask me about them, but I don't have anything to say," Aeron stood and began poking around the room, touching things.

"That's okay. We'll talk about something else. You know we have something in common."

"What's that?" she circled around behind Lee's desk.

"Well, the name you picked. Aeron. You know when you and your foster mother saw me, you thought I was going to be a man because my card says Dr. Lee Edwards. Well, Aeron is a man's name, too."

"Yeah, but it's spelled different." The girl sat in Lee's desk chair and spun around.

"Yes, it is." Lee preferred working with adults. They could be just as frustrating as children, but they didn't sit in your chair trying to annoy you.

"But not the way you think."

"What do you mean?" Lee asked.

The child picked up a pen lying on the desk and wrote AERON in capital letters across a letter Lee had been writing.

Lee got up and went to her desk. "It's an unusual spelling. Where did you come up with it?"

"I don't know." Aeron bounced up from the chair and started pacing again. "It was in my dream."

"So you do remember parts of your dream?" Lee immediately knew her tone was too triumphant. She regretted how it would sound to the girl. But Aeron didn't seem to be paying attention.

"Someone gave it to me."

"Can you remember who?"

"No. I thought you weren't going to ask me any questions," she said in the snotty voice of a young child.

Lee sat behind the desk, letting the girl wander around the room. They were both silent for several minutes.

Aeron looked at the old pictures, the antiques. It seemed so familiar, she thought. It was as though she'd been here before.

"Do you live here by yourself?" the girl turned abruptly to Lee.

"Yes," the woman hesitated, not used to being at the receiving end of questions.

"So you don't have any kids?"

"Not yet. I've never been married."

Aeron spun an old-fashioned globe sitting on the corner of the bookcase. "You will have. Two. Two boys." The words came out of her mouth before she could stop them.

"Now, is that a guess," Lee said trying to sound playful, "or is this something you know for sure?"

The girl stared right into Lee's eyes. "I know for sure." Her tone was so serious that bumps rose on Lee's arms. She had the most uncanny feeling that the child was right, that somehow, she *did* know. But she quickly dismissed these thoughts.

"Well, it certainly would be nice to have two boys. But to tell you the truth, I'd like to have a girl."

"So what else do we talk about?" Aeron returned to the sofa, lying across it with her feet resting against a silk pillow.

"You can talk about anything you like. I'll listen. That's what I do; I listen. I'm good at listening."

"Dora doesn't want me to remember my dreams. No one does. But they're close—they're getting so close I can almost see them."

"What can you see? Tell me anything you like. Whatever comes to your mind."

"It's never anything clear." She tried to sound indifferent as if none of this really mattered much. "Sometimes I'm flying. I've told all the therapists that. They say everybody flies in their dreams . . . it doesn't mean anything." She looked at Lee for a response but none came. The indifference went out of her voice as she continued. She so desperately needed someone to talk to.

"I'm not me when I fly." She got up and slowly moved around the room as she reached for the images of her dreams. "I'm a bird, a hawk. It feels so free. I don't have to be part of this earth anymore. I can soar up in the clouds and travel as far as I want to. And I can see all sorts of things below. But I always wake up screaming."

She stopped herself. "You know it won't change anything if I tell you all this. It never does any good."

"It's different now," Lee said, moving closer to the child. "Before you couldn't remember, or you didn't want to remember. Now you do. Something has changed. Maybe the dreams have messages for you that will help you learn about yourself. Just tell me whatever images come to your mind."

"There is a woman who floats in the air. She spoke to me."

"What exactly did she say?"

"Just the name, Aeron. She told me to take it. That it would protect me."

"Maybe she's right," Lee said.

Aeron looked at Lee. She was different; she really did listen—not just with her ears, but with her intense eyes, her open hands, and her entire body, which leaned towards Aeron, not away.

Aeron sat back down on the sofa. Images fell into her mind from her dream. They were like apples hanging in a tree in the sky, waiting to be picked from her night world.

It was a careful balance. Lee didn't probe too much and Aeron didn't recoil. When Aeron was leaving, she turned to Lee and said, "Oh, that tree out front? That big oak you've got? That branch that goes over your roof could fall in a big storm this winter." And then she left.

A chill went down Lee's neck.

Lee followed Aeron out the door and then invited Dora Wilkes to come in for a few moments.

"I think it went well. She's a very special child."

"Did you figure out why she's waking up screaming every night?"

"Not yet. In the first few sessions I need to build a sense of trust with her."

"That won't be any easy task. I've been trying to do it for five months. I don't know that she trusts me anymore than the first day she came into our home. She's always pushing me away."

Lee looked at the anxious woman sitting on her sofa. "But you love her, don't you?"

"Oh, that's for sure."

"But do you love *her*—or just having a child in your home, a daughter?"

"You mean, like it could have been any little girl?"

"Yes."

"Well, I don't know." Dora was confused by the question. Maybe it was true that she had wanted a child so much that she was ready to love the first one who walked through the door. "She sure don't make it easy to love her. She's got a mouth on her, that one. But I know that's just the surface. Underneath, there's got to be some sweetness. If I just squeeze the fruit enough, I think I'll find it."

"After a few sessions, I think we'll try hypnosis on her to see if we can get at those dreams."

"The social worker told me they'd all tried that before and it didn't work."

"Maybe it didn't work then, but she's older now. The most important thing is that she wants to remember."

"Did she tell you she crossed over this summer? Just about three weeks ago."

Lee was puzzled. "What do you mean, crossed over?"

Dora was embarrassed. She didn't like talking about such things. "Well, you know—became a woman?"

"Ah," Lee said. "She got her period for the first time?"

"You know, we don't even know when her birthday is. They told us that sometime in June she'd turn thirteen. We just picked a day to celebrate. Somebody ought to make that permanent, you know, set a date for her birthday."

When Dora and Aeron left, Lee made a note to have the oak tree in the front yard trimmed before the rainy season.

On the first day of school, Aeron was grateful that Dora had given her the name Wilkes. She could hide in the back of the crowded room and withdraw into her own world.

At lunchtime, the girls congregated in cliques throughout the cafeteria. Most of them had lived in the same town since their birth, so a new kid was left to find her own niche however she could. The conversations were a buzz around her. Many of the girls had crossed that invisible bridge from childhood into adolescence over the summer. Twelve had become the magic age of thirteen. They were teenagers.

"Hi. Are you new here?"

Aeron stared blankly at the two girls who stood in front of her. She had had too many first days in schools to trust these early approaches. Sweet faces and smiles could hide a desire to tease her and make her the butt of their jokes. A new kid was an easy target.

"So, what's your name?" said the perky blonde girl with the long ponytail.

Her name—such a simple question, but never before, not for her. Now, after all these years, she finally had an answer, the real answer. She had a name.

"Aeron," she said with pride.

"Where are you from?"

The sweet taste disappeared. This question was much harder to answer. Where was she from? And if she thought of a good answer to this question, there would just be another question, and another, and she could never find the answers to all of them. They would never know who she was, and she wouldn't either.

No words came to her. The old patterns were returning. But this time she wanted it to be different. She had a name like everyone else did—she could be one of them. She could have friends. She wanted these girls to like her.

She smiled as warmly as she knew how, and said to the blonde, "You're in my second period English class, aren't you? You have Mrs. Stevens?"

"Yeah!" the girl brightened up. "She's supposed to be really cool. Lots of fun, you know, not very strict. Doesn't give much homework."

"Oh good," Aeron said. "I hate it when they make you read all the time." Reading was Aeron's only joy. She had learned to lose herself in the mystery of fiction when she was a very young child. But she didn't think she could gain many points with these two girls if she admitted her passion for reading.

"Oh God yes," said the other girl. "You're lucky you didn't get Mr. Zimmermann. He makes you read all the time. I'm stuck in his class."

"Want to eat lunch with us?" the blonde girl asked.

"Sure," she said, taking out the sack lunch Dora had packed for her. When she unwrapped the bologna sandwich on Wonder Bread, she saw them lift their eyebrows and exchange mocking smiles. She wanted to throw the sandwich in their faces and run away. Not this time, she thought. "Shit," she said loudly. "Can you believe the crap my mother gives me?" She tossed the sandwich into the trash. "Let's get a dog from the machines." The snickers left the two girl's faces. Aeron reached in her pocket, praying she had the money to pay for the hot dog. Three quarters, just enough. For the moment she could still appear cool in their eyes, not a geek who ate homemade sandwiches and took the bus to school from the poor section of town in the empty foothills.

They sat on the grass together, the three of them, and ate. Other kids could look at them and see that she was no different then they were. She was one of them, not the crazy girl who had hallucinations, haunting nightmares, and a shrink.

The blonde chatted on about the cute new boy in her history class. Aeron tried to concentrate on what she was saying, but she couldn't stop her mind from seeing the young girl's face age before her eyes. The lips became tight and wrinkled, the eyes sank into their sockets, the skin under the chin sagged. Aeron pushed the future away. Not now, she begged silently. Leave me alone.

• 4 •

LOOKING OUT HER OFFICE WINDOW, Lee Edwards sat at her desk. A thick brown smog had rolled into the valley hiding all but the peaks of the San Bernardino Mountains. When she had moved to San Bernardino six years ago it had been during the winter, and the air was crystal clear. The impressive mountains behind the city soared into a blue cloudless sky. Snow capped their tops. She could hardly believe this was Southern California. It was a welcome change from the urban intensity of New York where she had gone to medical school.

She hadn't been prepared for the summer view, when an inversion layer of air held the heat in, baking the air and turning it to smog. But now it was already the middle of November, time for the smog to leave, and for her mountains to return. She hated these days when the heavy air crept into her mind and clouded her thinking. She longed to open the bay windows and breathe cool mountain air into her lungs before returning to the waiting stack of work on her desk. The notes and taped transcripts from her six sessions with Aeron sat in the middle of the mess. Yellow highlighter marked the memories that surfaced from the child's dreams. Visions were breaking through into Aeron's consciousness every night now. They poured out of her mind as if they were eager for an independent life.

At the top of a clean notepad, she wrote "Dream Memories." Then she began listing the images so that she could explore each one of them separately. The hawk was the primary one. It appeared to Aeron in many ways. Most frequently she herself was a hawk in flight. But then there was the female creature that seemed to be half-human, half-bird. Lee looked at her Audubon bird book to see if there was a species of hawk that was similar to the one in the girl's dreams. As she turned the pages, she wondered if the word the girl heard could have been *heron* instead of Aeron.

The Breath of Juno

Then there was the river of white women. Water images appeared frequently in the child's dreams as did visions of the moon. It was all so confusing. There were too many mysteries to unravel. What did the girl's dreams have to do with the hallucinations she experienced when she was awake? It was in the fourth session that Aeron had told her about the fantasy that had taken over her body during the preacher's sermon. And if that wasn't enough to figure out, every once in a while the girl seemed to think she had the ability to look into the future.

Lee looked at several children's fairy tales she had gotten from the library to see if any of the images could have come from a story Aeron had been told when she was very young. First she found a strange English tale about a princess who asked for the moon as a birthday present from her Father, the King. He told her it was impossible to bring the moon down to the earth. On the night of the child's thirteenth birthday she disappeared. The next day all of the King's court could see the princess' face shining in the moon.

She found several other stories from cultures all over the world where a child or a woman appeared in connection with the moon. The fairy tales led her further into books of myth and legend. Lee thought she could read all day and never finish the stories that had been written about goddesses of the moon. It was fascinating, but still she didn't know if they had anything to do with Aeron's dreams. The bird woman, she guessed, represented her mother. The recurrent dreams might be an effort to connect with the mother she had lost so early in her life. That was the logical explanation. But there was very little that was logical about this girl.

With their dozens of dog-eared pages, books by Jung and Freud that Lee hadn't referred to since medical school surrounded her notes. Both of these fathers of modern psychology had their own ideas as to the meaning of symbols in dreams. She studied them looking for answers. Aeron had described herself as flying in most of her dreams. Lee knew how Freud would interpret that—he felt that flying images were common in young girls coming into sexual awareness. They could represent the "letting go" involved in orgasm, a sense of freedom and release. But in Aeron's case, Lee thought, the flying sensations might represent something different. It was a puzzle that she had to think through one step at a time.

The child's life had been a chaos of one foster home after another. Maybe the dreams allowed her to escape into another world where she could feel more in control. But when Aeron flies, Lee reasoned, she is transformed into the body of a hawk. Lee turned to Jung to see what he had written about flying dreams. She read his words carefully out loud. 'The bird flying dream may represent the peculiar nature of intuition working through a medium, an individual who is capable of obtaining knowledge of distant events.'

Lee thought of the day she had first met Aeron. The girl had predicted with such certainty that Lee would have two sons. That definitely qualifies as a distant event, Lee laughed to herself. But what does the hawk symbolize? If the archetype dream visions are universal symbols, she concluded, they will appear in the mythologies of all cultures.

She read all the myths she could find about hawks, and everywhere she found similar meanings. The hawk was seen as a messenger sent by the gods or ancestors to bring heightened awareness, to wake up the deep sleeping mind, to call back the memories that lie just below the threshold of consciousness. In Native American myths the hawk was a totem that carried enormous responsibility because it had vast vision and the shrill cry that could pierce the unconscious.

In one book she came across a painting of a god with the head of a bird. The caption read, *Egyptian God Thoth, associated with transcendence.* On the next page was a photo of a small sculpture depicting a hawk-like bird with outspread wings and sharp talons but the face was that of a young woman! It startled her. Was this the vision Aeron had seen in her dreams? The caption under the photo plate read, *Small carving of winged goddess, found throughout the Roman Empire, Circa 200 A.D.*

If Aeron's dreams were the gateways to her inner life, it could be a mystical and terrifying place. The girl lived in a complex world. Lee didn't know if she could even begin to unravel it but for the moment the task felt wonderfully exciting.

Lee closed Aeron's file reluctantly. Beginnings were full of promise and the belief that she could make a difference in the direction a person's life would take. Her initial optimism usually began to fade when a client with deeply entrenched behaviors failed to show any progress. Unlike most of her colleagues, she didn't believe therapy should be a way of life. She gave herself a time limit for each client. It could be anywhere from six months to three years, depending on their problems. If she felt that they were becoming addicted to therapy and not learning to cope independently, she would suggest they stop coming. But Aeron was showing signs of improvement. She was doing well in school, making friends, and getting along better with her foster family.

Lee decided to take a walk into the mountains. Rigorous exercise bored her, but a casual walk helped to clear her mind. She would rather sit on a lake and admire the mountains than spend the day climbing to the top of them. She didn't see her body as something that she had to work on to maintain. It was simply the casing that held her thoughts and ideas. Heredity had blessed her with a strong well-formed body, and for that she was grateful.

She walked up the Angeles Crest Trail with the sun baking her head. The thermometer outside had registered only eighty degrees when she had started, but now it felt like it was over 100. Something was different these last few summers. The sun seemed hotter. It hurt her eyes and burned into her brain differently than it had in past years. Maybe it was something about the thinning ozone. All this greenhouse effect stuff, she thought, as she moved slowly up the mountain trail.

When she got up to the ridge, she looked down at the valley full of smog and wished that she could soar miles above it as Aeron did in her dreams.

WHEN AERON ARRIVED for her weekly appointment, Lee explained to the girl that she wanted to hypnotize her. The girl's medical records indicated that it had been tried many times before and failed to produce any useful results. But Lee felt there was something there, ready to come out now, asking to be heard.

"Are you afraid of being hypnotized?" Lee asked as Aeron laid down on the couch.

"No, I've done this lots of times before." Aeron knew it wouldn't work. She would just pretend to be asleep, then make up a story or two.

"I want you to know there's no reason to be afraid. I'm right here. And you can wake up anytime you want to. Are you ready?"

"Uh-huh."

"I'm going to take you back as far as you can remember. Just relax, take a few deep breaths, and listen to my voice. I'll be your guide, carrying you back in time." Lee's voice drifted in the air like a soft summer cloud. Aeron felt her body becoming lighter. She tried to move her fingers, but the message never left her brain. Lee's voice pulled her farther away from conscious thoughts.

They traveled together back through time. Lee asked Aeron to recall specific times, a Christmas, a vacation, and to tell her where she was and who was with her. It was going well, so Lee decided to take the plunge and go all the way back to Aeron's earliest memories.

"Now I'm going to take you back to when you were four years old. It's your fourth birthday party. Can you tell me all about it?"

Aeron crossed her ankles and swung her legs back and forth. "No birthday," she said, biting her lips. "I haven't got a birthday."

"Can you see a cake with four candles on it?"

"No!" Aeron said banging her arms against the couch.

"It's all right." Lee waited until Aeron's body relaxed. She knew there was no official birthday in the girl's records, but she had hoped that the early foster families would have picked a day to celebrate it anyway.

"Aeron, we are going back a little further. You are three years old. It's a lovely summer morning. You are going outside to play. What do you see?"

The corners of Aeron's mouth turned up. Then the small smile spread to her closed eyes, giving her the look of a young child hiding a secret. Lee gave her time to get fully inside the moment she was reliving.

"Can you tell me where you are? Is there someone with you?"

Aeron opened her eyes, looking directly at Lee. "Sara, will you read me a story?"

"Yes, honey. What story do you want to hear?" Lee answered her.

"The one about the moon."

"Can you hear Sara reading the story?" Lee whispered.

The child fell silent, closing her eyes slowly, as if she was falling into a deep sleep.

"Is Sara your Mommy?" Lee said softly.

Aeron rocked her head from side to side.

The Breath of Juno

"What does Sara call you?"

"Eve." The smile returned to her face.

"Is that your real name—Eve?"

Aeron shook her head again.

"Let's go back a little further. Before you met Sara. When you lived with your first mommy. Do you remember the name your mommy gave you?"

The girl nodded. But at the same moment her eyes popped open and her body became tense.

"Can you tell me your name?"

"No! Never!" She lashed out at Lee, pushing her away.

Lee decided not to press her. She gently guided Aeron's arms back to rest comfortably at her sides.

"Can you see your mommy?"

Again she nodded.

"And what does your mommy look like?"

Aeron ran her fingers through Lee's long brown hair. "Red hair."

"She has red hair like you?"

"Yes."

"And what's your mommy's name?"

"No."

"You don't want to tell me, do you?" The child shook her head violently. "That's all right; you don't have to say anything unless you want to.

"Now go to the last time you saw your mommy. Let's visit that day, okay? Just tell me where you are, what you see and hear."

"Mommy reading to me . . . ."

The child's face tightened with fear. Her eyes popped open. She was seeing something approach from above. She whispered, "Who are they, Mommy? What do they want?"

"What's happening, Aeron? Talk to me," Lee said firmly. "Tell me what you see."

"Three big black birds coming down to take me away. Stop them!"

"Keep talking to me and they can't hurt you. What kind of birds do you see?"

"Black birds. Black arms." She screamed, "No! Stop! Let me go! Let me go!"

Her arms flailed as if she was trying to free herself from the grasp of someone lifting her up into the air. She became more and more terrified.

Lee was worried. It was time to bring her back.

"Aeron, now listen to me. You're going to wake up when I count to three. You're going to come back to me and be thirteen years old when I count to three, all right?" Lee reached out and put her hands on the child's writhing body to calm her and counted to three.

The child became relaxed and quiet. She closed her eyes once again.

"All right, Aeron. You're thirteen years old now, and you can wake up whenever you want. You can open your eyes and wake up whenever you want."

Slowly Aeron opened her eyes, but she didn't focus on Lee.

"Are you awake?"

"Yes."

Lee could tell by the tone of the girl's voice that she was still hypnotized. "How old are you, Aeron?"

"I'm thirteen."

The voice was thinner than Aeron's, with an accent that Lee recognized as being from the Midwest.

"Aeron, where are you?"

"Who is Aeron?"

"I'm sorry. What is your name?"

"Amy . . . Amy Talbot."

"Do you know where you are, Amy?"

The child began to shiver violently. She hugged her small body with her arms and curled up into a ball. Lee had no idea what was happening. She took a throw blanket from the back of the couch and covered the child.

"It's cold. So cold in here."

"Where are you, Aeron?"

The girl huddled under the blanket. Lee realized that Aeron wasn't listening to her voice any more. She was afraid of losing control of the girl.

"Amy," she said firmly, shaking the girl. "Tell me where you are."

"So cold," she said, her eyes darting around the room. She was in a wood frame house. She was searching for firewood but it was all gone. The wind was blowing between the thin planks that formed the walls. She wore only a gray wool dress that hung to her ankles.

"It is the coldest winter ever. They all say it." She grabbed a tattered blanket from the bed and draped it around her body. The house shook violently when the wind slammed against its side. Her body was rocked about like a helpless doll. A little boy not more than three years old ran screaming to her side. Her fingers caught in the torn edges of the blanket, and as she opened her arms they were like wings, sheltering her brother beneath them. They huddled in the corner of the room as the wind howled all around them.

"Lookout!" she screamed, raising her arms to protect herself and the boy as the glass blew out of the front windows. She was crying and whispering at the same time. "We'll be all right." But even as she said the words, she could see through the broken windows. "The wind is taking the roof off the sawmill across the road! Now the water tower is falling down!"

Lee didn't know what to do. She had no idea where Aeron's mind had gone. When the child spoke of the cold winds blowing through the house, Lee could feel them herself. The hair on her arms stood straight up.

"It's so cold," the girl cried. "They told us when we came here it was the coldest place on earth."

"Tell me where you are!" Lee demanded.

The girl lunged forward, reaching for something in midair. She had seen the kerosene lantern fall off the table. She rushed to smother the flames with the blanket. "Bodie! . . . this is Bodie," she shouted.

Lee's mind ran wild. The only Bodie she had ever heard of was at the foot of the eastern Sierra range in California. It had been a ghost town since the turn of the century. It was abandoned after the Gold Rush. What was this child talking about? How could she know anything about living in Bodie.

"Amy, I want you to tell me what year this is."

"It's '79."

1979, Lee thought. That was a year before Aeron was born. She had to bring the child out of this trance now.

"I'm going to count to three now, and when I do, you're going to wake up as Aeron and be thirteen years old," she said firmly. "Do you understand me?" She began counting. "One . . . two—remember when I get to three you will be fully awake. It will not be 1979 but 1993. You will be Aeron and you'll be thirteen years old."

When she got to three she clapped her hands abruptly, inches from the child's face, and Aeron's eyes snapped into focus. It took a few seconds for her to recognize Lee.

Lee breathed a sigh of relief. "Are you all right?"

"I'm fine," Aeron said. "Why? What happened?"

"You don't remember anything?"

"No. Did it work? Do you know something?"

Aeron saw the terror in Lee's eyes and pulled away from her. "You know something! What did I say? Tell me! You promised me you'd tell me everything."

"I will." Lee was torn by her promise to the child and her fear that the trauma of the experience would confuse and terrify her. She made her choice quickly. "You remembered all the way back when you were three years old. You said you saw a woman who you called Sara, and she called you Eve. Does that mean anything to you?"

"People called me lots of things . . . Eve, Evie, Evelyn, Emily. But I don't remember a Sara."

"Well, it's only our first try. We'll do this again at our next session and you'll remember more."

"Only if you promise me you're going to tell me everything."

Lee tried to look as relaxed as she could. "Yes," she said, "I'll tell you everything that happens under the hypnosis."

She hoped she was doing the right thing. Later on she would tell the girl about the brief memory she had of her mother, of the black birds she had seen attacking her. But first there was the more vivid experience of Amy Talbot to deal with.

When Aeron left, Lee sat alone in her office, trembling. She tried to think of logical explanations for what had happened. Perhaps the child had read about the town of Bodie in a history class, and it was merely a fantasy confused with a memory. Or maybe she wasn't talking about the California ghost town at all but another place with a similar name. She played the tape she had made during the hypnosis over and over, looking for clues. Who was Amy Talbot? Aeron's file had notes about the possibility of multiple personalities. Maybe Amy was one of these. But Amy was the same age as Aeron, so she wasn't a personality that had split off when the child was young. Was she a part of Aeron?

The Breath of Juno

Lee felt completely over her head. She had no experience working with multiple personalities. She felt she should refer Aeron to someone who was an expert in that field. But now that the girl trusted her it seemed wrong to abandon her. She had already been abandoned too many times.

The coldest winter ever—violent winds, freezing temperatures. Tomorrow she would go to the library and look up the history of Bodie to find out when the coldest winter on record was.

Amy Talbot's shivering blue lips haunted her.

· 5 ·

THE SAN BERNARDINO COUNTY LIBRARY was humid. Perspiration beaded up on Lee's back as she read the history of Bodie, California. The town had boomed during the Gold Rush in the 1800's. At its peak there were thirty mines working and over 10,000 people living in this isolated high desert town below the eastern slope of the Sierra Nevada. Prospectors came, often with their young families in tow, to make their fortune in gold. The town was abandoned in the 1920's when the gold ran out. What remained of Bodie had been designated a state historic park in 1962.

The more she read, the more convinced Lee became that this was all crazy. Aeron could never have lived in Bodie, California. She reviewed the notes she had made from the tapes of Aeron's hypnosis session.

First she had thought that Amy Talbot was evidence of a multiple personality. But then, she reasoned, there was a simpler, more logical explanation. Aeron had been called by so many names in all the different foster homes that it was possible she had lived with a family by the name of Talbot early in her life, and they had chosen to call her Amy. The Social Services's file showed no foster family by the name of Talbot, but there were lots of gaps in the her history.

Lee decided to take another tack. She asked the librarian for the microfilm records of the National Weather Service and began scrolling through them, looking for towns whose names sounded reasonably like Bodie and that reported 1979 as the coldest winter on record. Two hours later she had still found nothing. She left the tiny viewing cubicle and went to find the vending machines in the corridor to get a cup of coffee. Leaning against the wall, she drank the weak black liquid, giving the muscles in her back a chance to relax.

The problem, she realized, was that Aeron's dreams and her real memories had melded into one another so that Lee could not distinguish between the two. Perhaps, she thought, what she'd uncovered in the hypnosis were bits of the girl's dreams rather than authentic memories. Somehow she had to figure out how to separate the two. She tossed her empty paper cup into the trash container and went back to the long library table where her notes were laid out.

The hours rolled by without her noticing. She couldn't remember when she had been so excited by her work. She felt like a detective looking for clues, trying to put together the pieces of a puzzle that were just beyond her reach. And always there was a piece missing or lost under the table.

She found a turn of the century map of California in the Geography stacks and looked for the town of Bodie. It was just off of what was now Highway 395, the route that ran north along the east side of the Sierra Nevada. Maybe, she thought, she should take a few days off. A vacation in the mountains would do her good, and a little side trip to Bodie could be arranged.

But this is ridiculous, Lee thought, as she stuffed her papers and books into her briefcase. What am I going to find there? A town that has been dead for almost 100 years? But still, the idea of it drew her. What the hell, she said to herself, as she left the library. It would be fun—I've never been to a ghost town.

EARLY ON THE following Friday morning she drove her red Range Rover east to the junction with Highway 395 and turned north. Five hours later she stopped at the imposing courthouse that was the Mono County seat. Inside she found a massive entrance hall without a single person to fill the space. She wandered around looking for life. Behind a door marked "Records," a young man was sitting with his feet on a desk, reading a paperback. Lee politely asked him if he could look up the records of the *Bodie Standard,* the newspaper that had been printed in Bodie in the 1800's. He jumped to attention, happy to have a task to perform. He guided her to the microfilm reader on the second floor and stood enthusiastically behind her as she loaded the machine.

"Thanks, I can manage by myself," she said, hoping that he would get the hint. Reluctantly, he smiled at her and left.

She began looking at the last issues that of the *Bodie Standard.*

Then it hit her! Under hypnosis, Aeron had said that the year was '79. At the time, Lee had assumed that the child meant 1979. It never crossed her mind that she could have meant 1879!

Lee scrolled back in time to January, 1879. She read the headlines of each paper. When she got to February 18, she read something that stilled the breath in her lungs.

"The coldest winter on record. Bodie's temperature drops to 30 degrees below zero. Winds over 100 miles per hour."

She was stunned by what she was reading. 1879! . . . the coldest winter on record! A person could freeze to death in a matter of moments if left unprotected. Bodie, California. How could Aeron have possibly known these things?

She returned the microfilm to the clerk who was back reading his novel. He tried to strike up a conversation, but she was eager to get going. She got in her car and continued north towards the abandoned town. As she drove, rational explanations ran through her mind. Aeron could have read about this in school. They could have studied it in California history. Perhaps she lived in a town not far away, and the history of Bodie was common knowledge. But all these possibilities couldn't keep the fear away. It settled into Lee's backbone and crept down into her legs and feet as she pressed against the gas pedal and moved closer to this mysterious place.

After eighty miles a road sign announced the turnoff to Bodie. The sign indicated it was east, ten miles off the highway. At first the road was paved, but soon it disintegrated into not much more than a wide dirt path. There were no other cars on the old road. In front of her was nothing but desert, and in the distance the profile of the White Mountains. Behind her were the eastern slopes of the High Sierras.

When she finally reached Bodie, she saw scattered buildings that remained in a state of decay all over the flat desert. She had read that the ghost town was open to visitors and often quite crowded in the summer, but now in late November most of the tourism had fallen off. She parked her car in the visitor's lot which was empty and walked down to what would have been the main street of a booming town one hundred years ago.

The town was amazingly big, and then she remembered that at its height, over 10,000 people had lived here. Many buildings still remained. She peeked inside homes with their rooms carefully roped off so that visitors could not disturb what was left of their furnishings. She explored the Church of Redemption on a small street north of the center of town. When she came out the back into the bright sunlight, she saw a structure she recognized. It was the sawmill that Aeron had described under hypnosis! Could Aeron have lived in one of these houses? The idea was so absurd, she couldn't entertain it for very long. She was an analyst—she had a trained logical mind. And yet, she was filled with the sensation that she was totally outside her realm. She wished that one of the dozens of abandoned saloons was still open so that she could stop in for a drink.

Just beyond the perimeter of the town she found a sign still tacked in the earth that read Masonic Cemetery. Behind it were many remaining headstones and plaques stuck in the earth. She walked among the stones, looking down at the graves that had sat in this abandoned desert for so long, and read some of the inscriptions.

Henry Leonard, Born 1868, Died 1871. Joanna Bell, Born to Lester and Mary Bell, 1873, Died 1885. So many died so young. Children, she thought, they brought children to this place, to this freezing cold hell, and they died here while their fathers looked for gold. It made her angry to think of all these graves filled with wasted lives.

She walked further. A small headstone with worn writing caught her eye. She bent down on her knees to see it more clearly. Dirt obscured the inscription. With her scarf, she cleaned the surface of the stone until she could make it out.

Amy Talbot, Born 1866. Died 1895. She could hardly believe what she was reading. Lee was so shaken that she couldn't move. The numbers ran through her mind. Born 1866. In 1879, she would have been thirteen years old. Amy would have lived here during the coldest winter on record.

Lee couldn't bring her mind to accept what was in front of her. There must be a logical explanation for this, she thought, but she couldn't imagine what it might be.

Sitting in the dry desert dirt, she stared at the stone in front of her. 1895. Amy Talbot had been twenty-nine years old when she died in this Godforsaken place in the middle of nowhere. Who was Amy Talbot? And what did she have to do with Aeron?

Goose bumps raised up on her flesh. How could Aeron know of

this young woman's life over one hundred years ago?

Trying to understand, Lee sat at Amy Talbot's grave for over an hour. There were so many gaps in the record of Aeron's life. Perhaps someone had taken her to visit Bodie, Lee reasoned. The girl had seen the grave of Amy Talbot and remembered it, and now she was fantasizing that she had lived there. It made sense. It was possible. But then how could she know about the coldest winter on record? Could she have read about the abandoned town in a history class? But her sense of that winter had been so vivid, so specific. She had seen it all happening. How could she have known about the houses, the sawmill, the water tower—especially since so much of it was destroyed now.

Lee looked around her at the soaring High Sierras on one side and the White Mountains on the other and thought how the winds must howl through this empty place in the middle of winter. She remembered how frightened Aeron had been when she had said that she was freezing, that the windows had blown out, that all the wood was gone.

How could anyone have survived a winter like that? Lee got up from the cold ground and walked down the dusty streets, peering once again into the abandoned houses. Which one of these had Amy lived in? Or had her house burnt or blown away long ago?

The structures were so flimsy they didn't look like they could keep out the wind, let alone the freezing cold. Lee tried to imagine what it would have been like to live here during the days of the Gold Rush, a real Wild West town.

As she walked back across the high desert to her car, she was haunted by a nagging fear that the mystery was deeper than anything she could understand or was prepared to confront. She was out of her league and she knew it.

What would she say to Aeron at their next session? Should she tell her about the trip to Bodie, about Amy? It would be unfair to hide it from her at this point. And yet, she was still a child. How would Aeron react? The girl had never had any religion or beliefs to hang onto throughout her whole young life. Aeron was proud of the fact that she was an atheist, that she didn't believe in a god. Lee didn't know how she'd respond to this kind of information. She herself had been frightened by the incomprehensibility of it.

The Breath of Juno

When she was off the dirt road and back on the main highway, she heard a horn blaring behind her. In her rearview mirror she saw a huge semi-truck closing in on her, threatening to run her off the road. With its horn still roaring, it swerved to the left to pass her. An oncoming car blocked its path. In the last second the giant truck narrowly squeezed by her. When she could catch her breath, she thought how fragile life was, how easily she could fly off the road and vanish in the desert. Life was far too fragile to exist on more than one plane. It was hard enough holding a being together in one lifetime. What of the conscious mind, the soul, or the spirit could travel from one life to another?

IT WAS A MISTAKE to let Lee Edwards hypnotize her. Aeron paced the tiny bedroom, furious at herself. Now this doctor knew something that she didn't know. Something took place during that session that Dr. Edwards didn't tell her about. All the others had only known she had blackout periods. None of them saw inside her visions. Not until now. Would this woman doctor think she was insane? Would she put her back in a psychiatric hospital where they would give her the drugs that made her forget, made her numb and empty? She remembered it all from when she was nine years old. With smiling faces, grotesque in the glaring fluorescent lights, they had stuck needles in her arms and pills down her throat. They wanted to peel back her skull so that they could look inside her brain for the people who they thought lived within her. If she wasn't careful, they would reach inside and rip out her memory, leaving her an empty shell—flesh and bones covering a hollow darkness. She had to always be on guard to keep them out—never again let any of them know what she saw. It had to be a secret, or they would keep her locked up forever.

They had tested her for paranormal powers too, asking her to move spoons with her thoughts, to predict what cards would turn up next from a deck. She failed all their tests until they finally gave up believing she was psychic. Even if she knew the answers, she would never tell them. And anyway, it was not a thing she could control. It happened in an instant. Walls would dissolve, leaving her in a field of wheat or on a mountain top. The faces of women, men, and children wrinkled and withered or grew young and smooth before her eyes. Maybe it was the future she was seeing or maybe the past. It was impossible to tell the difference.

It was late, almost two in the morning. She sat on the bed with her legs crossed. Dr. Lee Edwards had seen something that lived within her. Aeron had to know what she said under the hypnosis. Where had she been? She climbed under the covers and fought sleep as long as she could.

TUESDAY AFTERNOON AT three o'clock Aeron arrived for her weekly session. I have to sound perfectly normal, she thought, as she walked into Lee's office.

Lee thought the girl, who was dressed in her typical jeans and a tee shirt, seemed more relaxed than usual. She listened patiently as Aeron chatted on about what was going on in school and at home. The hour was half over before Lee decided the girl should know what she had said under hypnosis.

Lee stood, walked to the window, and with her back to Aeron, said, "Aeron, there's something I have to tell you."

"I know."

Lee turned around, surprised. "What do you mean, you know?"

"I can see it in your face. You know something. And you're afraid to tell me." Aeron mimicked the reassuring tone she had heard from so many of her doctors. "Don't be afraid. It's all right."

Lee allowed herself a small laugh. "Wait just one minute. Who is the patient here? Sometimes I don't know. You've turned things around so much I don't know where I'm at with you."

Aeron looked straight at her. To Lee, Aeron didn't seem like a young thirteen year-old girl any more. Her eyes were so deep and penetrating.

"You went to Bodie, didn't you?" Aeron said it simply, as if it didn't surprise her in the least.

"How could you know that?" Lee asked, astonished by the girl's question. "I didn't tell anyone I went. How could you know?"

"Don't look so frightened. You're as white as a ghost." Aeron was surprised to see the power she had over the doctor. "I can't tell you how I know. I just know things. They come to me." She was proud of herself and suddenly wanted to brag, to keep that look of surprise and even awe on the doctor's face.

"You're right, of course. I did go to Bodie. When you first came to my office, you told me that I would have two sons. Did you see that too?"

"I don't know. I just knew it. Maybe I saw it." Aeron began to regret her arrogance. She searched for words to make it all sound matter-of-fact. "It was just a guess. Maybe I see things in my dreams or get a feeling something is going to happen."

"So, you believe that you can predict the future as well as look into the past?"

"No!" Aeron said, all of her bravado gone. "I'm not crazy. I don't have any special gift."

"Then how did you know I went to Bodie?"

Lee no longer looked frightened. She stood, pushing her hands into her pants pockets. She wanted an explanation.

Aeron felt tired, tired of making up explanations. "I saw you driving up a highway and turning off on a dirt road. I saw a sign that said Bodie."

"Was this in a dream?"

Aeron searched for the right answer, the one that sounded the most logical and sane. "No. I don't think so."

"Do you know why I went there?" Lee went over to the couch and sat down next to the girl. "Last week, when I hypnotized you, you told me that your name was Amy Talbot, that you were thirteen years old, and that you lived in a town called Bodie that was freezing cold. I went there to find Amy."

It was Aeron's turn to be shocked. This was different than anything that had ever happened to her before. Amy Talbot. A whole person with a name! She didn't remember any of it. But Lee knew it all.

"You found her, didn't you?" Aeron said trying to sound calm.

"Yes. She died in 1895." Lee studied the girl's face for any reaction.

"Oh," she said, trembling. Then she got up so that Lee couldn't see the fear that was building inside her. She was losing control, letting this doctor, this outsider, know too much.

She turned to confront Lee. "Why did you go there?" she shouted angrily. "You want to lock me up again, don't you!"

"Is that what you think?" Lee put her hand on Aeron's arm expecting the girl to push her away, but she didn't move. "Look at me,

Aeron." She waited for her to lift her eyes. "I promise you that I won't recommend you be sent to a hospital. I went to Bodie because I want to help you. Amy was real. You didn't make her up. You're not crazy. If we work together, maybe we can discover how you know about Amy."

"Why should I trust you?"

"Because you need to trust someone. You've been alone with your secrets for too long. Besides, you're the one who can see the future. You tell me if I can be trusted."

"She's somewhere inside me."

"You mean Amy? Are there others?"

"I don't know."

"Amy lived one hundred years ago. How could you know about her? Could she be someone you dreamed about? Maybe you visited that abandoned town one time and saw the grave. You thought about her, and what it was like to live in Bodie, and then you dreamed about it one night. Do you think that's what it is, Aeron?"

"No." The girl was certain. "The dreams are different."

"You're frightened?" Lee asked gently.

Aeron folded her arms around her chest and lowered her head.

"It's all right to be scared. To be honest with you, Aeron, I was frightened to death when I saw that grave in the desert."

The girl looked up, her eyes wet with tears. "Do you believe in reincarnation?"

"No, I'm a skeptic by nature. I think there is another reason for these experiences you are having. We just haven't figured out what it is yet."

"Maybe it doesn't need to be figured out." Aeron was suddenly defiant.

"And maybe you weren't really hypnotized last week . . . could you be creating this puzzle for me?"

"I guess you could think that."

"If I am asking you to trust me then I guess I'll have to trust you. I'll help you remember what happened to Amy."

"I don't care about Amy. It's my dreams that I need to remember."

"But you *have* been remembering them. Look at this . . . I have reams of pages of your dreams. What does all this mean?" Lee put the notebook on Aeron's lap.

The Breath of Juno

"I don't know. That's your job."

"I'm afraid this is all too complicated for me. Most of the people I see have garden variety problems. You are a whole jungle of possibilities. Maybe I should refer you to somebody who has more experience than me."

"No, I don't want to see anyone else."

"All right. I'll try, but I can't make any promises."

"Are you going to keep seeing me just because I'm a puzzle to you?"

"Well, there is that," Lee smiled. "It's exciting to be a detective instead of a boring office psychiatrist. But Aeron, I really do want to help you."

A good detective, Aeron thought, looking at Lee's notepad. That's what I need—a detective, not a doctor.

• 6 •

It was dangerous to go out into the dark by yourself. Anything could be out there. When Dora warned her about all the terrible things that could happen to a thirteen year old girl who insisted on sneaking out late at night, Aeron ignored her. The terrors that Dora talked about didn't frighten her. As she walked north towards the foothills at two in the morning, she pictured the gruesome scenes Dora described in order to scare her. She could hear Dora's voice in her head as she moved further from the house.

"A stranger could follow you, put a knife to your throat and shove you to the ground. Someone in a passing car could pull out a gun and shoot you for no reason at all. This world is full of crazy people and terrible violence. It's in the papers every day. It happens so often no one even blinks anymore. A man loses his job and kills ten people in a McDonald's. Crazy people come out at night. Even way out here in this little town you've got to keep your doors locked and stay inside at night."

But all Dora's stories could never compare with her own private terrors. It was no longer the dreams that drove her down through the house, out the back door to the empty fields. It was the visions that took over her body during daylight. She had stopped thinking of them as hallucinations and had begun to call them her Shadows, because in some strange way they belonged to her. In the empty field she could think and be alone with the night. There she could remember the Shadows that crept into her body all the time now, ever since she learned of Amy Talbot three weeks ago.

She came to this place to learn how to push the Shadows away before they took root in her mind. There was always a warning before it happened . . . her fingers would become cold, then numb. The sensation would spread throughout her body. Each time when it began she imagined a warm light covering her body, hugging her skin. Then she would slowly breathe in until her lungs thundered against her heart. She saw the air fill her whole body as the light expanded into a weightless bubble that provided her with a second skin . . . a skin they could not break through. And it was working. The hallucinations, as Dr. Edwards still called them, were coming more frequently, but now she could push them away.

When she reached her safe spot in the field, she sat down with the sagebrush on the cracked parched dirt. But before she could begin her night ritual a tingling sensation crept up her spine. Something was watching her, waiting for its moment to attack her. There had been no warning. The hard ground disappeared, and suddenly she found herself sitting on the rickety porch of a rotting cabin. The open field vanished and she was surrounded by tall trees in a dense woods. Rain fell, striking her skin like sharp needles. In the distance two faces took shape in the thin starlight, forming from the white cloud—two identical faces—each a perfect reproduction of the other, hanging in the black sky. Two women with wrinkled faces, gray hair, and dark eyes. They moved towards her, their disembodied faces gliding through the air. Her hands flew to her face and raced over her body. To her amazement she was still herself. The hands were her hands and the skin her own. But something was different. She was no longer a thin girl, but a young woman with a mature body.

They continued to come, calling to her by name, both mouths moving in unison. *Aeron,* they murmured. *Let us in. It's not safe to hide from us. You can't hide from us.*

Aeron jumped to her feet, but she couldn't force her legs to run. This vision could not be controlled or pushed away. For the first time since the Shadows had come to her, she felt that her life was in danger. Death wasn't a stranger in the night, like Dora imagined, but two old women who carried it in their whispered cries.

The faces still called to her, repeating her name until she could feel them breathe their voices into her—through her ears, her skin, her eyes, they came into her and then vanished from her sight. The rain stopped as instantly as it had begun. The clouds grew dark, then evaporated into thin air. The cabin disappeared. She was back in the rocky field.

Fear invaded her sanctuary. Her mind whirled as she ran towards home. The identical faces had not come from the past but from the future. She was a mature young woman in the vision, not a girl! They were out there waiting for her, waiting to hunt her like an animal alone in the woods.

"LOOK AT THESE scores! Lord, I knew she was bright as a whip but even the school says they never seen a child test so high." Dora laid the letter from Aeron's teacher on the kitchen table in front of Bud. It was an unusually warm night in January. The kitchen, with its east-facing windows open, was the coolest place in the house.

The California education system was receiving national attention for its rapid decline in academic standards. Selected schools were running knowledge tests to see just how bad the situation was. The eighth grade students at Aeron's school had been tested right after the beginning of the school year.

"Read it, Bud. It gives me the willies. She's a regular Einstein." Dora cut herself a piece of blackberry cheesecake she had made that morning and sat on the old wooden chair next to Bud. The chair quivered with her weight, threatening to come apart at the joints.

"I'll read it tomorrow. It's too late to talk about this now."

"Here," she said picking up the letter. "I'll read it to you." She read the letter slowly, carefully pronouncing each word as one not used to reading anything out loud:

Dear Mr. and Mrs. Wilkes:

I would like to arrange a meeting with you both at your earliest convenience.

As you know, our test program was not what we would call an IQ evaluation, but an exam to determine the extent of the children's knowledge. Questions were asked in the subjects of geography, history, language, and science.

We were all quite disturbed to discover that over sixty percent of the children could not locate Germany or France on a world map. Many thought World War II took place in the 1800's. On the whole, the results of the test were appalling, which makes your daughter Aeron's scores stand out even more. Her knowledge in each of the subject categories was at or above college level. Her history score

The Breath of Juno

was almost perfect.

In light of these outstanding results, we would like your permission to test Aeron further. At the very least, she should be placed in our program for gifted children.

I'm looking forward to meeting you both. You must be extraordinary parents to have so cultivated the mind of your daughter.

>Sincerely,
>Ms. Julie Arnet, 8th Grade
>McKinley Junior High School

"You didn't tell them that she is just our foster child?"

"They didn't ask." Dora was defensive. She wanted to think of Aeron as her own child, but she knew that no child of hers would be scoring at the college level.

"Well, I'm not going to that school and meet with this Ms. Arnet."

"Oh, Bud. You got to come with me. I'm embarrassed to go alone. It's not like they're gonna give us one of those knowledge tests."

Bud's broad shoulders slumped down in defeat. "What have we gotten ourselves into here. We don't know the first thing about raising a child and this one is no normal child."

Dora looked at her husband of twenty-five years. She knew they were in water over their heads with this girl, but once she set her heart to something, he would never oppose her. Fate had not been kind enough to give her a baby, but whenever she looked into Bud's sweet gray eyes she felt blessed beyond deserving. He was a good man. Making her happy was the most important thing in his life.

"Don't worry. It's good that she's so smart. She won't have to ask us to help her with her homework." She rested her hand on Bud's arm. "I never told you, but the first week in school, she showed me a paper that she wrote for English class. When I asked her who somebody Brontë was, she said, you're so dumb. You don't know anything."

"Such a snotty mouth on her. I hope you told her off but good."

"I told her that from where she sat it probably seemed that way. Bud, it must be hard for her too, living with us. Sometimes I get the strangest feeling that little thirteen year-old girl is older than I am.

You just wait," Dora said, pouring her husband another cup of coffee. "Being smart is good, but it's got nothing to do with love. We are all she's got for parents. She needs us as much as we need her."

"She never listens to us. Didn't you tell her to go to bed? It's 11:30 on a school night and she's still banging on that piano."

"I'll go talk to her."

Dora cut a piece of cheesecake for Aeron. The girl was sitting in the living room at the old upright piano, picking out a melody with one finger. The tune was familiar; it took Dora a few moments to place it. She stood silently in the doorway, listening.

"That's lovely! However did you learn that piece? That's The Moonlight Sonata you're playing."

"It was in some movie I saw on T.V.—I don't think I got it right."

Dora sat on the overstuffed couch across the room from Aeron. She had learned that the girl was more comfortable when there was a distance between them. It had been a mistake to give her so much affection from the very start. It was as if Aeron had an invisible wall around her. When Dora reached through the wall to hold her or even just to touch her arm, the girl became tense. Things were better between them ever since the therapist had told her that Aeron didn't trust displays of affection. To her they were empty demonstrations of caring that could be withdrawn without notice. Lee had suggested that Dora back off a bit and give the child room to breathe. It was working. When she stopped smothering her with love, Aeron relaxed and talked more freely.

"You got a real good ear if you could pick up that melody just from hearing it played once. Just a few more notes and you'll have it. I got some music in the piano bench," she said cautiously. "If you want I'll show you a few chords and things. Maybe give you a lesson tomorrow after school. That piano just sits there. Nobody plays it much any more."

"Can you play?"

"It's been a long time. I haven't played that old thing since my mother died five years ago. I'll give it a try if you want."

Aeron got up from the bench, inviting Dora to sit down. Dora picked a book of Mozart sonatas from the bench and placed it on the stand. Her plump hands hung over the keys, trembling slightly. Then they fell naturally into the piece as if she had been practicing it for weeks. Her body swayed gracefully in time with the melody. She closed her eyes and lifted her head as her fingers danced across the keyboard.

Aeron was delighted. She looked at Dora and saw someone she had not yet met.

"It comes back," Dora said when she finished the piece.

"That was wonderful. Do you really think you could teach me?"

"You pick things up so fast. I'll bet you can learn to play in no time."

Aeron could never tell Dora that the talent wasn't her own, that it came from a Shadow who had taken over her hands in this very room. How could Dora understand that she had played the piano in a time when people gathered in drawing rooms at night to entertain one another.

"Did you take lessons?" Aeron asked Dora.

"My mother taught me when I was about your age. She had an ear just like you. She'd hear a song once and she could play it. She never read music. Got me a teacher so I could learn, then I taught her. It was real nice. We'd play together and sing most nights."

Aeron tried to picture Dora as a young girl sitting with her mother at a piano. The image made her feel lonely and envious. Dora had something she would never have, a mother.

"Sometimes I wonder if my mother is still alive. If she is, would she want to see me? Why doesn't she try to find me?"

This was the first time Aeron had mentioned her mother. Dora didn't know what to say. "Maybe she did try to find you. That file of yours is a mess. I think God himself would have trouble finding you."

"But why did she give me away? I can't remember her or my father—if I had one."

"I can't guess why she gave you away, child, but I bet she had some pretty important reason. I also bet that it broke her heart to do it."

"She didn't have me long enough to really love me."

"Time's got nothing to do with love, child. She most likely loved you before you were born. I don't know what dreams haunt you at night, but I do know that somewhere your mother is dreaming about you."

Aeron looked so sad. Dora wanted to hug her and hold her—to

make up for all the years the girl had lived without a mother, but she held back. Let her come to me when she wants to, she told herself.

"I can't imagine what it would be like to grow up without a real family," Dora said carefully, "without knowing that somebody loved you for who you are no matter what you did, that there was always somebody there for you. It must have been terrifying to grow up so alone. You're a brave girl. I don't know if I could have survived it myself."

Tears came to Aeron's eyes. "You always say that you love me. How can you? You don't even know who I am."

"Oh, child," Dora laughed. "I don't ever expect to understand who you are. I saw the scores on your knowledge test today. You know more about this world at your young age then I ever will. You're as deep as an ocean and I never even learned to swim. But God put you in my care for a reason. You came to me and from that first day I saw the sadness in your heart. They just dropped you on our doorstep like you was a package to be delivered. I figured you'd been dropped too many times. You needed a place to rest your soul. I wanted to be that place. To give you a home. It was easy to love you. I loved you before you even got here."

Aeron walked to the piano bench and put her arms around Dora's neck. Dora hugged her back. And for the moment she felt safe in the cave of this woman's embrace.

WHEN DORA WENT to bed, she found Bud falling asleep. She lay down next to him. Their bodies fell naturally into one another. Her broad back fit against his chest. His arm dropped over her shoulder. She felt his hair softly touch her neck. She waited until he was almost asleep, then sliding her hand over Bud's arm, she whispered, "I called Ms. Arnet and told her we would see her on Friday after you get home from work. Is that all right?"

"Whatever you want." In seconds, he was asleep.

She lay awake, listening for sounds from Aeron's room. For the past two weeks there had been no screams in the middle of the night. She was relieved that the terrifying awakenings had stopped, but she still listened for them every night. Frightening as they had been, the nightmare patterns were predictable. They happened every night between two and three a.m. Then, without reason, they stopped.

The Breath of Juno

Deafening silence now haunted the house. Sometimes she thought she heard the floor boards creak and she knew that Aeron was walking around the bedroom. Dora forced herself to stay in bed and not rush up the stairs to check on the girl. Finally Dora closed her eyes. She told herself that the worst was over, that now they could start becoming a regular family.

AERON'S HEART POUNDED against her breast. Her arms grew long and slender, her flesh was pierced by thousands of sharp feathers. Her powerful wings pulsated as she took flight.

She soared above the clouds, moving effortlessly in the thin air. Riding the warm currents, spiraling upward, breathing in the rich light of the full moon, then diving back to the earth, her wings tucked to her body.

She was no longer an alien presence riding inside the body of the giant creature. She had become a hawk! Its body blended with her body. Its wings, its eyes, its breath were all hers now. She was no longer afraid of being carried away against her will. She was the hawk's will and she went wherever she pleased. The freedom and the power were thrilling.

With each breath she was lifted higher until she could see the curve of the earth bending the horizon. Time lost all meaning. In one moment she soared over towering mountains and the world beneath her was white, covered in a blanket of snow. An eternity of seconds later she swooped down to a meadow that was green and yellow, filled with the scent of wild marigolds, blackberries, and lilac.

As she crested a mountain range she saw the moon dip close to the earth. She hovered, silently waiting for the miraculous vision to appear, the woman that spoke to her always promising that she would find her home. White light came rushing at her from the great globe. It surrounded her, caressing her body, breathing itself into her through her skin. The powerful wings that had carried her through time vanished—human arms replaced them! For an instant she felt she would fall through the sky and crash to the ground, but she discovered she no longer needed the wings to fly. She floated without effort in human form. Her hands moved in slow motion as if undulating with an underwater current.

Beneath, she noticed a river flowing through an ancient forest of oak and cypress trees. She floated down to see it clearly. The river became a line of women dressed in white robes moving silently between the trees. Each woman was carrying a candle despite the full moon. The silence was broken by the gentle sound of humming. A soft chant. The women in white gathered in a clearing and formed a circle. The candles were placed one at a time in the center as the chant grew stronger.

Her body trembled as she saw a baby not more than a few hours old brought to lie among the flickering lights. She descended closer to the circle of women, watching the helpless infant squirming in the center. Then, to her amazement, the women lifted their bowed heads and looked up at her as she came towards them from the sky. Her fear vanished. A feeling of complete peace came to her. The full moon was breathing behind her, pushing her gently down to the earth, to the center of the circle. The chanting filled the night sky. There was wonder and worship in the eyes of the women as they gazed at her. Looking down at herself, she saw why they were in awe. Her body was a globe of white light. But as she approached the earth, she was transformed. Part human, part hawk!

Understanding filled her. She was the wonder and the power of the night, able to see all that lived below her. The hawk woman of the moon had appeared, and it was she herself!

The women were chanting to her. "Blessed goddess. Watch over us. Breathe life into this child. Breathe life into the soil. Bless us with your power."

She placed her hands on the baby's tiny face. A wind swept through the forest. The girl-child stopped crying, stopped breathing. The mother rushed to her side, lifting the baby to her breast. The forest filled with the cries of the women.

WAKING, AERON COULD still hear them calling to her. She clearly saw the last vision of her dream. A mother holding her child, whispering over and over, "She is alive, she is alive."

The fog that usually surrounded her when she woke from a dream was gone. She got out of bed and walked over to the window. The new moon was a thin cup hanging high in the sky, only a few days old. The vivid dream came into her. It was sucked in whole in a single moment. It flooded her senses as it filled her memory. With brilliant clarity, she saw and felt it all. The women she had seen had been there in the forest for as long as she could remember. It was always the same. They had been waiting for her to see them since she was a child.

She opened the window and breathed in the cool night air.

"It's all here," she said out loud. The world that lived inside her was no longer beyond her reach. After haunting her for years, the dream was finally revealed to her. The curtain over her subconscious was lifted. She was as free as the hawk. She was the strange and beautiful spirit of the night, the hawk woman of the moon. The struggle to possess her inner world was over. No longer would she be haunted by the visions of the night. The magic of the spirit belonged to her now and not she to it. She would know its needs and its desires. She would feel its power. It was more than an end.

It was the beginning.

The Breath of Juno

PART II

*Spirit of the whispering moon
Cover the land
Grace me with your power*

• 7 •

1998: Highland, California

SPRING, THE SEASON OF THICKENING smog and dense morning fog, had come to California. Skinny palm trees choked in the polluted air, their fronds hanging limp, brown, and sickly.

It was Saturday morning late in May, 1998. Aeron was alone, walking west towards the outskirts of Highland. The abandoned field where five years ago she had spent so many night hours when she was thirteen, was now home to a processed papers warehouse. Black smoke poured from the cylindrical venting tubes six days of the week, making the air in the foothills of the San Bernardino Mountains taste of soot, dust, and acid chemicals. She covered her mouth and nose with her hand as she passed the plant.

When she needed to escape from the simple comfort of the Wilkes home and the routine of her ordinary life, she walked to the edge of town. There she caught the red bus that wound up the long mountain road to the rural communities that rested on the mountain's crest. During the week it carried workers home after their days in the crowded valley. But on Saturdays there were plenty of empty seats.

Aeron stepped aboard and went to the back. A few more stops and then they began curving up the Rim of the World—the name the highway had been given because it was carved from the side of the mountains. She remembered a rare clear day, years ago, when she could see hundreds of miles from the Rim of the World. But now, in May, once they had reached an elevation of two thousand feet, the valley below was covered in a blanket of smog and smoke. As they climbed, Aeron watched through the rear window as the entire valley disappeared.

Palm trees vanished and were replaced with yucca plants and scrub

The Breath of Juno

brush. The hillside gradually steepened, turning into a fragile mountain composed of enormous boulders towering over the highway. Loose rocks fell onto the road as they passed. The fierce cliff seemed to be eroding before her eyes. What had taken millions of years to form had been twisted, ripped, and bent in the last five years by frequent earthquakes, fires, and floods that ravaged the mountains.

The bus stopped in three towns at the top of the mountain range; Running Springs, Arrowhead, and Big Bear. She got off at her usual stop, the National Forest in Running Springs. From there she could hike miles into the woods and never see another person.

She knew that once, hundreds of years ago, Indian tribes had made these lands their home, living among the rocks and lakes of the high country. Knowing that their footprints were buried somewhere in the same dirt and dust that she walked upon made her feel at home. There was a family here for her, long disappeared. She could sense them watching her whenever she came to their domain, but whoever they had been, they kept themselves hidden from her. She was a visitor on their soil—the soil that they had earned with their blood hundreds of years ago. The soil that they claimed even now, when no trace of them remained.

As she walked the rarely used trail behind the springs, she ached to disappear into an earlier time here, when the sky was perfectly blue and the air was as clean as the sea once was.

She grieved for the people who had disappeared and left no mark upon this land. Everything should leave a trace, she thought, evidence that it existed. Nothing should disappear without leaving a message from the past. It had fascinated her when she had learned that the astronauts who walked on the moon in 1969 left footprints that are still there today. They had not eroded . . . not been blown away by the wind or destroyed by time. They were eternal evidence that men had walked upon the moon's surface and looked down upon the earth from the heavens.

But what evidence did we leave of our lives on this earth? Our buildings, our technology, our paper processing plants? Alone in the mountains, she felt that she was living at the wrong time. That somehow a mistake had been made, and that all the Shadows that visited her were calling her back to another place, another time, where she could find herself and finally feel at peace.

All through high school she had struggled to be ordinary, to be a part of the lives of her classmates even though so very little they did seemed natural or comfortable to her. The girls had their romances, and she had heard the boys bragging about their conquests. But she had felt distant from it all. She hid her virginity like a shameful habit that she could not shake off.

In another month she would be eighteen years old. The exact day of her birth was still unknown, so four years ago Dora Wilkes had picked a day to celebrate. Eighteen and still a virgin. Only Dora would see it as a virtue. She wanted the warmth, the caresses, and the kisses of the young men in her class as much as the other girls did. But when they approached her, her skin turned to ice and she pushed them away. She could not bear to let them invade her privacy.

Too many of the Shadows had invaded and taken over her body. They would keep coming, possessing her mind, living inside her skin. At least their invasion she'd come to know and understand. They were *of* her. But to allow a boy to take her in his arms and possess her was more than she could bear.

And yet she was a woman, full-grown. And in spite of her mind, her body yearned to be touched, to be joined to another.

It was almost three o'clock. She had lost track of time as she wandered in the woods. Soon she would have to find the trail back to the main highway and catch the bus down the mountain so she could get home before dark. How she wished she could continue walking, following the stream until she vanished into these mountains, never to return to the constant charade of her ordinary life.

At the head of the stream was a rock outcropping where the water cascaded down to the deep pools below. Squat manzanita bushes, their peeling purple branches crawling like snakes out of the ground, struck at her skin as she climbed. Once at the top she could see for miles around. Nothing stirred. Not so much as a ground squirrel caught her eye.

How could she demand that the native people who once lived here come back to her? On an impulse she spoke out loud to the empty land.

"I know you're out there. Why don't you come to me? I've looked for you for so long. You're out there . . . watching, waiting. I want you to come to me." Tears came to her eyes as she shouted to the vacant landscape. "Show me how to feel what you feel, to taste what you taste."

Everything was silence.

Just as she was about to climb down off the rock and start home, she thought she saw a slight shift in the light as if the sun had moved behind a cloud. But there were no clouds in the sky. From the corner of her eye she saw something move. Then a shape emerged from behind the rocks.

A young man, bare to the waist, led a white pony. He was perfectly formed in every detail. None of her visions had ever appeared so vividly. He had to be real, a boy from Running Springs, but he was barefoot and wore his black hair long and loose. A loincloth was all that covered his body.

Aeron's hands flew to her face. She checked her own body. Her red hair that she wore short, cropped close to her head, was now hanging in a single braid all the way to her waist. She could feel its weight as it lay against her spine. She reached around and pulled the braid over her left shoulder—the shining hair in her hand was jet black! Her jeans and t-shirt were gone and in their place was a beaded dress made of buckskin. This time instead of fear she felt enormous excitement—they had come. She was ready to give herself back to them.

In a single swift movement, the boy and the pony became one, galloping towards her. When he was just beneath the rock cropping where she stood, he called to her by name.

"White Feather—ride with me." His voice echoed in the mountains, pounding repeatedly in her ears.

She climbed down from the rocks and allowed him to lift her thin body onto the horse's bare back. He slid her into the envelope of his body. Her dress rode up, revealing her long naked thighs—dark-brown and strong. As she held the mane with her hands, the boy touched the pony's flanks with his bare heels and they ran off over the rocks.

The horse thundered beneath her thighs and the boy's hard body pressed against her spine. The three of them were one animal, flying together across ancient land. His arms went around her waist, pulling her closer to him. His hands reached up to cup her breasts.

When they reached a grassy knoll between the rocks, he pulled the horse up with a single tug on its mane and dismounted, bringing her gently down with him.

He lowered her to the damp grass, untied the leather straps that held her dress together, and softly pressed his lips to her breasts. His breath felt hot against her skin . . . his tongue circled her nipples. She grabbed his hair, pulling his face to hers, pressing her mouth to his. He tasted of salt, and she was hungry for him. His kisses moved down her body. Their naked legs twined together. She ran her hands down his back as he gently slid inside her. Their bodies moved in unison. The branches of the trees above her began to spin faster and faster. She felt herself tumbling uncontrollably, falling into nowhere—disappearing.

Then she was alone, lying on the grass next to the stream, her jeans and tee shirt, her short red hair, returned. Her body felt moist and warm—this time it had been so real. She could hardly believe that he was gone, and that glorious moment belonged to someone else and not to her. To know the feel of a man's skin, to have him inside her. Would she ever be able to feel those things again?

She closed her eyes trying to remember the touch, to bring back the moment. All she could feel were her own tears. It had all been a fantasy—all of it was fantasy. She would never possess her own life and live in her own body. She would never feel love unless she was in the hands of a Shadow. She longed for the boy to take her again, to make her feel, to carry her with him to his vanished world and never return her to the body that lived in the valley below.

She knew it could never be. For there would always be the other secret that lived within her. Since that wondrous night five years ago when the dream of the hawk woman came to her full, she had known that something extraordinary lived within her. Silent, cocooned somewhere within her body, she believed that it was slowly transforming itself—growing as she grew. Waiting to be freed. Waiting to give her its power.

But now, with the memory of the boy's touch still on her skin, she resented the hawk's hold on her body. What use was it to her if she couldn't find what she had always wanted?

Her own identity, and love.

· 8 ·

THE LONG LINE OF YOUNG WOMEN dressed in black robes snaked their way up towards the platform. Dora and Bud Wilkes sat proudly in the third row of the auditorium, waiting for their moment. Names were called one by one, in alphabetical order. They had to wait almost to the end for Aeron Wilkes to be announced, and the red-headed girl with shining green eyes and a mortar board cap stepped up to the stage. She accepted the diploma, smiled at Dora, and joined the rest of her classmates.

It was June 14, 1998, a day for a double celebration. The high school graduation had fallen on the same day that they had designated four years ago as Aeron's official birthday.

A mother's pride filled Dora as she watched Aeron take part in the ceremonies. Throughout the girl's high school years, teachers and counselors had pushed Dora to allow Aeron to skip courses and even years since she was so much more advanced than her schoolmates. But they could not break Dora's resolve.

She was convinced that Aeron's exceptional intelligence was only one part of her personality. What she needed more than anything after her scattered background of moving from one foster home to another was to stay in one place with the same group of friends over the critical teenage years of her life. In the long run, Dora had been right. Aeron had made friends in high school, and for the first time she had remained with one family.

Aeron had been chosen valedictorian of her class. And now as she stepped forward to the speaker's platform, Dora trembled in anticipation.

For a moment the girl stood silent before the microphone, center stage. The large audience that had gathered at Highland High School to watch the summer graduation rustled nervously, waiting for her to speak. She could see inside their collective thoughts . . . they were worried that she had forgotten her speech. She wanted to speak, to release them from their worry, but there was something intoxicating in the absolute attention they gave her. Finally, she broke the silence.

"When we walk out of this room today, the members of this class of 1998 will become the caretakers for the beginning of the next millennium." With confidence and self-possession, her voice filled the large auditorium. She looked out at the faces in the audience and saw that they were mesmerized by her, more by her compelling voice than by the words themselves.

"The challenge that my fellow students and I will face is deciding in what kind of a world we want to live.

"What legacy shall we leave on this earth? We march into the future bravely, as though we are an army taking a field. Are we forgetting what happens to that field when we leave it? The members of this graduating class cannot do many of the things their parents and grandparents took for granted.

"None of us can drink fresh water from a mountain stream. None of us can lie on a beach in the afternoon without thinking of cancer. None of us can travel by air without worrying about radiation from the sun. What have we done to our home? Will all our progress smother us until this small planet is no longer able to breathe under its own weight? Have you taken us down a path with no return, robbing us of our future?"

The audience nodded as she spoke, their heads bobbing up and down like dolls with spring necks. They were toys, little puppets that she could move with her will.

The power was overwhelming as she realized she could bend their minds with her voice. She had expected to be frightened by their attention, instead she was enthralled by the control she felt. She looked into their eyes and she knew that whatever she said, they would listen and believe.

All through high school she had worked to be one of the group, to not stand out from everyone else. She had learned to hide herself from her classmates and even her teachers by saying what she was expected to say and by pretending that she understood much less than she did.

Now that her moment in the spotlight had come, the voice within her refused to hide. What began as a simple graduation speech broke free into a passion that had throbbed inside her for as long as she could remember.

As the words flooded from her, she smelled the damp earth at night. That and her dreams were her only unbroken memories from childhood. She had belonged to no one, especially not to Dora's God. She belonged only to the smell of the earth, the light of the moon, and to the spirit within her now waking from hibernation. Pulling the audience into her vision, she enchanted them with the music of her voice.

For years she had pushed away the Shadows, the visions that haunted her, but in this moment she had become the one who could push her vision into their lives. The power burned within her. If she allowed it out she could make the faces that sat so reverently age, wither, and turn to dust before her eyes.

The walls of the auditorium disappeared, and she was speaking to a multitude in an ancient marketplace. Women who carried their wares in wicker baskets dropped to their knees. Men in short white tunics stopped bartering and fell silent. Children gathered at her feet. She opened her arms and as they spread out, her limbs became wings broad enough to cover them all. They were like fragile shells beneath her mighty wings. She could crush them with a single move, or she could be merciful and grant them grace.

Reluctantly she pushed away the vision, releasing them, giving them back their will.

The moment passed so swiftly—it was no more than a brief pause in her speech. The auditorium returned and the ordinary faces of hundreds of proud parents smiled at her as she finished speaking.

"We, the class of 1998, promise that we will walk more softly on the skin of this fragile earth."

Applause thundered through the auditorium.

After the formal ceremony, the room was a chaos of hugging and congratulating. Aeron worked her way through the crowd of friends and teachers who were complimenting her speech. She found Dora and Bud still in their chairs. Wet tissues lay all over Dora's lap. Bud put his arm behind the woman and patted her back. When Dora saw Aeron break through the swarm of people and move towards her, she pulled her body from the seat.

"Don't cry, Dora—this is supposed to be a happy time," Aeron said, wishing that just this once she could bring herself to call Dora 'Mother.' It would give her so much pleasure. Over the last four years Aeron had grown to care for this kind woman, this woman who had loved her even when she was bitter, angry, and cruel. Still she couldn't give her the one word that she knew belonged to someone else, 'Mother.'

"I'm only crying because I'm so happy. Oh, child! Listening to you speak up there in front of all these people was better than listening to the best choir on earth. You filled this place with divine music. Sometimes I think you must be an angel that God put in my keeping. He knew that I would keep you safe."

The Wilkes family joined the party on the front lawn of the school. A giant cake sat in the center of a long table. The blue and gold icing was beginning to melt in the summer heat, but the words could still be read: *Congratulations to the Class of 1998.* The young men and women were already leaving to celebrate at their own parties. A small group of Aeron's friends were begging her to hurry and come with them.

"Go along now, child. This is your night to celebrate with all the young people. You don't have to stay with us any longer."

Aeron was reluctant to leave. It would be one of their last times together for many months. Tomorrow afternoon Dora and Bud were driving her to the Los Angeles airport where she would board Global Airways. Eight hours later she would be in Paris. Her French teacher had put in the scholarship application to the School of International Living at the beginning of her senior year. The teacher had been astonished at how quickly Aeron mastered the language . . . she could speak French like a native before the first semester was over. Reading and writing came more slowly and her accent was unusual, still the fluency was amazing. A full scholarship had been awarded for the summer following her graduation.

"Aren't we forgetting something here?" Bud said as Aeron removed the black gown, revealing the slinky red dress with the low neckline that she had cajoled Dora into buying for her.

"Oh Lord, yes we are." Dora reached into her worn gray purse and found a small box she had wrapped for Aeron. "I know we said we would celebrate your birthday tomorrow, but I want you to have this for tonight."

Aeron opened the box. Inside was a gold hawk charm on a tiny necklace. It had green jade eyes . . . its wings were spread wide in flight. "Oh, Dora this is beautiful."

"It's a double present, for your birthday and for graduation. You always talked about that hawk in your dreams. I think maybe she's watching over you. Sort of like your own private guardian."

Aeron remembered that when she first came to the Wilkes home she had thought of Dora as a goose too heavy to migrate with the flock. Maybe it wasn't a cruel way to see her at all. Native people had looked for kin in the animal world, selecting totems to guide them and help them find their identity. The hawk was her totem. Perhaps the goose belonged to Dora.

Aeron turned to the quiet man standing with his arm around Dora's shoulders. She knew that Bud Wilkes had grown fond of her in spite of all the trouble she had caused with her strange ways and her terrifying dreams.

"Will you put this around my neck?" she asked him.

· 9 ·

TWO DAYS LATER AERON WAS LIVING AT a pension for students on the Rue d'Arcole on the Left Bank. She was in Paris, totally on her own for the first time in her life. She would be attending college-level classes taught in French three days a week at the International School. Jet lag had played with Aeron's internal time clock. After twelve hours of sound sleep, she woke to discover that the dawn was only just breaking. Aeron dressed quietly and tiptoed out of the room so as not to wake her roommate.

The city was almost empty at this hour. She wandered down the narrow road, taking in everything. The new day's first glow crawled down the grand walls of Notre Dame. This was the City of Light, so far from Highland, California. She wanted to see it all! A few early risers began to venture into the streets. A woman with four inch platform shoes, a tight leather skirt, and fading make-up was heading home. A painter was setting up her easel to catch the morning light.

Aeron crossed the road to walk along the banks of the Seine. As she approached the river that split the city in two, she noticed a gradual change in the light. Instead of becoming brighter as the dawn turned to morning, the sky seemed to darken. Down the bank a vendor was hauling in produce for his stall. As Aeron approached him she thought he looked strangely out of place. His baggy, torn pants looked rough as if they were made of old burlap. His face was that of a young man, but there were large dark circles that looked like the marks people called liver spots on old people. The handwoven basket he carried was full of rotten, wormy apples.

Repulsed by the moldy fruit, chilled by the sickly young man, she turned to walk away. Coming towards her in the other direction were two children holding hands, a boy of about eight and a girl not more than four. They were dressed much in the same manner as the man had been. The girl child wore a long dirty skirt made of a rough linen. The boy wore tattered pants. Both children were barefoot. Their faces were marked with black spots similar to those of the vendor.

Who are these people, she thought. Then the familiar sensation returned, the cold and then the numbness in her fingers that had come to her so many times in her life. Then she knew—she had been here before. She had walked this street at some other time in some other body.

She looked down at her own body to discover that she also was barefoot . . . dressed in a heavy long skirt and torn white blouse. Her hands were wrinkled and swollen . . . the knuckles puffy and stiff. She walked to the river's edge to look at her reflection. Her eyes were a soft brown, her hair a dusty gray; the face of a woman beaten by time and hardship stared back at her. It was a face she had never seen before, yet she knew it was her own. This woman looking at her from the murky water was a Shadow that lived within her, a Shadow who had once lived with bones, flesh, and breath. A woman who had walked upon this earth at a time when people's bodies turned black with the pox and the fruit was full of worms.

Across the river she could see Notre Dame. The steps that had been empty just a few moments before were now covered with people—destitute, starving people. A priest swinging a container with incense walked between the beggars. Children and old women grabbed for the hem of his long black robes, pleading for help.

"Alms for the poor."

"Please, Father. Have you no mercy?"

She saw the priest make the sign of the cross, not for the benefit of the beggars at his feet, but for his own protection. Then he pushed the ragged people away and hurried up to disappear behind the grand doors of the cathedral.

She knew without thinking that the year was 1326. Her name was Jean-Marie. She was a fifty-two year-old widow who had never born a child. The black plague had ravaged her beautiful city of Paris for over thirty years. She had survived while thousands had died around her.

Jean-Marie crossed the bridge over the Seine to the steps of Notre Dame as she did every Sunday morning. She carried a basket of stale bread and moldy cheese. When the child and old woman pulled at the bottom of her skirt, she opened the basket and offered them food.

They took it hungrily and stuffed it into their gaping mouths. The women on the steps took her offerings, turning their eyes away from hers. They were ashamed.

Before the plague had invaded their city, they had laughed at Jean-Marie right to her face when she told them what was coming. She had said a dark time would come when a black cloud would cover the city. She had stood on the steps of Notre Dame warning the people to go home and wash the floors and walls of their homes; to scrub the streets; to keep the disease from sneaking in through back alleys until it penetrated the very heart of their city. They had laughed at her, ignoring her crazy words.

She was a weird one, always making predictions, telling even strangers what would come to pass in the years ahead. When her predictions came true they called her a witch, a daughter of the devil who had no right to speak to them on the steps of God's own cathedral.

She had washed and cleaned her own home daily, making it inhospitable for the rats and mice that roamed the streets. In spite of all her precautions, her husband had fallen under the curse of the plague and died in agony in 1321. She had called upon all the spirits that she knew to spare her husband the terrible suffering, but she didn't have the power to change his fate.

When he died in her arms, she wished herself dead as well. She couldn't imagine her life without him. She had fed him, cleaned him and held him, yet she did not develop the illness herself. She was immune to the disease that ravaged everyone around, and for that the women on the steps of Notre Dame hated her even more. They took her bread and cheese, then turned their eyes in shame and envy.

Jean-Marie entered the cathedral, walking to a small nave behind the pulpit. There was a peaceful statue of the Virgin Mary, her right arm reaching down, her palm formed in a graceful cup. Jean-Marie sat at her feet and look directly up into her eyes.

"Our Lady," she said. "I've come to ask you to spare the people of Paris. Give them peace and escape from this plague that haunts them. Lift this illness from our earth. We are sick and dying. I ask for your help, good lady. Please protect us. Make your land well again."

From her basket she took a single feather, striated in black, gray, and white—the long tapered wing feather of a hawk. She reverently placed it in the outstretched hand of the statue.

"I BEG OF YOU, Notre Dame, sweet Juno, do not abandon us now."

The moonlight filtered through the lacy curtains, waking Aeron. She lay in her soft bed in the pension. It was the middle of the night, and she had no memory of how she had gotten there. The clock next to the bed told her it was two in the morning. Her roommate was asleep in the bed across the room. How long had she been gone?

When the Shadows came they could take her away for days, but when she returned to her own body and looked at the time, she always discovered she had been gone for only a few hours. She pulled off the light feather comforter and looked down at her body covered in a white cotton nightgown. When she put her hands before her eyes she saw that they were soft and young, the hands of an eighteen year-old girl.

She went to the window and looked out at the moon. When the Shadows came into her, she had learned to accept them. Not to fight them when they took possession of her mind and her body. They were part of her—her memories and her friends. She hadn't been afraid of them for many years. Yet when it was over and she came back to the present, she felt confused, incomplete, as if pieces of herself remained in another world. She had to pull them all back, one at a time, to collect herself as a whole being once again. The Shadows came to her in pieces. Rarely did she remember so much as tonight. Jean-Marie she had seen whole—an entire life had come into her memory.

Aeron grieved for Jean-Marie's sad spirit. She was a barren woman who wanted more than anything to have a child. She lived until she was seventy-three years old, outliving all her family and friends by more than two decades. A strong woman, she had fought the plague throughout Paris. Her weapons were her prayers, her gifts of food, her nursing, and her kind words. When she died, the church arranged for her to be buried in the cemetery behind Notre Dame.

Aeron could see the stone that marked the grave in her mind. *Jean-Marie Gallisone, Born 1273, Died 1346.* Even as Aeron saw the stone in her mind, she knew that the marker no longer existed. The gravesite had long ago disappeared.

There was something important to remember from this Shadow.

Something she had to bring back with her into this life. She tried to picture Jean-Marie praying at the foot of the statue of the Virgin Mary. She listened to hear Jean-Marie's exact words. Slowly they came back to her. "Lift this illness from our earth. We are sick and dying. I ask for your help, Notre Dame."

Notre Dame. Of course, Aeron realized, Our Lady. But there was more. She had said something else.

"Sweet Juno, do not abandon us now."

Juno! Jean-Marie had called the Virgin Mary by the name Juno. Aeron returned to her bed and slipped under the quilt. She sipped the wine that she had left sitting on her bed table. She knew who Juno was—she had learned about her in philosophy class. She was a goddess worshipped by the Romans, the wife of Jupiter, the protector of women and the fertility of the earth. Why had Jean-Marie called the Virgin Mary by that name . . . Juno?

Aeron was beginning to feel the old torment when questions she couldn't answer pushed against her. For so many years now she had felt that she was in control. She had made peace with her dreams and also with the Shadows. Whenever a Shadow wanted to come into her, she could feel it moving towards her and, if she chose, she could deny it access to her body. She could stop them at the gate of her mind, refusing to let them enter her body. Throughout high school she had pushed the Shadows away. She didn't want to make room for them in her life. When the Shadows came to look for her, she could sense their coming; she could taste them, touch them, and feel them before they were all the way inside and she would tell them no. I will not let you enter, she told them, and they obeyed, leaving her alone, staying dormant inside her.

But Jean-Marie had forced her way inside Aeron's mind this morning on the streets of Paris. She would not be stopped. It was as if she wanted Aeron to see this city as it had been almost seven hundred years ago. Was the power to push away the Shadows disappearing? Would she be haunted all summer by lives coming into her without her consent? She tried to sleep, to let the experience with Jean-Marie be forgotten for the night.

For the first time in many years she began to feel the old fear. The fear she had known as a child when the dreams came to her unexplained in the middle of the night, waking her with her own screams.

The Breath of Juno

The fear that Shadows might start to come into her from places all over Europe. Shadows that could find her now. She wondered how many memories lived within her. She had known only those who had lived in America—lived and died in the last three hundred years. How far did they go back? Were some even more ancient than Jean-Marie?

Lying on her back, hands clasped over her chest, she stared up at the gray ceiling. If they pressed to come inside her, how could she stop them? Should she try to stop them? Maybe they were there for a purpose. They could have secrets to share with her, now that she was an adult and old enough to listen to their mysteries.

Let them come to me, she thought, spreading her arms across the bed like the wings of a bird. Silently she formed the words.

Take my body if you must. I won't fight you any more. But I want something in return. I want to know who I am. How can I know so much about Jean-Marie's life and so little about my own past? What good is this unnatural vision if I can't see myself?

Her vision blurred for a moment, then the ceiling dissolved, allowing her to look directly into the black night. Fear circled her spine, squeezing like a snake constricting its prey.

Someone was watching her! Listening to her thoughts.

Was it them! The disembodied faces with mouths that spoke in unison to her?

She had first seen them in the empty fields that lay in the shadow of the San Bernardino Mountains. They had glided towards her, forming from the clouds. Two faces, identical in every aspect. Since that night they had appeared to her only three more times. Each time they had whispered her name, then begged her to let them in. Whenever she got the uncomfortable feeling that she was being watched by some unseen presence, she thought of the twin faces glaring so intensely at her.

Could they hear her now?

What terrible mistake had she made? Had she called them up and invited them to invade her body?

But the twin sets of dark eyes did not appear. The gray ceiling returned. Still the fear danced around her spine. She could not shake the sense that someone was watching her. Someone who had been searching for her all her life.

Who is looking for me? *Mother.*

She softly whispered the word she never had permission to speak: Mother. Is it you searching for me?

Turning on her side, she curled up into a ball, knees tucked to her chest, arms hugging her legs.

Please find me, she whispered. I'm waiting for you.

She closed her eyes and tried to bring back a single memory of her mother, one image of what her mother might look like. Nothing came to her.

Just as she was falling asleep, somewhere inside her head she could faintly hear the sound of her mother laughing . . . .

· 10 ·

THE GIRL WAS ALIVE! HE COULD FEEL HER POWER calling out into the night. There was no doubt. She was the one. After all the years of waiting, soon he would find her and it would all be over.

Father DeCarlo looked out at the calm sea from his private quarters on the third floor of the monastery. He wanted to call in a wind from the west to churn up the water, so that its agitated state could match his own excitement. It pleased him when nature reflected his own emotions, when the rain, wind, and heat seemed to wait upon his moods.

It was dawn on June 22, the morning after the Summer Solstice. The priest removed his long white night shirt and stood naked before the open window. The moist air caressed his thin withered body. He did not think it a sin to take pride in his body, even now at over eighty years old. These moments, when he was free and unadorned, were a great source of pleasure to him.

He gently touched his perfectly smooth chest. Not a hair was allowed to grow on his sacred flesh. If his hand found even one blond hair, he took a tweezers and plucked it from his skin. He had to be clean and pure—of God and not of animal. Men with hair on their faces, their chests, their backs disgusted him. They were no more than beasts who couldn't cleanse themselves properly. He had to prepare himself well, for this was a great day.

THE VILLAGERS CALLED the monastery that sat like a castle on the far north end of the island The White Fortress. From the sea it appeared to glow when the afternoon sun struck it with harsh unforgiving light. The White Fortress had stood facing the blue of the Mediterranean for almost two hundred years.

Except for the inhabitants of the fortress, the sparse population of Isola di Pantella lived on the south side and rarely ventured to the private lands surrounding the stark white buildings. Most of the villagers had lived on the small island since their birth . . . fishing and farming much as their ancestors had for hundreds of years. Only twenty miles wide through its middle, the island was an isolated world sitting halfway between Sicily and Tunisia. Rome lay four hundred miles north over the sea, however few of the natives of Isola di Pantella had ever been to Sicily, let alone the grand city of Rome.

Even the north side of their island was foreign to them. They knew the fortress was a monastery that housed a remote and ancient brotherhood of monks who had broken from the Church of Rome. The doors to the main entrance stood twenty-two feet high and were made of hand-carved wood. No one on the island could recall when they had last seen those massive doors open. Occasionally children stole up to the empty hills so that they could spy on the monks in black robes as they worshipped on the grassy slopes that faced the sea. As if by some unspoken law, even the children soon learned that they were not to disturb the monks or talk about them in public. Safe under their covers late at night, the children whispered to one another about the things they had seen, strange things that were at once both frightening and exciting. If they repeated any of what they saw to their parents, they were scolded and told never to go to the north side of the island again.

The adults tried to put the fear of God into their children to keep them away from the monastery. "They may look like ordinary monks, but they are powerful men who will pull you inside their White Fortress and never let you go, if they find out you have been watching their secret rites." But their threats only served to inflame the curiosity of the young.

RELUCTANTLY FATHER DECARLO came away from the window and began putting on the clothes that he had carefully laid out for himself. The first layer was a silk undergarment, a tunic that covered him from his neck to his ankles. He slipped it over his head, letting it slide down his body. The cool feel of silk next to his skin gave him a tingling sensation that he enjoyed. Next came the gown of white linen, still a soft fabric but with weight to it. It hung loosely around his body until he gathered it together with the polished silver belt he fastened about his slim waist.

He had a collection of outer garments to choose from—robes of different colors and weights. Today he put his arms into a red velvet robe. A black cape went over his shoulders, and then the chain he always wore was placed around his neck.

The pendant that hung from it was a pyramid with a single eye in the center—the ancient mark of the Brotherhood of Sidon, the sign of the true prophet. It pleased him to know that the All Seeing Eye had become a symbol used by civilizations throughout time. So many religions and nations revered the power of the third eye. The mark of the Sidon was everywhere. Even now it appeared on the currency in America without anyone knowing its rightful origin.

Once dressed, Father DeCarlo was ready to go and speak with his monks. His monastery could not have been further from the bosom of the Catholic Church. They told him that the prophecies of the Sidon were opposed to the teachings of the Catholic Church, the one true religion. When the church declared the monastery a dangerous pagan cult and instructed Father DeCarlo to abandon the rituals and beliefs of the Sidon, he ignored them, holding his monks to him with his own power. The church scorned him, excommunicating him and his followers.

Yet Father DeCarlo had always felt himself a devout Catholic. Now he knelt before the altar in his own church, making the sign of the cross.

"Lord," he prayed, "you have brought us all to a time of enlightenment. Help me deny this spirit that will take us back to chaos and darkness."

He believed with all his heart that the Son of God had brought eternal life. But he also believed the words of the Sidon, and that almost 2,000 years ago the women who worshipped the Roman deity, Juno, had persuaded their goddess to breathe her power into the body of an infant, a girl-child, making herself immortal in human form.

The prophecy the Sidon had written so long ago predicted that this spirit would be reborn one hundred times, moving from one home to another. In each lifetime the spirit would mature, until in its final mortal life it would have immense power.

But now it would all come to an end.

The girl who now carried the Breath of Juno had revealed herself! She was alive. And close.

For years he had prepared his monks for this moment—instructing them on the difficult task before them. He had to be sure of them. They could not lose their courage or be taken in by the girl's power. Years ago, selected monks had been told to dress as secular men and go to Rome where they were taught by experts to handle the weapons they would need if they were to succeed. But now that the time was upon them, they would need more than weapons— they would need all of their resolve and their faith in the words of the Sidon.

The priest walked down the spiral staircase to the chapel where his followers were waiting patiently for him. This morning he would pick those who would search with him, but all of them had to understand the gravity of the message he had seen in the shadow of the bones. He walked among his monks who bowed their heads as he passed and took his seat at the front of the chapel.

"Brothers, many mornings I have spoken to you of the danger that lies still dormant inside this girl. But now you must come to both feel her power and understand it." He spread his arms to them as if he could encircle them with his wisdom.

"If we are to be the instrument that denies this ancient prophecy, we must know in our hearts that what we do is right.

"The power she carries is a disease . . . a virus that will infect millions of people . . . everyone on earth, if it isn't stopped. She will spread it first into the unconscious of unsuspecting minds, then it will break through to consciousness. People will lose their sense of reason and behave like primitive animals who live only by their base instincts.

"The Prophecy tells us that if the power is alive in the body of a mature woman in the year 2000, the end of the second millennium, it will reclaim the earth for the powers of nature. The age of man will be at an end.

"The women who worship Juno are waiting for the millennium, for this spirit to bring what they believe to be a natural order back to the earth. They think that mankind has lost its way and can no longer survive without the power of Juno.

"To understand what the women of Juno believe you must watch the ants that make hills in the grass. They are working together by instinct, not intelligence . . . working for the good of the species. That's what this power is!

The Breath of Juno

"We are talking about an entire evolution of the human species. Those of us who refuse to behave like animals will become incapable of adapting in this new world. In time we will become obsolete. We will all be tossed back into the dark ages. A time of chaos and godlessness."

His voice rose with his passion until it thundered against their ears. "It is our destiny to possess this earth, our God-given mission. We have come so far since we lived in caves like animals, and we continue to progress, to earn our birthright. Soon we will be as gods, able to control all of our domain. The future shall be ours, for we are more powerful than this spirit that cowers within the body of a fragile female. But when we do battle with this entity, remember it is a mindless force, a primitive thing."

He grasped the pendant that lay over his heart. "We have our intellect and the eye of eternal knowledge—our power is greater than hers!"

Father DeCarlo looked at the faces he had filled with terror as he spoke his words. They would serve him well.

• 11 •

THROUGHOUT THE SUMMER THE Shadows demanded that they be allowed to invade Aeron's body, until she begged them to leave her in peace. Still they came, at first from London, Rome, Krakow, Athens. She recognized the cities as she walked through them in another time, in another body. Then from farther away—Constantinople, Kyoto, Macau. They came across the miles and across time to give her their lives, to tell her their stories. After each visit she would wake in the middle of the night in her pension, and she would remember it all.

They crowded into her mind, each finding a corner, a small crevice, where they could settle in and make a home. Each Shadow's visit left her feeling more alone and frightened. She was terrified that she would never own her body again. The freedom that she had experienced when she first arrived in Paris was gone. When she woke in the black of night, she felt she was a vessel created to hold the spirits of dead women. Once they were gone, she was hollow. They had eaten the marrow of her bones and the retinas behind her eyes.

And always she felt that someone or something other than the Shadows was watching her—able to hear her thoughts, but still unable to find her body. The sensation grew stronger every day as it came closer. She had to get away—but where could she run when she didn't know what she was running from. A dangerous power was hovering just beyond her view. It wanted her and her Shadows. It wanted her very life!

There was only one person she knew who could understand what was happening to her—who might be able to help her. She had to leave Paris now before it was too late. She had to go back home to San Bernardino to see Lee Edwards, the psychiatrist who had first helped her discover the Shadows.

* * *

The Breath of Juno

AERON SAT IN LEE'S comfortable study, talking aimlessly about her summer. They had developed a strong attachment over the years even though Aeron no longer was Lee's patient. But Aeron could not bring herself to explain the real reason for her visit. How could she ask for the help of this woman who analyzed everything, who never trusted her own instincts, who always looked for absolute answers? How could she tell Lee about Jean-Marie and the identical floating faces that haunted her?

How could she explain that she had come to believe that the faces belong to living women—two identical women who were watching her, who knew things about her early life she didn't know herself. There was no time for hypnosis or therapy now. She wanted help from Lee, not counseling or advice. If these women intended to harm her, she had to find them before they found her.

Could she trust Lee? Discovering Amy Talbot in the cemetery in Bodie had been too much for Lee's practical mind. She had tried to find a rational explanation, but Aeron knew that the mystery still haunted Lee. If she told her about the Shadows that visited in Paris and about the twin faces, Aeron was afraid Lee might think she had gone mad.

Lee interrupted her thoughts.

"Aeron," Lee leaned forward and took her hand, "you didn't come here to tell me about the sights of Paris. I remember the terror in your eyes when I first hypnotized you five years ago. It's back, isn't it?"

Aeron began to cry with relief. Yes. She would tell everything to this practical woman who lived with both feet in this world. The pain of holding her secrets alone had become too great—there was no one else who could listen to her bizarre tale. If she was going to disappear into the Shadows or be abducted by two old women, at least she wanted a friend in this world to know where she had gone. They talked into the night. Once she started, Aeron couldn't stop. The memories came flooding out, drowning them both in a bottomless voyage.

Lee didn't believe or deny. She just listened.

When Aeron finished, Lee asked the question Aeron had been hoping to hear. "You want me to help you find these twins?"

"You found Amy Talbot," Aeron implored her.

"This is a bit more difficult. I have no idea where to begin."

"I think they want me to find them. At first all I saw was their faces calling to me," she shivered with the memory of the eerie floating faces. "Then they started showing me more."

Aeron hesitated, afraid to go on.

"Lee, I know where they were born. I saw it! It was terrible."

"Was this a vision you saw or a dream?" Lee gently put her hands on Aeron's shoulders to calm the girl.

"I was there . . . in the hospital room. It happened to me the night before I left Paris. I was in my pension looking out the window. When I turned around I found myself standing in the corner of an operating room, watching."

Aeron dropped her head.

"They were born connected," she whispered as if she was terrified the twins themselves could hear.

"Siamese twins?"

"Yes. First one head pushed out, then beneath the head, coiled around the fragile neck were two tiny feet. They slid out together, two babies, lying head to toe, joined at the middle. All tangled and welded flesh. I saw it clearly; then I was back in my bedroom again as if nothing happened."

"Do you remember why you were in the hospital? Are you a doctor or a nurse in this vision?"

"It's not a vision," Aeron insisted. "I was myself! The nurse's name tag read 'Rockfalls Memorial Hospital.' That's where they were born. I know it!"

"So you think these babies are the gray-haired women that haunt you. That would mean that they would have been born sixty or more years ago."

Aeron's heart leapt. Whether Lee believed her or if she was just intrigued by the mystery didn't matter. Lee was going to help!

THREE DAYS LATER Lee took Aeron to the main branch of the San Bernardino Library.

"There are five small towns named Rockfalls in the United States. I think you will be most interested in the one in southern Illinois," she told Aeron with the excitement of a detective that has just discovered a solid clue. "I think I found your twins."

The Breath of Juno

She pulled up the microfilm from Illinois' *Rockfalls Gazette*.

"April 15th, 1934. Siamese Twins Born Head to Toe"

The dramatic birth was headline news featuring graphic photographs of the tiny babies. Rockfalls wasn't just a dot on the state map. It had a respectable population of 25,000; yet according to the Gazette, none of them had been born connected to a sibling in anyone's memory.

"It's just like I saw it!"

"Their names are Mattie and Nellie Sheppard," Lee told her.

Names! Aeron could hardly comprehend that her apparitions had names.

"According to these news stories the whole town must have been hungry for news of their fate."

Lee showed Aeron the many articles written about the twins. Each story speculated about the meaning of the unnatural birth. But the reports had a dark, menacing undertone.

It was 1934. These babies with their twisted abnormal bodies had become a symbol of a world abandoned by an angry god. The articles spoke of fear as a pollen carried by winds across the country. People breathed it deep into their lungs, then retreated to their homes, hiding from a world at the brink of despair. A leader, they heard, was coming into power across the ocean in Germany—a leader that many dreaded would seek to rule the world. Some believed he was born of the devil—the anti-Christ who would leave the bodies of millions in his path as he marched towards power.

Their future was dark. Without savings, without jobs, without hope, the articles revealed that people were looking for someone to blame. They were looking for omens to help them understand why their comfortable lives, full of promise, had disappeared. They looked, in the same way people had looked for centuries, for signs to help them understand how they had offended powers beyond their knowing.

The townspeople of Rockfalls, Illinois didn't have to look far. The deformed female twins became their scapegoat.

Three months after the birth there was a story about the operation performed to separate the infant's bodies. No one expected the

Siamese twins to survive, so when the doctors emerged after a six-hour surgery and announced to the waiting press that the operation was a success, people were shocked. It had been easier than they had expected, the physicians explained. The babies shared no organs and only one major artery. The severing had been accomplished. Both infants would thrive.

An editorial told how guilt had haunted people's homes as they waited for news of the operation. Deep in an ancient part of their minds, the article read, many people believed that if the offensive babies died, their death would expunge the world of the dark cloud that hung like a permanent night in the sky.

After the separation of the twins, the stories became even more threatening and bizarre. The infants, they claimed, were born of a sorceress, a witch, who was rumored to have midnight rituals under a full moon. She and her twisted offspring were evil. They belonged to a secret society that worshipped a pagan goddess. There was a single reference to the ancient deity they venerated—Juno, a goddess worshipped by the Romans.

Aeron was stunned. "Jean-Marie, the Shadow in Paris who took me to Notre Dame, she called the Virgin Mary, Juno! How are these Siamese twins connected to Jean-Marie? She lived over seven hundred years ago."

Lee searched her mind for a rational explanation.

"For some reason it seems you may have developed a telepathic communication with these twins. Maybe you are getting these visions from their minds. This Jean-Marie could be part of a mythical legend that the twins believe to be real."

"No, Jean-Marie *is* real! She lived and died in Paris during the Black Plague. I didn't make her up and neither did they. I must find these twins."

"I've already tried," Lee said with disappointment. "I searched all the information directories in the area. I called churches, banks, newspapers . . . everything. There are no traces of the Sheppard family left in Rockfalls, Illinois. It is as if the mother and the daughters just vanished sometime in the early 1970's."

"They haven't vanished! They are out there somewhere watching me! Why are they watching me?" She grabbed Lee's arm. "If we can't find them then you have to help me find my mother."

Aeron began to cry. "She is the only one who can help me understand all of this. I feel her out there! I was right when I knew the twin faces belonged to living people. My mother is living too.

"She's alive," Aeron whispered, almost to herself. "She's waiting for me to find her."

• 12 •

1972: RockFalls, Illinois

Mattie and Nellie Sheppard had turned thirty-eight in the Spring of 1972. They worked next to each other as tellers at the First National Bank on Franklin Street in Rockfalls, Illinois.

In 1954, when they were twenty, they had moved out of their mother's home and rented an apartment together. Suspicion spread. Spontaneous conversations started up at bus stops and Dairy Queen stands. Wherever people gathered, Mattie and Nellie, who had become known as the "depression twins," were the topic of discussion.

"It's unnatural for two single women to take up housekeeping together" . . . "Not to mention that they are sisters!" . . . "I heard that they sleep in the same bed, always with some part of their bodies touching" . . . "Some say when they are asleep they can join their flesh again as it was in their mother's womb" . . . "It's downright evil" . . . .

Over the years the town's interest in the two women waned without any strange events to fuel the fire of curiosity.

But the twins did have secrets.

They had a unique ability to communicate with one another without words. It didn't feel unusual in any way to them—it was just part of their lives together. Reading each other's mind was a daily occurrence. They could feel each other's thoughts, remember each other's dreams, and literally talk to one another even if they were separated by miles. Whenever someone noticed their special telepathy, they masked it so as not to become objects of curiosity.

They also had another secret that they carefully guarded. Once a month, when the moon was full, they went to their mother's house at midnight to meet with a small group of women who were members of the Juno Society. There they participated in a ceremony that had been a part of their lives for as long as they could remember. They knew only what their mother had told them about the purpose of the gathering and what they had secretly read in the journal she faithfully kept on the night table at the side of her bed. When they were teenagers their curiosity about the Juno Society drove them to read parts of the thick journal.

They learned the Society had begun long ago and spread all over the world. The members were of all faiths—Christians, Jews, Buddhists, Muslims, as well as people who did not believe in a god figure at all. Apart from their separate religions, the followers of Juno paid monthly respects to another power or spirit. What these people had in common was their belief in the magical forces of nature.

Like ancient people from the beginning of human time, the followers believed in powers that lived outside their own religious teachings. For them the earth itself was a living entity, and the moon was her guardian.

Juno was the name the Romans gave to the queen of the heavens, the goddess who watched over the earth, keeping it healthy and fertile. In Roman mythology she was the protector of women. The Greeks had called her Hera. In some native cultures she was known only as the hawk woman of the moon. She had a thousand names given her over time by a thousand different peoples—but her name was unimportant. She was a spirit that existed in the collective unconscious of people everywhere. For thousands of years women had gathered on the nights of the full moon to honor the goddess and to ask her to look after the earth.

In the early 19th century the Juno Society had actively worked to bring together all these groups of people. Most of them had been forced to hide their meetings and ceremonies for fear of being called pagans, witches, heretics, or worse. The Society came to them offering a larger identity and the protection of a secret, well-organized league with powerful networks that could unite them. For Mattie and Nellie the sole purpose of the ritual was to honor the powers of nature and to respect the well-being of the earth. The monthly ritual meant the gentle hum of chanting, soft shadows cast by the full moon, and the safe feeling that they were connected to each other and to the whole earth in a magical way. When they had been children, whispers that their mother was the head of a witches coven, that evil things took place in her house, hurt them and made them angry. Now as adults, they ignored the small-minded people who were frightened by anything they didn't understand. Still, by unspoken agreement, neither Mattie nor Nellie ever discussed the midnight meetings with anyone.

It wasn't until July of 1972, when the twins were thirty-eight years old, that they came to understand the deeper significance of the midnight meetings. It was then they learned that the Juno Society had another purpose.

When they arrived at the midnight meeting, they found two old women who had never been there before. They wore ankle-length dresses over their thin frames. Marian Sheppard introduced them to the group as "guardians."

"Let us celebrate the night as we always do," she said. "Then these visitors will tell us why they have come."

The thirteen women went out into the secluded garden behind Marian Sheppard's home. One by one they took long white candles from a wicker basket that had been placed in the center of the grass. Marian tucked a tiny baby's blanket into the empty basket, then went back into the house. The women created a circle around the basket and waited patiently, watching the night sky. Marian lit a wooden taper from the flames in the fireplace and carried it to the garden. Shielding the flame from the breeze, she went around the circle, lighting the candle each woman held. Then she lowered the flame to the wicker basket, setting it on fire. As it burned, the women formed a line with Marian leading them. They were a snake winding through the grass, their candles bending together as they moved. Marian danced at the head—a slow graceful dance—her arms undulating up and down like the heavy wings of a powerful bird. Softly they began to chant as they placed their candles around the burning basket.

Mattie and Nellie followed the others, but for the first time they felt out of place at their mother's moonlight dance. The ancient words of the chant the twins had learned as early as their nursery rhymes suddenly seemed strange and foreign. Tense anticipation stole the serene grace they had come to expect from the communal prayer. Silently they shared their fear that something was about to change, robbing them of the calm they had always known in their mother's home. They could feel it coming.

The Breath of Juno

When the chanting ended the women stayed seated on the damp grass waiting for the visitors to speak. The faces surrounding the sisters looked as though they had been touched by a frost rather than warmed by the mid-summer night air. Faces with the crevasses of time etched around eyes, at the corners of mouths, lines in once smooth brows looked stark in the moonlight. The sisters felt ashamed of their still full cheeks and unwrinkled skin, of their hands, moist and as yet unlined. Secrets were about to be spoken by the elders to women experienced and old enough to hear them. They were almost forty themselves, but in the presence of these women they felt like children again. They wanted to run away before words, not meant for them, fell inside their young ears and took root in their minds, leaving them forever changed.

"Friends. So good to be with you all and to mix our voices with yours." The white-haired woman spoke first with a thick Italian accent. The sisters exchanged a quick glance—they thought she must be well into her eighties. She trembled slightly, pushing her words away from her thin lips as if without this effort they would stick in her mouth, refusing to become airborne.

"We have traveled a long way to be with you tonight, to share a most important discovery. We come from the Mother Home of the Juno Society. We have been 'guardians' for forty years but only now has our task become urgent. We are here to tell you that, as it was predicted, a girl-child has been born in the new world here in your country on June 12, 1959. We have been watching her for the last thirteen years. She has just crossed the threshold into womanhood. The women of Juno believe that she may be the one to carry the spirit into the next century."

The sisters looked to their mother to help them understand, but Marian was intent on every word the old women spoke. She seemed to forget her daughters were there. They were indeed children who were being left out of the adult secrets. Why were these old women secretly watching a young girl? What were "guardians?" The simple ritual they had shared with their mother and this small group of friendly women had suddenly taken a seemingly sinister turn. They searched each others minds for clues to help them understand the old woman's words. None came.

The second visitor, a frail stick of a woman, said, "The Prophecy tells us that it will be a young woman who will take us over the bridge, perhaps between eighteen and thirty years of age, but nothing is certain. This child born in 1959 will be forty-one in the year 2000. Perhaps too old, but we must protect her as if she is the one. We cannot know how her life will unfold."

"Where does she live?" Marian asked.

"In the desert of the Southwest. In Arizona. Her name is Paula Campbell."

"Does her mother know who she is, that she is being watched?"

"No, not yet. There has been no reason to tell her this early. Even if *they* have found her, we don't believe they would ever take action against a child this soon."

They sat talking on the grass until two in the morning. The women who had known each other since they were children had many questions for the visitors. The sisters remained silent. Their curiosity was not as strong as their fear, so they didn't interrupt the conversation.

Just before the gathering ended, one of the "guardians" turned her attention to the twins.

"In our eagerness to share our knowledge, we have forgotten that you may find our words strange and confusing. Soon enough you will know what all of this means. Please trust us as you do your own mother. Some of the talk must have been frightening to you. But we can't hide the truth . . . there are dangerous times ahead of us. It is not a small thing we speak of in this quiet garden tonight. Much is about to take place on this earth. It was essential that you be here tonight because it is your destiny to play a great role in all that will happen over the next thirty years."

When she said the word *destiny,* the sisters stared at one another. The idea of having a specific destiny was alien to them. Their lives were defined by small accomplishments and low expectations. Grand dreams didn't hover in the recesses of their minds, gnawing at the contentment they had always taken for granted. They had been born in Rockfalls and just assumed they would spend their lives in this quiet town which sat peacefully against the banks of the Mississippi River. Destiny was something associated with whole nations or great leaders. It had nothing to do with two small-town girls from the heartland of America who worked as tellers at the First National Bank on Franklin Street.

The Breath of Juno

* * *

BY THE TIME EVERYONE left it was past three o'clock in the morning. The twins lingered, waiting to talk to their mother alone, waiting for clues that would help them understand all the secrets they had heard that night.

"Girls, it's too late for you to go home. Why don't you stay here? We'll talk more tomorrow."

The sisters went upstairs to the bedroom they had shared for most of their lives. The twin beds were neatly made, anticipating their visit. Nightgowns and towels were laid out. It had been expected that they would be spending the night. They undressed, got under the sheets, and began to whisper to each other as they had every night when they were children.

"What do you suppose she meant by our destiny?" Mattie asked.

"I don't know. It's strange. Why are those old women watching a young girl that is halfway around the world from their home?"

"Did you see Mother's face? It was as if she were in a trance. Do you think she has known about this for all these years and never told us?"

"They all seemed to know about it—as if they had been waiting for this day all their lives. They were so excited."

"Maybe. But I think they were just as afraid as we were. I've never seen them all so quiet."

Just then, Marian opened the door to their room.

"My girls," she said softly. Although the twins were now thirty-eight year-old women she would always think of them as her girls. "I know this conversation tonight has left you with many questions. I won't be able to answer them all but I promise that I will tell you everything I know. Go to sleep now. We'll talk tomorrow."

"Why did they come to us? What role are we supposed to play in all this?" Nellie wanted answers now.

Mattie supported her sister's refusal to let their mother leave the room without first answering their questions. "What is a 'Guardian?' Are they actually spying on that poor mother in Arizona and her child? What are they trying to learn?"

Marian realized that her daughters would never be able to sleep until she told them the whole story. She walked to the window and opened it so that a cooling breeze could fill the stuffy bedroom.

"It is time you both knew everything. Perhaps I should have told you the legend years ago. I always thought there was plenty of time. I never knew when it all would actually begin . . . when the 'Guardians' would come into our lives."

She sat on the rocking chair under the west window, and together the sisters felt themselves moving back in time. They were young children again and their mother was rocking back and forth, telling them bedtime stories. She hadn't read from books, but created her own tales, making them up as she went along. From the depths of her imagination she had created a world in their bedroom filled with princesses that had wonderful powers, dragons as wise as any human, and rivers that were so deep they could almost touch the earth's center.

The girls had hung on her every word, begging her not to stop when she said they could hear the rest of the story the next night. Lying in their twin beds, they had felt safe with their mother's voice spinning magic in the darkness.

Now, they felt the same nervous excitement they had known when they listened to their mother's tales so many years ago. But tonight they were hearing a tale more fantastic than all those stories invented for their young minds. A story that began in the ancient Roman empire just years after the birth of Christ: a story that had traveled through the centuries waiting for this moment in time to explode into action; a story that would change and dominate the rest of their lives. The full moon shone through the open window, casting long shadows against the far wall.

As their mother spoke they understood what the old woman had meant when she said it was their destiny. They saw how everything came together . . . how they had been moving towards this ancient story their whole lives. Thoughts and fears mingled inside their common mind as they understood why it was inevitable that they play a part in their mother's tale.

The dawn was beginning to break when Marian finished telling them why they had been chosen to protect the spirit. The three women sat in silence as the room slowly filled with light. They waited as if the returning sun could burn away the night's story, turning it into a haunting dream instead of a waking reality.

Finally Mattie spoke. "Are we now the 'guardians' of the child?"

"Yes. You need only watch her from a distance. It is believed that she will start remembering now that she is of child-bearing age, but we don't know when she will understand who she is. There is little that we can know about the girl's mind or how much she will remember of the past. Some people at the Mother Home believe that she will have a complete memory . . . all of it will survive intact. There is no proof that this will be the case. I don't believe it myself. It is just too incredible to imagine.

"The child will be watched as she grows. If any attempt is made to harm her, you will be required to protect her."

"Who are they?" Nellie asked. "Why do they want to destroy the child?"

Marian came to sit at the foot of Nellie's bed. "My girls, how I wish I never had to tell you this part of the story, but I know that I must. You need to prepare, so tonight I speak the words that have not been spoken outside the Mother Home for a thousand years.

"They are older than the Juno Society, called by a name more ancient than all the great pyramids of Egypt. Even tonight the guardians were careful not to speak their name. It is from them that we know of the prophecy. You must know of them as one day they will know of you. They are the *Sidon.*" She pronounced the word as though the very sound had the power to cut into her tongue. "They began as a secret order of priests in Babylon who watched the heavens, not as astrologers do today but with the skill of our modern astronomers. It is said that their ancestors go back to the beginning of time, that they built the great stone circles found all over the British Isles. The one that remains today is the famous Stonehenge. They built these places to predict the journeys of the moon, the sun and the planets.

"In the time when Babylon was the center of civilization, they practiced their arts on a sacred burial field outside the city walls. That place was called the field of Sidon, so they took its name for their order. The bones of the dead were broken into pieces, and the priests prayed over them as they studied the night sky. By the time of the Roman Empire, the prophecies of the Sidon had become so powerful that even the greatest emperors, Julius and Augustus Caesar, believed the predictions as strongly as they believed the words of their own oracles. The Sidon Brotherhood found a new home in the heart of the Empire, in Rome itself.

It was written that the Sidon predicted that the two great planets, Jupiter and Saturn, would pass over one another causing a brilliant light that would appear as a single star. Under this star, they said, the son of a god would be born, bringing a new faith to rule the land and all the days would be counted from his birth.

"For many years after the birth of Christ, they continued to look into the future. The prophecy I told you earlier tonight was written by the Sidon long before the women of Rome began to gather and worship the goddess Juno."

"Are there still priests living today who follow the beliefs of this Sidon?"

"Yes, they live, as does the Juno Society. Beliefs as old as these never die. They are handed down from one generation to another. The priest that leads this Brotherhood today believes that the prophecy must be denied, no matter the cost."

"Do they know who we are? Where we live?" Mattie asked, feeling the danger.

"I doubt they know of you . . . not yet."

Marian saw the fear in her daughters' eyes. She grieved for the burden that had been placed upon them without their consent. She had hoped that they would have many more years to enjoy the daily routine of their lives before they were called upon to retreat from their own lives and become the guardians of another. From the day they came from her womb connected to one another, she was fearful that they had been chosen to be the last guardians. When the first signs of their telepathic abilities emerged, her fears were confirmed. At first they read only each other's minds, but by the time they were ten they could sense events that were about to happen.

They were hardly aware of their unique talent—it was natural to them. Mattie could relate the contents of a letter before it was opened. Nellie could see the black funnel of a tornado whipping through the sky long before it actually crossed the Illinois cornfield. One day they would be required to use those skills to defend and protect the keeper of the spirit.

Marian closed the drapes to keep out the bright sun. "We'll talk more later." She left the twins' bedroom and went down to the kitchen to sit alone. Tomorrow her daughters would begin a journey that would take them far from the only home they had ever known into a future where they would be in constant peril, relying on their special instincts to stay alive.

· 13 ·

THE NEXT MORNING MARIAN SHEPPARD GAVE her daughters the letter that was to change their lives. It was written in broken English, long-hand, with beautiful round strokes.

> Our Dearest Sisters,
>
> The time comes for you. The Breath of Juno lives. It is now you go to the girl-child who is chosen. Born on the day of the midnight sun, June 21, 1959. Thirteen years old she is now. She is called by the name Paula Campbell.
> Now the remembering will begin for her. The power of Juno will take the veil from the past.
> The dreams too will come to her as the spirit rises within her. She sees the hawk fly from the moon as all the others have. But now she begins to remember the dream.
> It is still much time until the year 2000. We do not think you are in danger now. Though we cannot be sure of this, so please take care. Be aware of everyone around you. Your mother told you of those who seek to destroy her. They will also destroy those who protect her.
> You will need all your psychic powers for the journey ahead of you. You must remember how to look into future to protect the child and yourself. Once you are close to the spirit, you will see inside the girl's mind. Her visions will become your visions. Trust your instincts. You would not be chosen guardians if you did not have special sight.
> We hold you close to our hearts and pray for your safety.
>
> Tamara of the Mother Home

Inside the letter were two pictures of Paula Campbell: one as a baby and the other taken recently.

Her body had grown naturally over the years, but the child's features remained constant. A stubborn cowlick made the brown hair stick out at odd angles. The eyes were set too close together, giving her a pinched looked as if she were perpetually looking down at her nose which was too large for her narrow face. None of the pictures had caught the child smiling. She held her mouth tightly closed with the corners turned slightly down, and there was always a look of dread in her eyes.

Nellie and Mattie were silent. For the first time in many years they breathed in unison, listening for each other's thoughts. Remembering, the letter said, would make this girl vulnerable to detection by the Sidon.

"Are we supposed to just disappear? We've got to tell the Bank that we're leaving."

"What do we tell them? We don't know how long we will be gone or even if we will be coming back."

Mattie read the letter over to herself. "How can they know that we will be able to read this girl's mind and look into her future? I haven't done it in years."

Nellie looked at her sister. "We just did it, Mattie. We can still become one."

"Yes, we used to do it all the time. Maybe they are right and we will be able to see once we're near the child."

Nellie began to plan. "We'll tell them at work that there has been a death in the family and we have to take a leave of absence."

"To tell the truth, I don't know if I believe in this prophecy," Mattie confided. She took Nellie's hand. "Do we have to do this? It is a dangerous thing they are asking us to do. If the Sidon tries to harm the girl, how can we prevent them? We can read minds, but we can't stop bullets."

"Are you saying that we shouldn't go?" Nellie looked at her sister's face, tense with fear.

The twin sisters, still identical in appearance, sat looking into each other's thoughts, searching for an answer.

"I don't think we have a choice," Nellie said. "This has all been decided for us a long time ago."

Mattie knew it too. Now that the future had taken root inside their minds, they were bound to play their part in it.

* * *

WHEN THEY ARRIVED in Phoenix, they were met at the airport by a young woman who drove them to an innocent-looking white adobe house with a cactus garden in bloom in the front yard. "This is a safe house. It will be yours for as long as you need it."

"And just how long do you think that will be?" Mattie asked.

The girl avoided the question. "The Campbell family lives in the brown house at the end of this block."

A growing look of anxiety engulfed her face. "I have to go now. I'm sorry. I must leave."

They settled in as best they could, filling the pantry and refrigerator with groceries. At night they allowed their minds to reach down the street into the brown house at the corner and up to Paula Campbell's bedroom. After a few days they were able to feel her thoughts and look inside her dreams. Only once in the first three weeks did they actually see her. She was getting into a gray Pontiac and driving off with her mother.

They knew without looking into the child's frightened thoughts that she was being taken to a doctor. Her mother was trying to find someone who could help her child. The girl was reclusive, with hardly any friends. And every night she was tormented by dreams that woke her with her own screams. Her thirteenth birthday had made things worse. Images from the dreams crept into her waking mind. The twins could see them all with great clarity.

The child's dreams always began the same way. A line of women dressed in white robes moving through a woods, and then the ceremony that looked much like the ritual the twins had taken part in ever since they where children. Then the vision turned menacing and violent. The child was transformed into an enormous bird of prey, a vulture, that flew just above the trees in the forest. The full moon cast its wide black shadow against the cold ground. When the women below gathered in a circle around a baby placed in a wicker basket, the vulture swooped down. Its wings surrounded the infant as it pecked at the soft head. Then its claws grasped the baby's flesh and carried it off into the trees. The women were left wailing below.

The images from the dream were coming to the girl all the time now. They shattered her mind and tore at her sanity. She hid in her room, stared out the window, and refused to eat.

Mattie and Nellie felt her terror and didn't know what to do. Something was terribly wrong. The girl dreamed not of the hawk as others before her had, but of a vulture. Their duty was to be her guardian, to protect her from the Sidon, but they didn't know how to protect her from herself.

On September 26, three weeks after they had arrived in Phoenix, the twins woke simultaneously at four in the morning. Their minds welded together as they felt the burn of a rope around their necks. It tightened, pulling the air from their lungs. Together they felt the breath go out of their bodies. They knew instantly what had happened. They had seen it in the same second that it took place. Paula Campbell was dead.

Stunned, they got out of bed, turned on the lights, and looked into the mirror of each other's eyes.

"Why didn't we see it before it happened?" Mattie said, feeling a deep sense of grief for the child they had never met. "We might have been able to save her."

"We thought the danger would come from the outside," Nellie said, putting her arm around Mattie's shoulder.

"Still, we had no premonition, no vision of her taking her own life." Mattie buried her face in her hands. "Her life was in our keeping and we failed her. It's been too long. We can't see into the future clearly anymore. Our psychic abilities are useless."

"Maybe it was already too late. Maybe it has been too late for many years. Her destiny might have been outside of our control." Nellie tried to comfort Mattie. "The dreams and the memories broke her mind into pieces, driving her to despair. She wasn't strong enough to hold all the chaos that was going on inside her."

"We felt the child's torment. Even without our future vision, we should have been able to see where it would lead. We failed her and we failed the women of Juno."

The sisters sat together in silence until dawn broke. Sadness and the belief that they should have prevented Paula Campbell's death kept them immobile. They cried when they felt Paula's mother climbing the stairs to her bedroom, opening the door . . . they held one another closely as Paula's mother saw her limp body hanging . . . a thin clothesline twisted around her neck. They heard a mother's piercing scream and watched her faint.

They didn't go outside where they knew an ambulance would be sitting in the Campbell driveway as a small group of curious neighbors gathered in front of the house.

They closed their minds to the future, pushing away even an image of their own destiny.

Later that afternoon Mattie looked out the window. It was a bright sunny day. "What happens to the spirit when the girl carrying it dies? Where does it go?"

"We can't know that," Nellie said. "Mother told us that the moment the life goes out of the girl holding the spirit, the Sensors can feel the breath as it moves, searching for a new home. The infant that will carry the spirit next will be born today, September 26, 1972."

She joined Mattie at the window. "She could be anywhere in the world." A gentle breeze rustled the leaves on the distant trees. Thin white puffs of clouds seemed to recede into the endless blue of the sky. "The Sensors will find her when she takes her first breath."

Mattie gazed at the cloudless blue sky. "A child born today will be twenty-eight at the turn of the millennium. Maybe you're right—Paula Campbell's young death was her destiny. Perhaps the spirit needed one more life to mature into its full power."

Nellie started to gather up their few things.

Mattie came away from the window to help her. "Do you think we will be asked to go to this newborn child now or will they wait until she is thirteen to call us?"

"It's the decision of the Mother Home. They will tell us what we should do."

Mattie already knew the answer to her question. When she closed her eyes, she could picture them both in a small boat traveling up a wide river someplace far across the sea. Sheep grazed on the grassy meadows along the banks, and in the distance craggy peaks cut sharply into the sky.

IN THE SMALL antechamber of a church just two miles from Paula Campbell's house, a small group of people were gathered. They had come together as soon as they had learned of the girl's death. They exchanged guarded glances, mutely waiting for Father DeCarlo to speak. He stood. His black robe hung formlessly over his lean body.

At fifty-six, he was already the undisputed leader of their sect.

"Last night Paula Campbell committed suicide," he announced. "This has taken us by surprise. We didn't know she could be so quickly destroyed by her own hand."

Brother Anthony, in his early thirties, was the youngest at the table. He had been the protégé of Father DeCarlo since he was a child in Rome.

"Whoever her 'Guardians' were, they cannot have had the gift of looking into the future or reading the child's mind."

"Perhaps not this time," Brother Martin said, taking a long pull on his meerschaum pipe only to discover it had gone out. He kept it in his mouth still because he liked to cup it in his hand. It gave him reason to pause, creating the impression of a church elder who weighed his words carefully before he spoke. He enjoyed these small meetings where he was seen as a well-respected man with cultivated tastes and literary sensibilities. He'd come a long way from his days in the cloistered monastery in the Mediterranean. "Her Guardians probably had no idea that she was going to kill herself or they would have tried to stop her," Brother Martin reasoned.

"Maybe we are overestimating the powers of these women," Brother Anthony said. "The whole society for that matter. It is now possible that the prophecy won't come to pass even if we do nothing. If the girls kill themselves when they start remembering, the power will be destroyed before it can become a threat. Perhaps no girl-child who inherits the power will live to be a mature adult in the year 2000."

"Maybe it is for the best," Father DeCarlo said, a tone of disappointment in his voice. "It may be that they will all die before they become women. The power may have grown too great for any of them to carry."

He didn't want to believe his own words—that it could end without him. Now that he was so close to the spirit, he burned with the desire to be the instrument of its destruction.

Helga Hydinger stood before she spoke so that her large presence could envelop the room. At fifty-two she was still an imposing figure. Both men and women stared at her, mesmerized by her stark ageless features. She wore a dark dress with a red scarf folding into itself repeatedly as it made its way around her neck. Her black hair streaked with strands of gray was waist length; it was a stallion's mane hanging wild and loose. As she spoke her hands formed a triangle in front of her chest, palms apart but fingers touching.

"With all respect, Father, that is too much to hope for. I lived among the women of Juno, carrying out my duties for most of my life. Several of the children have grown to maturity in this century. Paula Campbell was weak. The next child may have far greater strength.

"The prophecy comes from your own order of Sidon. You cannot believe it will be so easily destroyed. I felt this child the moment she was born in this country in the summer of 1959, but I could not know her destiny. I give you my word it will not end here."

"It's more than twelve hours since the child's death," Brother Anthony said. "Do you know where the next birth will take place?" he asked Helga. The woman made him uncomfortable. He never felt he could shake off the weight of her voice.

Helga knew that they were waiting for her to speak . . . that she alone would be able to tell them what had happened to the spirit that lived inside Paula Campbell. She felt a wonderful sense of power as they all watched her. She had been a Sensor for the Juno Society since she was thirteen years old. But in the late 1940's she had broken her vows to the Society and had begun giving secret information to Father DeCarlo.

She lowered her hands and rested them on the table, palms facing upward. In the center of her left hand, just below the index finger, there was a small angry red birthmark shaped like a crescent moon.

"Soon I will be able to feel the breath move so that we will know where it is born again," she lied. They would learn of the child's birth when she wished them to and not before. The child's life must always be in her hands first and last.

Helga had known the answer to their question the minute Paula Campbell had died. She felt the breath leave the girl's body like smoke from a withering candle. It freed itself from mortal life and sailed formless into the sky, searching for a new home.

It had crossed the sea to come live again in the tiny body of a baby, born September 26, 1972 in a small town in Wales, near Cardigan Bay. A baby christened Mary Alice.

· 14 ·

1998: Wales

Gavin Langley sat quietly, staring into the flames that glowed from the fireplace. January in Wales was a desolate time, bleak and gray. The long nights gave him too many hours to remember the past, to hear the sweet voices of those who had died so long ago. He was forty-eight years old, a man still in the prime of life, but he lived like a hermit aching for the past. Not a day went by that he didn't think of his young life when the world was full of promise, when everything was his.

It seemed to him as though it had all taken place in a different lifetime. Often he felt as though God must be punishing him for some unknown but unforgivable sin. They had been so happy until his wife died giving birth to their first daughter. Then eight years later the child had drowned in a tragic boating accident. That was eighteen years ago—1980.

He looked up at the grandfather clock as it struck nine, and stroked his full red beard. They would be here soon. He had so few visitors that when the old Father and the monk had first come he had welcomed them into his home. Traveling emissaries of the church, they had called themselves. Come to Wales to bring the word of God into the hearts of man.

He had never been a deeply religious man, and then the cruel loss of his family had turned him even further from God. For a reason he could not understand, he found comfort in the visits of these two holy men. They had been coming to him every few days for almost a month, always speaking kindly of the grace of God. For the first time in many years he allowed himself to speak of his daughter.

He thought it odd that they only came at night, especially now in the dead of winter when the roads could be so treacherous. But they seemed like dedicated men, so he didn't question their ways. They arrived just as the clock stopped chiming. Gavin invited them in and offered brandy.

As they sat by the fireplace the frail old priest turned to Gavin and put his wrinkled hand on Gavin's knee, patting it with his long fingers. Then in a scratchy quivering voice, he said that tonight he had much to tell the Welshman. He leaned back in his chair and began to relate his story, choosing his words carefully as if he were telling a wondrous tale to a child.

Gavin listened, wondering why Father DeCarlo was telling him this strange story. The old man painted a sinister picture of an ancient cult of women who worshiped a pagan goddess as their ancestors had two thousand years before.

"I know how this sounds to you," the priest said when he finished his tale. "But these things I have told you are not the fantasy of an old man. This is not just an ancient legend. These women of Juno deeply believe that the life of their goddess is threatened."

Gavin was confused by the priest's words. "And why, may I ask, are you telling me this?" His voice held the music of the Welsh hamlet where he grew up. "These women you speak of may be part of some kind of witch cult, but the truth be known, I can't see what this has to do with me. It happens in all countries. Followers, poor lost souls, who have been spit on once too many times by life, that's who joins these cults. That terrible night all those people drank KoolAid and cyanide because they believed their leader, Jim Jones, was god. Then there was that man in America, in Texas, who called himself Koresh. I'm sorry to say we are living in an age of cults. They are everywhere. So I ask you, what does this have to do with me?"

Brother Martin poured himself another glass of brandy. The years had not been kind to the monk. His arms and stomach had grown flabby, his skin had turned a jaundice shade of yellow, and dark moles had eaten into his forehead. He took a deep pull on his ivory pipe, then slowly allowed the smoke to escape from his mouth.

"These women believe that the power to kill the ancient spirit of their goddess Juno lives in chosen young girls." The monk clasped the silver cross that hung around his neck. God would forgive him for this deception. He watched Gavin's reaction as he spoke.

"By the end of this millennium, they believe one of these girls will grow powerful enough to destroy their goddess. It is crazy, of course, but they believe it so strongly that they have been driven to kill innocent children. Do you remember two identical twins, they must have been in their forties at that time, watching your daughter?"

Gavin turned white, as a vision of the perfectly identical faces came to him. Brother Martin sat back in his chair, pleased to see that he had touched the right nerve. Gavin had seen them watching his daughter, Mary Alice, ever since she was a baby. Whenever he tried to approach them they moved away. No one had known who they were or where they had come from. How could this monk know these things, things that happened eighteen years ago?

"What are you saying? Are you telling me that these women were from this Juno Society?" He feared that this insane story would resonate in his bones for all his life.

"Yes, they were watching your daughter for signs. They had to see if she was a danger to them."

"After all these years you come here to tell me these women you speak of had something to do with her drowning that night, that my daughter's death was not an accident!"

Brother Martin paused for a moment, sipping his brandy. He wanted to shock Gavin without panicking him. "The identical women you saw are assassins."

The two religious men were silent. Gavin scanned their faces. They were deadly serious.

"The murder of an innocent young girl? My daughter! No, I can't believe they would actually do this."

"I'm sorry to tell you that you are wrong." The priest placed a gray envelope on Gavin's lap, and smiled sadly. There was something terrifying in the simple expression—something that spoke of things outside of his control.

"You see, Gavin, not only did they kill your daughter, they have tried to kill another child."

"Open it," the other monk instructed.

Gavin's hands, surprisingly thin for such a big man, reached for the gray envelope. He opened it. Inside were pictures of a young girl, a child with brilliant red hair and green eyes not more than three years old. A single note clipped to the photo read, *July, 1983. Three year old girl. Born to Elizabeth Casey on June 22, 1980 in Lake Tahoe, California.*

"What does this mean?"

"An attempt was made on this child's life fifteen years ago," Father DeCarlo said. "Taking the life of a girl-child so young . . . it is not something that can be done without terrible regret."

"The girl in this photo is eighteen years old now," Brother Martin said, taking back the gray envelope. He wanted to move the conversation forward as quickly as possible. The fewer questions Gavin asked, the better. "You see, the child disappeared after the failed attempt on her life in 1983. She has been lost to us for fifteen years."

"How do you even know that she's still alive?"

"That we do know," the monk said with more confidence than he wanted to imply. "The girl is alive."

The absolute certainty in his voice irritated Gavin. After all the pain in his life, he had learned that there was very little that one could be certain of.

"She must be found now," the monk said.

"Why now?" Gavin was beginning to dislike this man with his definite statements and his brusque manner of speaking.

"What you don't understand, Mr. Langley, is that we have no doubt as to who this child is and that she has been marked for death." The priest's voice became soft and reassuring so that Gavin was reminded of the confessional of his childhood.

For a moment the room was silent.

"You can't be serious," Gavin said. "Gods, goddesses. This is not the dark ages, for heaven sakes. Nobody believes in these legends anymore, not even here in the back country of Wales."

"But they do," the monk said. "The women of Juno have many believers. It is not so difficult to understand. People everywhere in the world believe in some form of pagan religion. They just make light of them by calling them superstitions but they still play a part in people's daily behavior. Many buildings skip the 13th floor. Where do you think that comes from? It's pagan, Gavin. I can give you many examples . . . . "

Gavin was no longer listening. He stared at the flames of the dying fire and thought of Mary Alice. How had she died? All these years he had been haunted by that night. Drowned, she had drowned. But had she been alone? The familiar sensation came to him—the feeling that his daughter wasn't really dead but still out there somewhere—calling to him to save her.

Gavin stood. He wanted them to leave so that he could be alone. He had to sort this all out. How was this red-haired girl connected to his daughter?

"Where is this child right now?" he asked.

"We don't know."

"If she is who they think she is, does she herself know it? Is she aware of the danger you say she is in?"

"No . . . that's why we must save her," the monk said, warming his hands over the fire.

The two men made no move to leave. They needed Gavin and they didn't intend to leave until they had convinced him to help them. They had been unable to find the girl themselves. Father DeCarlo had always believed that she would not be able to hide from him—that she would reveal her identify to him before it was too late. But time was running out and still they had no idea where to search for her.

It had been Brother Martin's idea to bring Gavin Langley to their aid. The monk had convinced Father DeCarlo that they should find Mary Alice's father and do whatever was necessary to woo him to their cause. He would have the closest connection to the spirit. She might send him her dreams before anyone else, and through him they would find her.

As Brother Martin had hoped, Gavin was a man full of the vulnerability that only deep despair can bring. They needed only to show him that he was necessary to help them overcome an ancient force.

The priest softly reassured Gavin that this was a mission that would bring him back to life, free him from the sorrows of his past. He appealed to Gavin to help them save another innocent victim of fanaticism who was marked for death by the women of Juno. He carefully explained to Gavin that his brotherhood might not be able to find the girl by themselves and protect her from this insane cult of women, but with Gavin's help they could find her before the women of Juno did. Only *he* could recognize the twin sisters after so many years.

Carefully he allowed Gavin to realize that if he helped them, he might find the moment to avenge his own child's death.

They left Gavin Langley's home at midnight. The wind howled across the barren land but they didn't feel the cold. There was so little time left to find the girl.

Now, with Gavin's help, they would be able to stop her before her power grew beyond their mortal strength.

The Breath of Juno

PART III

*Vision of sorrow
Pierce the night
Death in the moonlight
Let the hawk take flight*

· 15 ·

1998: San Francisco

The thin outline of the Golden Gate Bridge broke through the dense fog lying across the bay. The two women sat on the grass at Fisherman's Wharf, drinking hot coffee from a thermos and watching the sun set in the mist. The island of Alcatraz, only a mile off shore, was barely visible. Tired after the seven hour drive from San Bernardino and from talking to one another all the way, Aeron and Lee let the silence of dusk rest gently against their bodies.

Aeron's need to find her mother had become even more intense. She had become obsessed with the belief that when she found her, all the Shadows would vanish. Her mother's love would fill her, leaving no room for the others. Her mother would put her arms around her, and she would be reborn.

With patient investigation, Lee had been able to uncover one clue—a place to start their search. A handwritten note signed by Sara Morgan, who Lee learned was the original case worker when Aeron was three years old.

Lee discovered that Sara Morgan had retired in 1988. Several obsolete addresses were in different data banks. The computer trail was a dead end.

"She must be deceased," the San Francisco Information Office had told Lee. "This is 1998. Nobody can hide from the information system and still be alive. She'd have to have no phone, no driver's license, no tax records, nothing."

"If she were dead, you could find that out pretty easily," Lee had said sarcastically. "It's hard for a dead person to hide from the Information Office."

"You got a point there, lady," he had chuckled. "We got everybody in these computers, dead or alive."

Not everybody, she thought, when she had hung up the phone. If they could find everyone, the country wouldn't be full of drug dealers, rapists and killers who walked the streets of every city undetected. If *they* could hide from the Information Office, surely one retired social worker could slip between the cracks. The challenge excited her—she was determined to be more clever than the Information Office.

Her tenacity paid off. Using a search of library card files, she located a Sara Morgan who lived in Bodega Bay, a fishing village about an hour north of San Francisco.

"It may be a worthless trip," she had told Aeron. "Even if this woman is the one we're looking for, she may not be able to tell us anything we don't already know. But I'm willing to take you up there if you want to go."

They had left the next morning.

THE FOG TURNED a dark red as the sun set behind the Golden Gate Bridge. Aeron stared at the San Francisco Bay—into the huge expanse of black water. It called to her, telling her to leave the chaos that was shattering her mind into fragments, to let the deep emptiness free her from the Shadows that now entered her body whenever they pleased.

Lee saw a familiar distant look in Aeron's eyes. For a moment she was afraid to break the silence—to bring the young woman back to the present. "Are you still in there?" she said quietly.

Aeron turned to Lee and smiled sadly. "Maybe I shouldn't have told you so much. If I'm quiet for a second, you think that someone else has taken over my body."

"Well, since it is still you, I think we'd better get going," Lee said. "I got us a hotel in the Marina. Tomorrow we'll drive up the coast to Bodega Bay. Do you think you'll recognize Sara Morgan when you see her?"

"I was three years old. You're the psychiatrist. You tell me. Will I remember all the people who took care of me when I was three?"

"None of the regular theories seem to apply here," Lee said as they tossed out the remains of their now cold coffee and got into the

Range Rover. "I can't make any predictions about your memory. There doesn't seem to be any precedent for you. You're the one that makes predictions. Tell me what will happen tomorrow."

"I have no idea," Aeron said simply.

"You know, in spite of all your memories and dreams, I am discovering that you are not always right about things. Do you remember when you first came to my office in 1993? You told me with such arrogance that I was going to have two sons. There was not a doubt in your mind that your grand prediction would come to pass."

"It's always been like that," Aeron replied. "From out of nowhere I'll see something, and I don't know whether it is going to happen in the future, or if I am seeing something that has already happened in the past."

"What exactly did you see that day in my office?"

"You. I saw you standing next to a window that looked out on snow-covered mountains. You were singing to two baby boys that lay next to each other in one crib."

"That's it? That's all you saw? Well, I'm forty years old and I don't have a man I want to spend the night with, let alone marry. I can't sing, and the San Bernardino Mountains haven't been topped with snow for almost five years. The weather service predictions are better than yours. They say that the whole earth is getting warmer every year. I don't think there will ever be snow on those mountains again. So it looks like you were wrong."

"It's still possible. Women are having babies even in their fifties."

"Maybe, but you have to admit that two sons is a long shot."

THE SUN DIPPED below the horizon as they reached their hotel. Once they settled into their room, Lee turned to Aeron. "You are such a puzzle to me. I get all these different parts of you mixed up. What do the Shadows, the memories that visit you from other times, have to do with all the terrifying dreams you used to have where you were possessed by a giant hawk? And how is it all connected with your ability to predict the future?"

"I used to think that the dreams and the Shadows were two separate things. That they didn't have any connection to one another. Now I don't know. The dreams don't frighten me any more. In a strange way, they fill me with a wonderful sense of power. It's almost as if I can control them, demand that they take me wherever I wish . . . show me what I need to see."

Her fingers gently touched the necklace that she had worn all summer, the gold hawk with the green jade eyes. My mother, she thought, will tell me who this voice within me belongs to.

That night Lee and Aeron slept in twin beds, talking like sisters rather than women who were separated in age by twenty-two years. They talked not of the extraordinary events of Aeron's Paris summer, but about little secrets that sisters share in the quiet of a dark room late at night. When Aeron asked Lee how she knew when she was truly in love, Lee wondered how such lovely innocence could coexist with the ageless intelligence housed inside this young body.

"I don't know if I am capable of falling in love," Aeron said. "There doesn't seem to be enough room inside me to hold that big an emotion."

"Maybe not yet. Once you get all these other people, these Shadows, out of the way, I know it will come to you. It will breathe into you like so much fresh air."

"Is that a guess or a prediction?" Aeron teased her. "How about you? Do you want to fall in love again?"

"It's three in the morning. The only thing I want to do now is fall asleep."

Aeron lay in bed, her eyes fixed on the plaster ceiling. She knew that she would become the hawk again tonight and that now, more than ever, she had to remember all that her sharp eyes revealed to her. The dream was her map into the future.

FLOATING CLOSE TO the earth, she sailed over a peaceful river lying between two lush meadows. She saw a herd of pure white sheep grazing quietly on one side of the river. On the other side she saw a flock of black sheep also peacefully lolling along the banks. She heard the bleating cry of a lone black sheep at the edge of the water. The call was answered by a single white sheep. It left the flock and entered the placid water, swimming to the other side. When it emerged on the far bank, it was no longer white but black. The new member was accepted immediately into the flock, and then it happened in reverse. One of the white sheep called with a throaty bleating sound and a black sheep entered the water and crossed.

She glided over the river, watching the movements of the flock until a wind suddenly whipped up the water beneath her. A rowboat carrying a single passenger was being tossed about wildly in the angry river. A young child wearing a white night dress was struggling to keep the boat afloat. The look of terror in the child's blue eyes seemed to call to her, to the hawk, for salvation. Her giant wings dipped, carrying her to the water's surface. She was too late. The swirling waves overturned the tiny craft and threw the child like a feather into the churning waters. Her long blond hair spread out like a lace fan, then sank beneath the surface.

As the girl vanished in the dark waters, Aeron felt herself being pulled away from the body of the hawk. They were no longer one creature. She was being ripped out of the hawk and sucked into the body of the drowning child!

Coughing, gasping for breath as the water filled her lungs, she desperately reached for the surface but was pulled down as if someone was grabbing her feet, yanking her to the bottom of the river.

For the first time in many years, Aeron woke to the sound of her own screams.

At first she didn't remember where she was—the sterile hotel room held no familiar clues. Then Lee's face emerged from the darkness. Aeron breathed in relief.

"I thought the dreams no longer frightened you," Lee said softly. Then she opened the heavy curtains so that the bright sun light would free Aeron from the dark. It was ten o'clock. The early morning fog had burned off, and the room was already beginning to heat up. Lee switched on the air conditioner.

"I was drowning. No, that's not right. I did drown . . . in an icy river." Aeron got out of bed and quickly dressed. "Let's get going. I must find my mother before it's too late. I feel she is in terrible danger."

TWENTY MINUTES LATER they were on Highway 1, traveling north on the rugged coast road to Bodega Bay and Sara Morgan. The heat pressed against the Range Rover. The climate of the San Francisco Bay area, once known for its cool, hazy summers, had changed rapidly in the last few years. During the summer of 1998 temperatures over ninety were not uncommon. Only the fog brought relief, when it rolled in at dusk and again at dawn.

The sea pounded the cliffs below them, each wave racing to the shore as if it were being hunted by an enemy just over the horizon. Two turkey vultures with their black wings and red heads swooped low, looking for a tasty breakfast of carrion. Aeron had a sudden picture of the disgusting birds picking at human flesh. She pushed it from her mind.

The fishing village of Bodega Bay had a few motels and a small wharf with bait stores and shell shops. Only a little over an hour from San Francisco, it seemed remote from city life. They stopped at a grocery store to ask for directions to the address of Sara Morgan's house. After all the searching Lee had done to locate Sara, it seemed ironic that the actual house was so easy to find.

Sara had no phone and there hadn't been time to write her a letter, so she had no way of knowing that they were coming.

"She may not even remember me," Aeron said as they approached the old gray farmhouse that was six miles outside the village. "It was fifteen years ago."

"Trust me, Aeron. You are not forgettable."

Lee pulled the Range Rover into a dusty unused driveway. "Well, this is it. Let's hope she has some answers. I would hate for the trail to end here. You don't have any last minute predictions you want to share with me, do you?"

"I wish I did." Aeron rested her hand on the door handle, but could not push it down.

"Aeron, that look of fear is back in your eyes. I can't pretend I understand who you are or what all these memories that haunt you mean. But I do know if you stop here, the fear behind your eyes will never come out."

• 16 •

THEY WALKED UP THE STEPS TO THE PORCH of the old farmhouse. Aeron clasped her arms around her chest to stop her body from trembling. Lee looked for a bell but there wasn't one, so she knocked twice against the door. For a moment they heard nothing from inside the house; then there were footsteps moving in their direction.

The door opened a crack.

"What do you want?" a low voice said suspiciously. "Are you lost?"

"No, we aren't lost," Lee reassured her. "We came out here to see you. You are Sara Morgan, aren't you?"

There was a pause, then the sound of a safety latch releasing. A slender gray-haired woman who looked to be in her late sixties stepped through the door onto the porch. She reached down for the glasses that hung on a chain around her neck. "Yes, I'm Sara. Do I know you?" she said, putting on the glasses.

She looked at Lee, then carefully at the young woman on her porch. Her soft brown eyes appeared tired and lonely. Then her mouth fell open. She recognized this girl!

"Oh, dear God." Her hands went to her face. "I don't believe it! You said you would find me again!" She wanted to reach out to the young woman who stood frozen before her, but she remained still, worried that she might frighten her.

"You are Eve, aren't you?" Sara asked.

Tears ran down Aeron's cheeks when the woman called her Eve. What her mind didn't remember, her heart had saved. She saw herself sitting at a dressing table as the strokes of a soft-bristled brush moved through her fine hair.

"I have never stopped carrying your sweet face, your lovely red hair, and green eyes around in my mind." Sara reached for Aeron's hand. "Do you remember me? You were so young, just a baby."

The Breath of Juno

"May we come inside?" Lee asked.

Stunned, Aeron allowed Lee to guide her into the living room. It all looked so familiar. She touched the tattered fabric that covered the old sofa. Purple flowers—lilacs. She bent and rested her cheek on the cool cotton flowers.

"I do remember you." Her lips quivered. "I remember the sound of your voice."

Sara smiled. "That's because I talked all the time. When you came to me I had been living alone. I used to talk out loud to no one. You were just three years old. I must have talked to you as if you were able to understand everything I said. Sometimes I thought you did understand it all. You were such an extraordinary child." Sara reached over to take Aeron's hands in hers. "If it had been up to me, I never would have let you go."

Aeron held the soft hands, wondering what her life would have been like if this woman had raised her. The loneliness of the years spent in foster homes without anyone to listen to her, to love her, came back to her like a tidal wave breaking over an unsuspecting beach. So many years spent in anger and bitterness, without a real home, until she finally was placed with the Wilkes.

Sara turned to Lee. "I suppose you are her mother now. How long has she been with you?"

Lee was taken back by Sara's question. In spite of the difference between their ages, Lee had never thought of Aeron as a daughter or herself as a mother.

"No. I'm not her mother." She was about to explain that she was Aeron's doctor. But she looked at Sara kneading Aeron's hands and instead said, "I'm her friend."

"How did you ever find me all the way up here?"

"It wasn't easy," Lee said. "Why are you living up here so far from civilization and without a phone?"

"Things are changing too fast for me in this world. I wanted to go backward instead of forward, to live some place that was quiet, where people couldn't find me. San Francisco has become a terrible place to live. The air is unbreathable . . . the streets everywhere are dangerous. Here it's quiet, and there's still time to listen to the birds sing in the morning before they're all gone. I came here to live what was left by myself. I decided we weren't going to win."

"Win?" Lee asked.

"They will take it all away from us with their greed and their arrogance." Sara's face turned red with anger. "They don't care what they do to this poor earth. They want too much of her and she isn't going to be able to keep giving them all they ask."

"Who is this *they* you are talking about?" Lee was beginning to think that Sara Morgan might be a little paranoid.

"They—the ones who make all the decisions—who think they know what's best for the rest of us. The ones who cut down our trees and dump radiation in our oceans. The ones who decide where all the abandoned children are to be stored. That's why I left. They took you from me, Eve. And after you thousands more came to me—homeless, desperate. More and more each year. I couldn't help them anymore—there were too many."

"You did help me," Aeron said, bringing Sara back to the present. "How did you know my name was Eve?"

"It isn't your real name. I gave you the name Eve."

Aeron was shocked. She'd always thought that was her birth name—the name her mother had given her.

"I named you Eve because you were so alone. You were sealed into your own world, and I thought if you grew up that way, you would feel like the only woman on earth."

"Please Sara, tell me how you came to know me."

So Sara began to tell her of the day, fifteen years ago, that had changed her own life.

"At first," she recalled, "I thought you were the child of one of the nuns from the convent, and that she couldn't bear the shame. But I could never believe in my heart that a woman who had dedicated her life to God could abandon a child."

"These nuns—they must have known where I came from. Or did somebody just drop me off at their convent when I was a baby?"

"I think they knew more than they would tell me. I pressed them. Finally the Mother Superior of the convent told me . . . " she hesitated, unsure whether she should tell Aeron the truth and bring fear back into her life.

"Please," Aeron implored her. "I have to know every detail you can think of. I have to find my mother."

"All right, then, I'll tell you everything I can remember. It isn't very much." She told them of her phone calls with the nunnery, conversations with the Mother Superior, and what she remembered of the police investigation. The words that stuck most profoundly in her mind were the Mother Superior's warning: "Her safety, her very life depends on our secrecy. I cannot tell you where she comes from. She is in the hands of God."

The day was hot and the sun baked the roof of the old farmhouse; still the three women felt a chill as Sara spoke.

"My mother must have brought me to St. Andrews Convent because she feared for my life. Who could have wanted to hurt me when I was just a baby?"

"One day," Sara continued, "I remember I took you shopping in a supermarket. A man with a long black coat walked by us, and you started screaming and pointing at him. You were terribly afraid of that coat. It wasn't the man you were afraid of, just the coat."

As Sara spoke, Aeron's mind was carried back into the past. Three men in long black coats flying down at her—black ravens grabbing her flesh!

Sara's gray hair turned a bright red, the wrinkles dissolved from her skin, leaving her face smooth and young. It was a face Aeron remembered! She was just about to cry out "Mother," when the vision vanished. Sara's face returned.

"Sara," Aeron heard Lee asking, "these nuns you speak of—is the convent still active in San Francisco?"

"No, it shut its doors long ago."

"Do you remember the names of any of the nuns? If we can find them . . . "

"I remember the Mother Superior. We talked several times. Her name was Sister Mary Katherine. They never have any last names. I don't know how we'd begin tracing her."

"Well, I do," Lee said, "the Information Office is a pain in the ass most of the time. But they're damn good at finding people, usually for their own purposes. We can tap into their banks. If you can tell me where the convent was, when it closed down, I bet we can trace your Mother Superior."

"You can't do it from here," Sara said. "I haven't even got a telephone."

"There were a few motels on the Bay when we drove in. Sara, will you come with us, spend the night, tell us everything you can remember? You and Aeron can talk, and I'll try to trace Aeron's convent."

The idea of leaving her isolated home frightened Sara. She didn't want to be a part of the world outside ever again. But it was this girl who had brought her back to life after Brad died—who had showed her that love was still possible, and now here she was, pulling her back once again. She looked at Aeron, the child she had known as Eve, and knew she would do whatever was necessary to help her.

"If you think that it's important, I'll come with you. Just give me a few moments to put some things together and lock up the house."

Before they left Sara went upstairs and returned with a tiny satin jewelry bag that she carefully cupped in her right hand. "Before we go, Aeron, I want to give you something. I can't get used to calling you Aeron. I still want to call you Eve. You had something when you came to my house—it was a bracelet. I kept it. I know it was wrong of me. Somehow I felt I needed to keep a part of you. It was on your wrist when the nuns brought you in. It was just a small thing, probably of no significance. I thought you might like to have it back."

She handed Aeron the delicate bag and asked her to release the clasp. The contents took Aeron's breath away. It was a tiny gold chain made for the size of a child's wrist. On it was one charm, a tiny thing, but she could easily make it out. It was a hawk in flight much like the one that Dora had given her.

She showed it to Lee. "My real mother gave me this!"

ONCE THEY HAD checked into the Inn at the Tides in Bodega Bay, Lee went to work on the telephone. She'd brought her modem, computer, fax, and videophone system with her. She was linked up to the information bureau in seconds and began searching for Sister Mary Katherine, Mother Superior, St. Andrews, San Francisco. Sara and Aeron talked while Lee worked.

The memory of Sara as she had been in 1983 was faint in Aeron's mind, yet she felt close to this woman, as if she had always known her. Without telling her anything about the dreams that had haunted her most of her life, she told Sara about the foster families that she had lived with for the past fifteen years.

"If I had known how they would toss you around so terribly, I would never have let them take you away. I would have stolen you myself and prevented you from going through all that sorrow."

Once again, Aeron thought how different her life might have been. She would never have known Lee, Dora, and even Bud. These people had come to mean so much to her. They were her family, and she couldn't imagine life without them.

Two hours later, Lee shouted, "I've got it! I've found her! She's still in San Francisco. She's eighty-three years old. I've got a phone number for her, and she's on the videophone system. Get over here! We're going to give the Mother Superior a call."

The three women huddled around the small screen that was now plugged into the modem. Lee punched in Sister Mary Katherine's phone number in San Francisco. It rang five times as the women waited anxiously. Then they heard it being picked up. "Hello?"

"Is this Sister Mary Katherine?" Lee asked.

"Yes it is. Who's calling please?"

"You don't know me. My name is Lee Edwards. I'm a friend of a young woman who was a three year-old child when she came to your convent some time in the early 1980's. She had bright red hair and green eyes. Do you remember her, Sister?"

The sister was silent for a moment, then sharply asked, "Miss Edwards, who are you?"

"As I said, I'm a friend of that girl. She's eighteen years old now, and she is looking for her real mother . . . her birth mother. We thought perhaps you could help us."

"I don't think so," said Sister Mary Katherine, her voice becoming nervous. "There's really nothing I can tell you."

Lee could tell that she was about to hang up. "Sister, please. You're on the videophone system. It would be easier if we could see each other's faces. The girl is here with me. Will you talk with her?"

There was no response, so Lee quickly activated the system. A moment later the videophone flicked on with Sister Mary Katherine sitting in her living room. Her face was carved by the unforgiving power of time. She placed a pair of bifocals over her squinting gray eyes and examined Aeron's face.

"Sister," Aeron pleaded with her. "I'm asking you to help me find my mother. You're the only one I can turn to."

"Child," the sister said slowly. "I was sworn to secrecy back then, promising I would take my silence to my grave." She paused, then went on. "Perhaps you must know now. You weren't with us for very long . . . only two weeks.

"Two women came to the convent late on a Saturday night. Of course, we let them in because they seemed to be in terrible distress." The faces of the two women were still etched in the Sister's memory. It was not only that they were identical in every respect, but that they seemed to look right through her, into her very soul. She pushed their images from her mind.

"They had a child with them," she continued. "I guess that was you. What did you say your name is?"

"Aeron Wilkes."

"Aeron, these women were sick to death from fear. We asked them to spend the night, but they refused. They said the child was in danger—that they needed us to save her life. The child was marked for death, they said. An attempt had already been made on her life. There would be another.

"The only way the child could be safe was to give her up and hide her some place where she would never be found. They wouldn't tell us anything else—not the name of the child, nor anything about her. We said they could not leave you with us—we were not equipped to take care of a child. One of them grabbed you in her arms and held you, then put you down. They both ran out the front door and disappeared. I never saw them again. I have no idea where they came from or where they went.

"We kept you for two weeks until we had time to decide what to do. It was these women's hope that we keep you in the convent, hidden from secular view, but you became so despondent. You withdrew deeply within yourself—you looked so frightened all the time, waking in the middle of the night, screaming. Something terrible had happened to you. Your life truly was in danger. We wanted to protect you—we feared that you would die in our care."

"Did these women tell you my name?

"No—and we could never get you to speak it either."

Aeron continued to ask the Mother Superior questions, but no more useful answers followed.

Aeron was visibly shaken by the phone call. Had one of those two women seen her mother? Why had she abandoned her? What could possibly have put her life in such danger when she was a child?

Sara put her arms around Aeron as she cried, "It's another dead end. What are we going to do now?"

Lee had to admit she had no more ideas.

"May I make a suggestion?" Sara said. "Why don't we all sleep on it. Maybe tomorrow something new will come into our minds."

Just before they went to sleep, Lee remembered something. "When I hypnotized you, the time that you went back to 1879 into the life of Amy Talbot in Bodie, California, before you went into her life, you talked about when you were three years old. It was the only time I got you to remember any of it. You told me that your mother was reading to you—then suddenly you were being attacked by black ravens.

"Three black ravens swooped out of the sky and were pulling you out of your bed. You were screaming so much that I tried to wake you from hypnosis. It was then that you went into Amy Talbot's life. Do you remember anything about that night?"

"No! I don't know," Aeron cried in frustration. "I don't know what any of this means." She pulled out the bracelet that Sara had given her with the hawk charm. "My mother must have known I was having dreams where I was flying as a hawk. She must have thought that it was a good symbol because she gave me this charm to protect me. None of it makes any sense to me."

As Aeron fell asleep, she tried to imagine herself a child of two or three years old, listening as her mother read to her. The brief vision she had seen of her mother in Sara's face came back. A light scent of pine filled the air.

"Show me where you are," Aeron whispered to the night. "Mother, I am coming to you."

WHEN SHE WOKE the next morning, Lee and Sara were already up, preparing coffee in the mini-percolator. Aeron was eager to tell them what she had seen in her dream.

"There was a vast oval-shaped lake beneath me. The long bank on the west side of the lake rose up to sharp snow-covered mountains. The opposite shore was completely different, it was flat and gray like a desert. The water was the most incredible color—more intense than a blue—a kind of emerald. Pine and fir trees seemed to be growing right out of white sand beaches. There was a bay . . . ."

Sara interrupted her, excitedly. "I think I know this place you saw in your dream!"

"What makes you think she dreamt of a real lake?" Lee challenged her.

"Because she described it perfectly. It can't be anywhere else! Aeron, you saw Lake Tahoe in your dream. There's no other lake with mountains on the west and nothing but desert on the east! The High Sierras are on the California side of Lake Tahoe, and the deserts of Nevada are on the east side. The state line runs right through the center of the lake. It's the biggest lake in the west."

"That's it," Aeron cried. "My mother sent the dream to lead me to her!"

"Lake Tahoe is only about four hours from here. Maybe we should go there," Sara suggested.

"You will come with us, Sara?"

"This is crazy," Lee argued. "We can't just get in the car and drive up into the mountains without knowing where we are going. I know Lake Tahoe. It must be one hundred miles around. What are we going to do—just drive around it until Aeron has another dream? We don't even know what we're looking for up there."

"We are looking for my mother," Aeron snapped. "The dream was sent to me for a reason."

"Aeron, this just isn't logical."

"Does everything have to be logical for you? Have you got any better idea what I should do?"

Lee had to admit that she had no more tangible clues as to how they could find Aeron's mother, so she finally agreed to allow Aeron's instincts to guide them.

As they left the motel, Aeron felt certain that she was destined to find her mother in Lake Tahoe.

· 17 ·

THE THREE WOMEN, BORN IN DIFFERENT generations and with no blood tie to bind them, shared a single purpose as they began the long climb up Interstate 80 to Lake Tahoe. The lake, famous for its beauty, sat in the stark glacier-carved Sierras.

When they reached Donner Pass, Aeron said, "I know this place. I've been here before! Stop the car. I want to feel the ground under my feet."

Lee pulled the Range Rover off the road to an overlook point. They looked down at the Truckee River that wound through the valley below them. Aeron walked toward the edge of the cliff. Sara started to follow her, but Lee held her back.

Even from this distance, the river was a mighty force. "We used to come up here all the time when I was a kid," Sara said. "My family had a summer cabin in the woods. In the Spring of 1988 I came to see what kind of shape it was in. The Truckee was only a trickle that year. Those were the long drought years of the eighties. All the grass in San Francisco went brown after six straight years of drought. People thought it would never end. Now it has been three years of flood with violent thunderstorms and hurricanes across the country. Thousands of people killed, billions of dollars of damage and still the government tells us not to worry. Nature can talk as loud as she wants to and still they don't get it. I hate to say it but I think it's too late."

"That's a pretty pessimistic attitude. You've got to have some faith in the progress we're making," Lee said. "Science always finds answers."

"So much is happening, things that even the best scientists thought wouldn't take place for hundreds of years," Sara disagreed. "The summers are hotter everywhere, even the winter rains are warm so that they bring floods to the mountains, not snow. I used to write letters pleading with the government to see what was happening. I felt like Jacob going to the Pharaoh and predicting that the years of feast would be followed by years of famine. At least the Pharaoh listened to Jacob."

"You have isolated yourself in that fishing village for too long. Things are being done," Lee said, disgusted with Sara's fatalism. "They're looking for ways to control all the changes in the weather. We used to seed the clouds to make it rain. Now they are learning how to seal them to stop the rain."

"That's just the problem. They are looking for ways to control the impact of nature's violence. What they should be looking for are the reasons that we made her so mad in the first place."

"I remember this valley," Aeron yelled to them. "Quick, come over here." Lee and Sara stopped arguing and walked to the cliff's edge. "I have been here before. I'm sure of it."

"In this lifetime or another?" Lee asked, forgetting that Sara knew nothing about the Shadow visits.

Sara was surprised when Aeron took Lee's remark seriously.

"I'm not sure if I'm seeing it from when I was a child, or if it belongs to someone else."

"I'm afraid you two have lost me," Sara said. "What are you talking about?"

Lee and Aeron looked at one another, not knowing what to say. "I think we should tell her," Aeron said.

"Tell me what?" Sara was beginning to feel uneasy.

"I wanted to tell you last night after we talked with Sister Mary Katherine, but I thought you would be safer if you didn't know everything about me. Now I'm afraid that we have already come too far together. I pulled you into this without warning you that we might be in danger."

Sitting on the rocks overlooking the valley, Aeron told Sara about the dreams and the Shadows. She expected her to be shocked, but Sara took it in without question.

"I knew then that you were an extraordinary child. I used to imagine that you were an alien from a distant planet. You often said things that made me feel you were an adult living in a child's body. The idea of reincarnation never came to me."

"There may be another explanation for these phenomena that Aeron is experiencing," Lee said. The idea of reincarnation was at odds with her rational way of seeing events. She still wanted to believe that if Aeron found her mother, she could face the vivid fantasies that took over her body so realistically and allow them to disappear. Even Aeron's strange connection with the Siamese twins would have a basis in logic.

Once Sara had spoken the word, *reincarnation,* Aeron knew that although Lee was her confidant and friend, she didn't understand and accept her as Sara did.

"This is getting out-of-hand," Lee said. "Here we are sitting on the top of Donner Pass talking about past lives. When you said you had been here before, Aeron, I hope you weren't passing through in 1846 with the Donner Party."

"What was the Donner Party?"

"My god, there is something you don't know about," she said sarcastically. "Then I forgot, you were living in Bodie at the time the Donner Party got snowed in up here and froze to death. They had to eat their dead in order to live through the winter."

"How horrible," Aeron said.

"We should get going," Lee said abruptly. "I don't want to be driving this mountain road at night."

"Lee, you're angry." Aeron put her hand on Lee's shoulder. "I know it's hard for you to understand all this. It's hard for me too. I know you're here to help me find answers."

"Right. So let's get moving," Lee stood and walked back to the Rover. Sara and Aeron followed her.

A short while later they stopped for sandwiches at a cafe in the town of Truckee, then drove the last ten miles to the lake. The night air pressed against Aeron's body as if each mile increased the force of gravity. Excitement and fear fought for control of her mind. She searched Lee and Sara's tired faces. They had no idea what lay ahead for them. The closer they came to the lake, the more she knew that she was guiding the three of them into a danger she could feel though not explain.

"There it is," Sara said as they approached Lake Shore Drive. "Lake Tahoe." Her voice quickly turned from enthusiasm to disappointment. "My god," she said, staring at the expansive lake.

"What's wrong?" Lee asked.

"It's been so long since I was here." Tears came to Sara's eyes.

"This lake used to be so beautiful. The water was emerald green . . . so pure and clean."

They drove along the shore in silence, gazing at the black still water. The setting sun reflected off its dense oily surface. Trembling, Aeron suddenly shouted. "I know where we are!"

"Good," Lee said. "Can you tell us where we go from here?"

"Turn right. We go south on the west bank of the lake for about eight miles. There will be a place called Sherwin Creek."

"You weren't even old enough to read when you left here. How can you remember the name of the town?" Sara asked, then she saw that Aeron's eyes were staring into the distance without focusing on anything. It was the same empty gaze she had seen in the child who first came to her home so many years ago.

Resorts and homes separated them from the water's edge for the first few miles, then the road curved, taking them close to the shore. The partial skeleton of an old wooden pier came into view, the moorings rotted with time.

"Stop here," Aeron cried when she spotted the remains of the pier sticking precariously out of the water.

Lee pulled the Range Rover over to the side of the road. Aeron quickly jumped out and ran to the pier. Lee opened the door to follow her. Sara took Lee's arm, stopping her.

"What's the matter with you?" Lee said pulling her arm free. "She'll fall right through that thing into the lake."

"She sees something out there," Sara said, watching the girl climb over the broken slants of the pier. "It is not our place to interfere."

Reluctantly Lee stayed in the car.

From the end of the pier Aeron saw a small rowboat bobbing in the gentle currents of the lake. It was a warm calm day. A young child sat in the stern as a woman rowed out further from the shore. Both the woman and the child had brilliant red hair that sparkled in the sunlight. The woman pulled the oars into the boat, and they drifted peacefully. Aeron looked down to discover she was wearing a cotton sundress and tiny sandals. The woman was reading to her from a book called *The Little Red Pony*. She giggled as the woman acted out the story.

Then she was standing on the edge of the pier. She was not alone. Across the lake a white mist rose from the water and slowly formed into two giant faces without bodies—the twins! She saw them sailing across the water towards her, calling to her, both mouths moving together.

"Kayla, let us in. Don't hide from us. Kayla, remember it all."

Who were they and what did they want from her?

The next thing she knew Lee was helping her climb off the dangerous pier and walking her back to the car.

"We must hurry," Aeron said, getting into the front seat. "I know where my mother lives. She's in danger! I've got to go to her."

Aeron directed Lee to Spruce Lane, a street that lay in the foothills just behind the town of Sherwin Creek. When they turned on to the lane, Aeron was eager to get out of the Rover.

"Park here," she said. "We'll walk the last half mile."

"It's already dark," Lee protested. "Why can't we drive right to the house? We don't even know if your mother still lives here. It's been fifteen years. She could have moved away long ago."

"She's here. I can feel her!" Her heart pounded against her chest. Nothing mattered now but her desperate desire to see her mother.

The three of them hurried down the narrow road, then Aeron guided them behind the few scattered houses to where the forest began. The ground was covered with fall leaves and pine needles. She told them to walk softly so as not to make any noise.

"If we are being watched," she had to explain, "we ought to come in quietly through the forest."

"Who could be watching us?" Lee asked. Even as she spoke the words, Aeron's fear flowed into her.

"There's a side door that goes into the kitchen, with a huge oak tree covering it," Aeron whispered. "That should protect us from being seen."

"You've come a long way from not knowing where your mother is, just yesterday, to remembering secret back door entrances," Lee whispered back.

"I'm not remembering it. I can see it in my mind."

They made their way through the forest until they came to the back of a small house with peeling green paint. Firewood was stacked up to the A-frame roof.

"There's lights on," whispered Sara. "What are you going to do? If you go to the back door, won't she be frightened?"

"You stay here. I'm going by myself. It will be quieter."

The two women watched Aeron move under the heavy canopy of sycamore trees. The low moon cast the trees in long shadows. Aeron moved quickly, hiding from the moon's light. When she got close to the side door off the kitchen, her sense that she was being watched grew more intense. She looked around for another way to approach the house. There was a window hidden from view by a large overhang on the roof.

She ducked under the overhang and looked in through the window. Inside was a child's bedroom. At first the room appeared to be empty. Then she heard soft humming, not a tune at all, but a low purring, as a contented cat would make. There was a down quilt lying at the foot of the bed. As she looked at it, she could feel its softness caressing her body. She could smell the scent of freshly washed flannel.

As she stared into the room, she thought she saw the blankets on the bed move. Then a small head raised up on the pillow—a child with brilliant green eyes! She looked into the girl's eyes and saw herself. She wanted to smash the windowpane with her fist, to climb in and hold the child until their skin and bones melted together making them one. The distance between them remained. She watched from the outside as a woman entered the room, sat beside the child on the bed, and with great animation told her a story. Aeron could hear the woman's low-pitched voice inside her head as clearly as if she'd been in the room. It was a familiar voice. She knew it as if she had last heard it only yesterday. The woman was her mother.

"Kayla," her mother said. "One more story and then it's bedtime."

Kayla. She remembered it now. That was the name the twin faces had called her on the lake. Kayla. It was all coming back to her so fast—living in this house with her mother, playing on the shore of the lake, taking out the boat on Sunday afternoons, watching the birds fish at dusk. She was home and she could remember all of it!

Her whole body shook as she watched her mother bend to kiss the small girl's cheek. When her lips touched the young flesh, she felt the pressure on her own skin.

"Mother," she whispered. Tears ran down her cheeks, as she stood outside the house in Sherwin Creek, California, watching a memory that had happened fifteen years ago as though it had been frozen in this spot, playing itself over and over again, waiting for this moment, for her to look through the window and see it happen!

"Kayla," her mother's voice repeated her name, and Aeron wanted to scream, "I'm here, Mother! I'm here! I'm your daughter, Kayla, and I am still alive."

The child giggled at her mother's story, clapping her hands in delight. When her small arm came out from under the covers, Aeron saw something shiny around her wrist. It was a bracelet—a gold bracelet with a charm attached—a tiny hawk, its wings spread in flight! The same bracelet she now held in her hand.

Just then a terrible thundering came from further inside the house. The bedroom door flew open, and the child's tiny room was suddenly full of men. So many of them in long black coats like hungry birds of prey swooping down on the child. They were everywhere, grabbing the side of the bed, holding her down. The child was screaming. She watched herself screaming from her child's mouth and realized that the same scream was coming from her own throat on the other side of the window.

She heard her mother shout, "Why are you taking my daughter? Stop! What are you doing?"

And the child . . . "Mommy! Mommy! Help!"

The red-haired woman threw herself at the men in the long black coats, pushing them away from her child. One of them viciously flung her away with his arm, and she fell against the wall, hitting her head against the steel radiator. Her body slid, lifelessly, to the floor.

"Mother! No!" Aeron screamed, pounding on the glass.

The child struggled to free herself. Aeron yelled, "Stop! Leave her alone! Let her go!"

Her screams brought Lee and Sara from where they waited in the forest. They raced down to the back of the house to find Aeron, her hands clawing at the glass, screaming.

Lights popped on throughout the entire house. A man in his pajamas opened the back door, holding a rifle. "What's going on? Who's there?"

Lee stepped between him and Aeron. "It's a mistake," she explained. "I'm so sorry. We're at the wrong house. Please . . . forgive her. She's fine. She was just frightened by something in the woods. So sorry to wake you up."

Sara pulled Aeron away from the window and back to the road, while Lee made their apologies as gracefully as she could. Once the three women were safely back in Lee's Range Rover, they tried to get Aeron to calm down, but she couldn't stop crying.

The vision she had seen inside the small house happened over and over again in her mind as though it would never end.

"She's dead," she kept repeating. "My mother is dead. She called me here. How could she be dead? I saw her in the house and before that, I saw her on the lake. It was the vision of her that brought me here. I thought she was still alive because I could hear her calling me. I was hearing the past. All these years I thought she was out there waiting for me, I've been seeing the past. She's been calling me from the past.

"She's dead. She died a long time ago."

An overwhelming sense of grief came to Aeron. Now that she could remember the touch of her mother's soft hand against her cheek, the fresh smell of her skin, the light sound of her voice—now that she could finally remember her mother's love—it was all taken from her. She would never again feel her mother's arms around her body, holding her, protecting her.

Aeron wanted to go back to the house, smash the window, put her arms around her mother and pull her out of the house before the men in the black coats arrived, before they flung her against the wall, leaving her lifeless on the floor. She wanted to go back in time, stop it before it happened, change the future from that moment forward. An intense pain of loss settled deep into her bones.

· 18 ·

"THEY KILLED HER," AERON MUMBLED. "AND NOW they want to kill me. They're still out there, looking for me."

The three of them sat in the Range Rover, uncertain of what to do next.

"Aeron," Lee said, "this is the house where you spent the first three years of your life. When you looked through that window, you might have remembered something that actually happened here. But whatever you saw, it happened a long time ago. No one wants to hurt you now."

Aeron ignored Lee's words. How could she ever make Lee understand that she was wrong. How could she explain why she knew with certainty that someone did want to hurt her now and that they were out there searching for her, waiting? That any moment, they would find her. They'd been looking for her all of her life—her, and all the Shadows that lived within her. Lee would never believe any of this. It could never make sense in her rational world. It was Sara who would believe, so she pleaded with Sara to understand.

"It isn't safe here. The men I saw in that room are still here looking for me. We have to find a place to hide."

Sara needed very little convincing. She seemed to know instinctively that Aeron's life was in danger.

"They know I'm here," Aeron kept saying. The image of the twin faces came into sharp focus in her mind. Somehow they were connected to the men in the cabin. "It wasn't my mother who sent me the vision of the lake or the memory of my home. It was them! They brought me here. They made me believe that she was still alive. They called me home to my mother, to show her to me. But what they were showing me was the past."

Lee tried to reason with her, but Aeron shut out her voice. How could she understand that things did not move through time in a logical way? Time wasn't a straight line. The terrible moment she had seen in that bedroom had happened fifteen years ago, and it was still happening now. She could feel it as profoundly as she could feel her own body.

"We must get out of here," Sara said, taking charge.

"Where do we go now?" Lee said.

"I don't know yet," Sara replied. "Just drive."

Aeron curled up in the back seat, pulling her knees to her chest, hugging her thin body, rocking up and back. She felt more lost and abandoned than ever before. Everything was in the past. All the Shadows that came to her brought the past. What did she care about the past if she could do nothing to change it—if she couldn't call back the one moment she had just seen inside that house and save her mother's life? She knew that the past she had seen was unalterable.

Aeron fell silent and started to shiver. Sara tried to get her to talk, to pull her from the trance that was taking over her body.

"What did you see in the bedroom?"

Aeron would not describe what she had seen, but thoughts raced through her mind. Whoever had come to take her as a child, whoever had killed her mother, was still out there now, looking for her, waiting for the right moment.

Sara put her arms around the girl trying to comfort her. Still Aeron remained in a world of her own. When she looked up at Sara's face, its soft features changed and doubled before her eyes. Sara's face was replaced by a two-headed creature—the twin faces attached to one body.

"No!" she screamed, pulling her body away from them. "They want to kill me! Stop them! Stop them!"

Lee had had enough of Aeron's panic. She had to do something—something logical, sensible. "Sara," she said, "I'm going to take her to the hospital in Reno. She's having some kind of breakdown. She needs help."

Sara knew that no hospital could help Aeron. She had remembered the child's frightened eyes when she had screamed in the market at the man in the long black coat when she was three years old. And now she seemed to be seeing the same image. The look of terror was the same in her eyes. She was reliving something that had happened, some great harm that had come to her and her mother. She felt the same overwhelming desire to protect the girl as she had when Aeron was a child.

"She doesn't need a hospital. She needs us," Sara said. "Even if whatever happened in that house took place a long time ago, it may be that Aeron's life might be in danger now. For that matter all of our lives. I know where we can go, where we can be safe for the night. Lee, please do what I tell you."

Lee was not about to take directions from Sara. She pushed her foot against the accelerator and turned on to the main highway, heading towards Reno.

The sudden jerk of the car woke Aeron from her trance. She understood Lee's intent. She remembered when she had stood before the auditorium of faces on her graduation, how she had been able to bend their minds with her will, how easy it had been to make them do what she wished. Now it seemed terribly important to bring Lee to her will. She sat up in the back seat and reached forward, placing her hand on Lee's shoulder, pressing firmly down. Calm, she thought, I have to sound calm.

"Lee, turn up the dirt road as Sara has told you." Her voice was low and hypnotic. "We are not going to Reno. We are going into the mountains."

Lee quickly took her foot off the accelerator and the car slowed. Instead of taking the turn that would put them on the highway, Lee veered to the left as Aeron had instructed her to do. Without speaking, she followed Aeron's will.

Sara was astonished by the impact Aeron's words had on Lee. Without a question Lee was doing exactly what Aeron told her to do. "There is a place . . . " Sara lowered her voice. "The cabin I told you about. I was there ten years ago, in '88. No one will know we're there." Sara began giving Lee directions, telling her where and when to turn. They drove west, further into the mountains.

As Lee understood that she was no longer in charge she relaxed, allowing Sara to take over.

Sara guided them from one unpaved road to another. Each dirt road became increasingly more difficult to steer through. Without any maintenance, the roads were turning back into the trails they had once been. Debris from fallen trees, rocks, and mud from heavy fall storms made the road almost impassable in spots. Twice they had to get out and move objects from their path in order to get the Rover through.

"It's amazing you can find this place yourself," Lee said as they reached yet another fork in the road, and Sara instructed her to go left. "It's a good bet no one else will be able to find us here."

"My family only used the cabin in the summer. This road was in a lot better condition back then. The cabin's been abandoned for years. It's pretty isolated up here."

Aeron was quiet. Each turn took them deeper into the wilderness, yet she still felt that they were being watched. They hadn't seen another car for over a half-hour, still she could feel the presence of someone following her.

It was two in the morning when they found the cabin. When Aeron got out of the Range Rover, another shock hit her. I've been here before, she thought. Right here at this cabin. Then it came back to her. Sitting in the abandoned field in Highland when she was thirteen, she'd had a vision of this place. It was the first time she saw the floating faces that called to her. They had shown her this cabin, this moment in time! They were a window into the future as well as the past.

Weeds crawled up the log walls, blocking the door. Their hands were cut and bleeding by the time they managed to clear their way inside. The full moon was their only light. All their work was rewarded with a rotten smell inside.

"Jesus," Lee said, putting the sleeve of her blouse over her nose. "It smells like air that's been trapped in a dark cave for a few thousand years."

"I boarded up the windows when I was last here ten years ago. There's a tool box in here somewhere. If I can find the hammer, I'll get the boards off and let some fresh air into this place."

"Are there any candles here?" Lee asked, longing for her own comfortable bed and the safety of her home in San Bernardino.

Sara found a box of candles and began lighting them from a book of matches Lee had in her purse.

Aeron, still shocked by all that she'd seen, took one of the candles and wandered to the back of the cabin. There were two small bedrooms with pairs of single beds in each. Between them was a door that opened on a narrow staircase. Aeron felt herself being drawn up the stairs one at a time, as if someone was in the room above waiting for her. The weak light of the candle guided her up the damp stairwell. Another door sat at the top on the stairs. She reached for the knob and twisted it to the right. The door slowly swung open. She took a step into the room. In the candle's light she thought she saw a shape—as if a figure were standing next to the boarded-up window. She went closer towards the dark shape.

Aeron stood frozen, too frightened to scream. Looking at her was a young child! She was moving her mouth, trying to speak, but no words came out. The child's long blond hair was draped over her shoulders, hanging against her white nightdress. Water was dripping from her body on to the wooden floor. She was soaking wet.

Her arms rose from her sides as she reached out to Aeron. Then a sound came from the child—a thin voice whispered, "I am of you. Father will come to you. Go with him."

Without thinking Aeron moved towards the child. She was filled with a desire to take her in her arms, to comfort her—to save her. Just as she was near enough to touch the child, the girl vanished. All that remained of her presence was the wet spot on the floor.

Limp, Aeron fell back on the musty bed. Her heart pounded in her ears. No more, she begged silently. I can't take any more. Without my mother, there is no one to make it all end. She pressed her fists against her eyes wishing she would never see any of it again. The vision had felt so real. She had wanted so much to hold the child. It was as if she had known her all of her short life. Who was she?

Then she remembered! The girl in her dream—the girl in the middle of the river struggling to keep her rowboat float. Aeron gasped as the memory returned . . . the suffocation, the desperate longing for air as she slipped deeper into the water. She had felt it with this terrified child when she had drowned. Was she really dead? Why had she appeared tonight in this desolate place? What had her words meant?

THE MOON SET AT four in the morning, leaving a few hours of complete darkness before the sun would burn into the sky once again.

When Sara and Lee fell asleep, Aeron walked outside on the rickety porch. The night was quiet and still. Nothing moved in the woods around her. The only vision that filled her mind now was the one she had seen through the window of the house on Spruce Lane. She played the scene over and over in her mind, each time believing that she could crawl inside the body of that three year old child, the child that she was, and change things so that the man in the long black coat who threw her mother against the wall would freeze, his arm outstretched in time. And her mother could still be alive today. No matter how many times the vision went through her head the outcome was always the same.

Looking in through the window, she could only see the long black coats flying around the room, not the faces of the men wearing them. Each time she replayed the scene in her mind, she was on the outside looking in. The hours passed and still she could not sleep. I have to get inside, she thought, I have to see their faces. I need to know who killed my mother, and why, and what happened to me that night.

Show me, she furiously demanded of the night. And then it happened. In a moment, she was through the window, inside the child, looking out from those tiny eyes, straight up at the black coats that hovered around her, looking into their faces.

In an instant they imprinted themselves on her mind, and she knew she would never forget them—the old man with the long pointed nose and close-set eyes, the one with the round face with thick, heavy eyebrows, and the young one with the thin mouth and pinched lips. These were the faces of the black coats, the faces who grabbed her small body, yanked her from her bed, and threw her mother against the wall. These were the faces! She knew them. She wanted revenge.

Her grief and her rage merged until they were one, tangible and black within her body. The anger grew within her until she could no longer house its power. It shot out from her body and soared into the dark night on the wings of a hawk. She sent it searching, searching for the black-coated faces who had taken her safety, taken everything except her life.

She wanted the great bird to rip the flesh from the men who had inflicted this terrible wound on her, taken her mother from her. She looked down at the earth, through the sharp hawk eyes, searching for them in the night.

They would pay.

· 19 ·

FATHER DECARLO WOKE IN THE MIDDLE OF THE night, his body burning with fever. When he opened his eyes, he discovered that his vision was blurry. Frightened, he sat straight up in bed, staring at the striped gray curtains across the room. They seemed to be undulating as if he was seeing them through waves of heat. He blinked, trying to clear his vision when suddenly the curtains disappeared . . . the entire wall vanished and before him was the bedroom of a child, a bedroom he would never forget.

He saw it all, happening again and again, his own hands pulling the child from the bed, the woman throwing her body between him and the child. And then the woman flying so lightly through the air, like a feather, falling to the floor.

Gasping, he pulled himself out of bed, stumbled to the bathroom and stuck his head under a stream of cold water, trying to clear his mind. Why am I seeing this now, he asked himself.

Then he understood.

This comes from her—I am seeing it as she saw it. He opened the heavy curtains and looked out at the black night. He imagined what she must look like now. He hadn't seen her since that night when she was three years old, and now she was a young woman of eighteen, and she was about to die.

When he was able to sit down on his bed, and breathe normally once again, he realized the importance of what he had just seen. She's there! She's at her mother's home! After all these years he had found her. It was just as he had always believed. Once the power grew strong within her, she would not be able to hide herself from those who were joined to the spirit, and he believed his connection to the spirit was deeper than anyone else. It was he that she searched for in the night with her pain and rage. In her innocence, she had betrayed herself to him. Excitement pulsed through his veins. He would find her in time!

He quickly called Brother Martin in Rome and discovered that the monk had had the same experience.

"So she has sent you the message as well," Father DeCarlo said, a slight tone of jealousy in his voice. He had been so certain that the spirit would come only to him.

"Our moment has come!" Brother Martin was eager to act. "We must gather our strength and go to her. It is time for Gavin Langley to play his part. I will send him to her at once. He will be our guide. She is of him. He will be able to find where she hides."

Father DeCarlo wanted to say we don't need Langley anymore, though now he couldn't be certain. They had gone to Langley because Brother Martin had believed only the father of Mary Alice would be able to feel Kayla's presence when the power began to fly out from her mortal body. If they had to use Langley to find her, so be it. But only he would be there at the final moment. He longed to look into her eyes before it happened, to see into the spirit that lived within her. He wanted to feel its power, to be as close as he could to it, before he destroyed its mortal home.

The end was in sight. After years of searching for the girl, for any clue of her existence, they had found her. Now it was only a matter of time until all of it would be at an end.

Father DeCarlo pulled off his silk nightshirt, opened the doors, and naked stepped out onto the balcony to look at the sea. A warm breeze caressed his flesh. He was eighty-two years old but he had never doubted that he would live to see it through. He had always known that God would grace him with the years and the strength to keep searching. And now he was to be rewarded with the final denial of the spirit's power.

There were so few of them left who still believed in the ancient ways, who still knew of the ancient prophecies. His greatest fear had been that the spirit could outlive them all, bursting forth into the next millennium after their deaths when no one remained alive to stop it.

He went to his desk and picked up *The Book of Sidon Prophecies* that he read every morning before he read his Bible. He turned the pages yellowed with age, hand-scribed by monks over the centuries.

The Breath of Juno

Words thought lost a thousand years ago, yet passed down from one holy hand to another. Here was the Juno Prophecy spoken by the brotherhood of Sidon, long before the birth of Christ.

Father DeCarlo rubbed the palm of his hand across his perfectly smooth chest. He was the last of the line. Others had watched to see the prophecies fulfilled. One by one they had come true over time. Other seers had looked into the future from the dark ages, and much of what they had seen had come to pass. The visions of Nostradamus were famous, but only the Sidon's voice echoed from the beginning of time.

GAVIN LANGLEY WAS IN Sherwin Creek by late afternoon of the following day. Ever since they had come to him in Wales, he had waited for this moment to arrive—his chance to avenge his daughter's death.

Brother Martin had called and told him to go to her—that he would find her in California, in the village of Sherwin Creek on the west bank of Lake Tahoe. His duty, the monk told him, was to keep the women of Juno from hurting the innocent girl he knew as Kayla Casey. Although the girl's mother had died in a car accident many years ago, Brother Martin said the girl believed that her mother was still alive. They had reports that she had now returned to her birth place to find her mother. It was his job to find the girl, and keep watch over her until the Brotherhood of Sidon could warn her of the danger and save her from the women of Juno.

Now, standing on the deck at the Iris Inn on the lake shore—now that he was deeply in the middle of this strange drama, he felt confused. Protecting the girl had seemed such an important responsibility when the priest first entrusted the task to him. He had believed the Father and the monk when they said that this cruel cult of women intended to kill another child.

As he watched the sun's first rays hitting the lake, he wondered if all of this was not the dream of senile old men. How was he supposed to find Kayla? Why had they chosen him?

The image of his own daughter, Mary Alice, came into his mind as it often did, leaving him sad and alone. Her innocent face burned into his heart, clouding his thoughts. Yes, he did want revenge for her young death. Even though it had been eighteen years since she drowned, he thought of her every day of his life. If she had lived she would be twenty-six years old now.

He knew that she had died alone, falling into the river from their tiny rowboat, but still he wanted someone to blame. He wanted to believe that the women of Juno had caused her death.

The Breath of Juno

• 20 •

Like a broad maple leaf she floats in a slow-moving stream, the water gently rocking her body, caressing her cool skin, swirling around her fingers. Gliding with the current, light as air. No longer solid but transparent liquid, she lives—breathes in a world beyond time. Spinning around, defying the current, she drifts upstream in a back eddy, circling without need of direction, without fear or care. The night sky, an endless canopy, glows in the halo of a full moon.

Above her, a single hawk hangs in the darkness, so still, as if by a string from heaven. Slowly it descends, growing larger as it approaches the earth. Then it hovers just above her, its wings wider than the river's banks. She is filled with wonder as the giant bird sails over her and perches on the branch of an ancient oak tree. The water ceases to flow. She lies motionless, marveling at the great hawk when suddenly it is transformed into the serene figure of a woman with wings for arms and skin of copper. The slanted eyes first appear to be coal black, but as the night light reflects against the irises, they turn a brilliant shade of green. The strange creature is cradling a baby not more than a few hours old in her winged arms.

She lowers her majestic head, placing her mouth over the child's face. The still forest bends with a gust of wind as the hawk woman's breath enters the infant's lungs. A cry pierces the night—a cry of first life.

THE LIGHT OF DAY leaked through the cabin's windows. Lee woke. The dream had come to her just before dawn. She could still feel the peaceful water holding her body. She looked at the others as they slept. She climbed out of bed and opened the cabin door to let in the morning air. The bright light caused Aeron and Sara to stir slowly as if waking from a deep sleep.

"I had the most unbelievable dream," Lee said, eager to tell them before the memory slipped away. "I was floating in a river, so quiet and calm. I wasn't in my body or any body really. I was the water! Then a hawk descended and changed into a spirit creature . . . "

Sara sat up, startled by Lee's words. " . . . a woman with feathers for skin. She held a baby with the birth blood still fresh on her forehead and breathed her life into the infant. Lee, we had the same dream!"

"Aeron," Sara looked at the still-waking girl. "You entered our minds while we slept. You have given us your dream!"

"There is a rational explanation for all of this," Lee insisted nervously.

"Then how do you explain the dream we shared?"

Lee paced the room. "I have to admit that it was one of the strangest experiences of my life. The dream was so vivid, as if I could reach out and touch the child. There is a type of dream telepathy that has been documented in medical literature. Just because we were all picking up the same dream doesn't mean that there was anything supernatural going on. Telepathy, mind-reading, even seeing events that took place hundreds of years ago, are all beginning to be understood in scientific terms. They are heightened forms of awareness that we all may be capable of tapping into one day."

"Lee, it isn't important how it happened. Why did you have my dream?" Aeron asked.

"It wasn't your dream. Aeron, please listen to me. You aren't sending us your dreams. And no one is hunting you."

"They are, and when they find me I'll know the meaning and the power of the hawk woman you saw in your dream. Since I was thirteen years old, she and I have been one. When I know who she is, I'll know who I am and why the Shadows come to me. They aren't just fantasies as you think they are, Lee. They come fully—I see their whole lives. Lee, you can't hide from my world. It will change you as it has changed me."

"I think we should leave here now," Lee said, frightened by the intensity in Aeron's voice.

"And go where?" Sara challenged her.

The three women got dressed in silence, not knowing what they should do next. Sara looked through the pantry covered in cobwebs and began pulling canned fruits and vegetables from the shelves. She placed them on the table in order of their expiration date.

"Well, if we are going to stay here any longer we need to get some food," Lee said, looking at the cans packaged in 1989. "This stuff has got to be full of either ptomaine or penicillin by now. The two might actually cancel each other out but I'm not willing to risk it. Sara, how about you draw me a map so I can get to town and then find my way back here. I'll get us some real food."

"I wish there was some way you could get in to town without taking the Range Rover," Sara said. "Someone might have spotted it."

"It took us hours to drive to this place. I hope you're not suggesting that I walk back to town," Lee said, rummaging through her purse looking for money she had stuffed in different compartments.

She looked at Aeron who was sitting cross-legged on the floor, her head in her hands. "Does this plan meet with your approval?" she snapped at the girl. "Can you look into the future and tell me if you see anything that I should know about for the next three hours?"

Aeron jumped up. "You look at me like I'm supposed to have all the answers. I don't know what we should do any more than you." Angrily, Aeron threw a can of Bird's Eye peas against the wall. It exploded, leaving green slime rolling down through years of dust. "I don't know why you all had my dream last night. There is too much happening too fast. If we don't slow down I'm going to come apart."

"You're right," Lee said, feeling ashamed of her own frustration and anger. This was much more then an uncomfortable adventure to Aeron. She had just come to understand that her mother had been dead for fifteen years, and now she believed that someone intended to kill her.

Lee put the Rover into first gear and started down the dirt road. She didn't feel fear for herself, but when she looked at Aeron's shrinking face in the rear view mirror, the dream came back to her—the sensation of drifting in endless time, of being immortal. It was a wondrous feeling. She said a silent prayer to a god or gods she didn't believe in to keep the girl safe.

GAVIN DIDN'T KNOW where to begin his quest, so he walked around the village of Sherwin Creek to get his bearings. At the far edge of the town he found a small market and realized he was hungry. As he stood in line waiting for the cashier to ring up a package of chocolate donuts, a container of orange juice, and a cheap bottle of white wine, he noticed the attractive woman in front of him. She was slim and athletic-looking. An unexpected desire to talk to her came to him. It had been a long time since he'd looked at a woman with interest. There had been a few short affairs since his wife died, but he had never been interested in making a commitment with any of the women he had gone out with. No one could replace his Margaret Ann.

When the woman glanced back at him, he saw that she was tense as if alert to a sudden danger. The brief glance gave him an opportunity to speak.

"I know you must think it a wretched sight, chocolate donuts and white wine."

She relaxed and smiled when she heard his Welsh accent. What a lovely smile she had, he thought, and there was such intelligence and eagerness in her eyes.

"Not to me," she said. "Today, that's my kind of breakfast too. Look." She moved the bread and fruit in her basket aside revealing the same brand of donuts and three bottles of wine. They both laughed.

He wanted to talk with her more. She seemed receptive to him. He knew that he was still an attractive man, even though he was approaching fifty. Women liked his weathered looks, his red beard, his ruddy complexion, the light wrinkles that had settled in around his eyes. But this was not the time nor the place for such feelings. "Have a nice day," was all he could think of to say as she took her packages and left the market.

As the cashier rang up his purchases, he opened the donuts and took a bite out of one. Outside, he saw the woman still loading her groceries into the back of a red Range Rover. He longed to offer her his help, but he turned away and walked back to his motel.

The Iris Inn was situated directly along the lake. His room looked out on the silence of the deep water, but he could still hear the sounds of traffic traveling south towards the gambling areas.

When night fell he uncorked the wine and drank two glasses to help him sleep. He woke at three in the morning with the strangest dream hanging in his mind. It pressed into his consciousness. He got out of bed and poured himself more wine. On the terrace of his small room, he looked out at the black lake, lit by the now waning moon. He felt compelled to remember the dream.

He had seen a black river churned up violently by the wind. That was an image he was familiar with. Whenever he thought about his daughter Mary Alice, he saw the river that had taken her life. Then the river brightened, its surface glistening with the moon's reflected white light. No longer water, but a bending ribbon of supple cloth.

A long line of women dressed in white robes softly chanting. He could hear the peaceful, soothing sounds of their chant. He felt a deep sense of calm come over him, as if the dream had woken him not from just one night's sleep, but from years, even centuries of sleep.

He went back to bed, closed his eyes and slept again. The ribbon of women returned to him. The river became a mountain stream. Just behind the stream was a decaying log cabin hardly visible in a thick woods. A young woman with her head bowed stood on the porch, her red hair shining in the moonlight. He called to her, and she lifted her head, revealing a face wet with tears. Then her sharp green eyes changed to a deep blue; the red hair became blond. She was no longer a young woman, but a child—his child! Mary Alice. She raised her arm and as it moved gracefully through the air, it became the wing of a giant bird. She invited him to ride upon her wing and carried him high off the ground until he could see the woods and the cabin a great distance below him.

The next morning when he woke he remembered seeing his daughter in his dream, and there was more. He had seen her! *Kayla.* He knew where she was! She had shown herself to him just as the monk suggested she might. He called Father DeCarlo to tell him that he felt certain he could find the cabin he had seen in the dream and that the girl would be there. They could go to her—protect her. The Father was deeply pleased with his dream, though he didn't seem surprised that the vision had come to Gavin in such a strange manner. The Father insisted that Gavin tell him exactly what he had seen—every detail.

"Wait for us, Gavin, we are coming. Do not go to her alone. You may be in danger. Tomorrow we will arrive and go to her together," the priest promised.

· 21 ·

Gavin cursed himself for his inaction. Why had he waited all day for them to arrive? A girl's life was at stake. He should have ignored the priest and gone to find her on his own. Instead he had spent the day in his room drinking wine and thinking about the past.

So many years living alone in the bleak rugged countryside of Wales had made him inert. He was disgusted by the man he had become—passive and indifferent to the lives of others. When the priest first visited him in Wales, invading his solitude, he had no interest in the world outside his home. He could never have imagined then that the fragile old man would pull him out of his seclusion and send him so far from his land. When this was all over, he promised himself, as he poured a fourth glass of wine, he would stay in America and try to make a new life for himself.

At dusk he went down to the lake to walk along the sandy shore. A warm wind came across the water, breaking the surface into foaming white caps. He had wandered a few hundred yards when he saw two figures in the distance. Coming towards him along the empty beach were two older women. Long skirts hung on their thin bodies swaying together as they walked into the wind. Gavin stared at them as if they were a mirage born in his mind. As they came closer he could make out their faces. They were identical! He was so startled that he froze in his tracks. Identical in every aspect—the twins! They were much older, but still he would never forget them.

They had haunted him over the years, whenever the frustration and anger he felt over his daughter's death came in despondent moods. He remembered them always in the background—haunting his daughter, always watching her—an innocent child.

These women had given a face to the fear the priest had planted in his brain. They had made it personal. His desire to stop the cult from killing Kayla had been borne of his need to destroy the identical twins who had played a role in Mary Alice's death. And now they were here, the same women, coming towards him on the shore of the lake.

They knew him as well. His heart pounded as he realized that his life might be in danger. Whatever they had done to his daughter, they could also do to him. Still he could not move. He wanted to face them—to finally know what had happened to Mary Alice. He stood, waiting as they came to him.

When they were only a few feet away, they both smiled at him at the same instant, as if their mouths were connected to an invisible ventriloquist's hands, able to move each of their features at the same moment, creating an unearthly effect.

"Gavin," Mattie said softly, "sit with us awhile. We have much to tell you."

The wind whistled in his ears, making him feel as though the woman's voice had come from inside his head. He wanted to put his fist into their faces, to see blood flowing from their wrinkled skin, to make them suffer the way he had seen his daughter suffer so many times in his memory. Then as if by an unseen signal, the twins pulled their long skirts above their knees and sat in unison on the sand next to him. He felt his own knees bend without his will, and he found himself sitting on the sand with them. A vision of them as they had appeared to him so long ago flashed before his eyes. The light brown hair he remembered had gone white in exactly the same places. Age lines framed their eyes at precisely the same angles. Not a skin flaw or an age spot deviated on their long narrow faces.

As he stared at them, his rage turned to confusion. "Who are you?" was all he could say, mesmerized by their harmless-looking, grandmotherly faces. "What did you do to my Mary Alice?"

"We were her guardians . . . sent to protect her." Mattie looked into Gavin's eyes with sadness and compassion. "We grieved for her as you did."

Gavin's anger returned with her words. He jumped to his feet. "Grieved for her! Who in heaven's name are you to grieve for my daughter. You didn't know her! I don't want your grief. I want to know what happened on the river that night."

The twins remained perfectly calm as he continued shouting at them, accusing them of killing his daughter.

"We don't know how Mary Alice died," Nellie said simply. "It was beyond our ability to see."

"What did you call yourself? Guardians!" Gavin roared into the wind. "Tell me now, what were you guarding my daughter against?"

"It is not us that seek to destroy the spirit. It is the Sidon, lead by the priest who first came to you," Nellie said slowly. "He has hidden the truth from you, using you to find her. And now they intend to take the life of the girl you think you are protecting."

"Why should I believe you?" he said, thinking they had come to him to find where Kayla was hiding. The thought was barely formed in his mind when Mattie spoke.

"We know where she is hiding. We have not come to you to find her."

"Then why are you here?"

"We have come to you," Mattie said, "because we need your help."

"My help?" Gavin said, incredulously. "God's sake! How can you be thinking that I will help you kill this innocent girl?"

"Your mission was to find Kayla for them, and you have fulfilled it. They no longer need you. We are the ones who need you. We come from the women of Juno as they told you. It is our duty to guard the spirit. We were selected to protect the girl."

"The child you saw in the photograph is now the woman they are hunting," Nellie said.

"Why would they want to kill her? She is no threat to them," Gavin challenged her.

"Yes, she is. They told you that we believe the spirit within Kayla would destroy the power of our goddess Juno. That is impossible," Mattie said, leaning towards him.

"You see," she whispered, "the spirit is Juno herself!"

Confused and frightened, Gavin looked away from her eyes, out to the black water.

"Now as the girl becomes a woman," Nellie spoke, "she will have the full power of the spirit. She was chosen to carry that spirit into the next millennium. It is the Sidon that wants her dead."

They would not bewitch him. "There can be no such spirit living inside this girl," he said with a certainty he didn't feel.

"It moves from one life to another. Kayla is the last of the line.

Now that the Sidon has found Kayla through you, they will go to the cabin where she is hiding. They will find her tonight."

"If you believe that, why don't you stop them?"

"We are," said Mattie, "we're talking to you."

"You're talking to the wind." He turned to walk away from these twin sisters who had haunted him for eighteen years.

"Seeing into the future can be more of a curse than a blessing!" Mattie called after him. "Just because we can see things that will happen doesn't mean we can do anything to alter the future. Once we both have clearly seen an event take place, there is little that we can do to change that destiny."

Gavin spun around and looked at her. "Then why are you talking with me?" he shouted at her. "If you are right and the Sidon is to succeed in taking the life of Kayla tonight, what can I do? If the future is written, why are you here?"

"They will not succeed." Nellie said simply. "Kayla will survive. We play a part in her survival and so will you. That's why she's been sending you her dreams."

The anger drained from his body as he struggled to understand the meaning of her words. "Sending me her dreams?"

"Yes. She sent herself to you in your dreams and you have betrayed her to the Sidon. The dreams are beginning to move out to all the people surrounding her. She is at the center of a circle, spinning outward, bringing more people into the circle with her."

Gavin could listen no longer. Once again he turned his back on the women. Nellie stopped him with a single word.

"Aeron." She pronounced it with a Welsh accent. "It's the girl's name. Kayla, the child they showed you when she was three years old. She calls herself Aeron."

"Aeron." Gavin repeated the word as though it had magical powers.

"Kayla now calls herself Aeron after the river in Wales. The name was given to her in a dream. The name was meant to be her shield. The armor that would protect her from you in this very moment. Kayla Casey was born June 22, 1980.

"Lord, what are you telling me?" Gavin said, trembling.

"Your daughter died three hours before Kayla was born. The spirit, the breath of the goddess Juno traveled across the sea to find a new mortal home on the same day your daughter drowned."

"God no! I won't believe it." He saw his daughter as he looked at the lake in front of him, his sweet Mary Alice only eight years old, her boat tipping over in the churning water, her body sliding into the river—the river Aeron! His daughter had drowned in the river Aeron. The visions of his dreams flooded his mind. Had Kayla sent him the dreams? What a fool he had been, blinded by his grief.

"That's why they came to me, the old priest and the monk! They believed that my daughter carried this spirit you speak of. They knew they could find the next child through me."

"And so they have," said Nellie.

Gavin could hardly believe the words coming from his mouth. "Then Kayla . . . Aeron . . . keeps the soul of my daughter, Mary Alice!"

• 22 •

The sky wore a shroud of black that was descending on the earth. A fierce thunderstorm threatened to roll down the mountains. Lightning cut through the darkness as Gavin drove up the dirt road beyond the north end of town. He knew exactly how to find the cabin, still he had to get there now before the storm broke. The priest could arrive any moment. Gavin's stomach twisted into a knot when he thought about how they had deceived him. He was determined not to let them harm the girl who carried on the soul and the spirit of his daughter. Aeron was not of his blood, still he felt part of her was of him. In a sense she was his daughter, and he wanted her to live.

Soft mud and boulders cluttered the road, making it difficult to get his car with its narrow tires up the dirt road. He had to stop continually to move debris from his path. If the priest could find the cabin himself, at least he would be slowed down by the mud-soaked road. Gavin wished he could destroy the road behind him, scattering fallen branches and rocks in their path, but the twins had told him there was no other way out—he had to return by the same road. The storm settled in, making it even harder to see the bends and turns ahead of him. The clear vision of this road that he had seen in his dream was now a chaos in the darkness. At each turn he could hear the voices of the twins inside his head, guiding him to make the correct choice. Rain began to fall, the black rain that came from clouds saturated with industrial waste.

Then, just as he had seen it in his dream, the cabin appeared in the woods before him. Afraid to drive too close and get stuck in the mud, he stopped the car, leaving the motor running, and pulled his coat over his head. A young woman came running through the rain to meet him.

"I felt you coming to me. I know who you are." She pulled him from the car. "They are coming for me, aren't they? They want to kill me," Aeron cried, holding on to Gavin.

He looked down at her face, searching into the green windows of her eyes.

"Yes," he said, putting his arm around her, "I am sent to take you away."

Aeron had been seeing a vision of this man coming up the road in the pouring rain all day. His face had so perfectly chiseled itself in her mind that she felt as if she had known the man in the mud-covered car for years. He was the father that the drowned child had told her would come. She knew that she could trust him.

Once inside the cabin he could make out her face in the candle light. He was not surprised that it was the face he had seen in his dream. There were two other women visible in the dim light.

When he came closer to the women he thought that he recognized one of them. She was the woman in the market that he had been so drawn to.

Lee remembered him at the same moment. Aeron had predicted that a solitary man would come to take them out of danger. Lee thought it another illusion. And now he was here!

"Who are you?" she demanded.

"I haven't the time to explain," he quickly told them, "even with all the time in the world I don't know if I could tell you. You must trust me, for you all are in grave danger. You must come with me. Now! The rear axle on your Range Rover is broken. You've got to come with me."

Lee felt a shiver go up her spine. The Rover had broken down a half mile from the cabin when she returned with the food the day before. "How could you possibly know that?"

How could he begin to tell them that two old women, the twins, had told him that the Rover was broken, and the girl had no way to escape—that they had seen it happen. These women would think he was crazy.

"He's right," Aeron said, ignoring Lee's challenge. "We've got to go right now."

With all three women in his car, Gavin drove down the muddy road, hoping to get back to the highway before the priest came for Kayla. Lee sat next to him in the front seat, Sara and Aeron in the back. He retraced his route down the mountain. The black rain pounded against his windshield, blinding him; still they were making good progress. Then in the distance he saw the headlights of a car coming towards them. There was no way to turn around and even if they could, where would they go?

Gavin decided to drive directly towards the oncoming car. Neither of the cars turned away as they pushed through the mud, advancing on one another. At the last instant Gavin swerved to the right, barely missing an oak tree. His wheels spun in the mud. They were trapped. The other car stopped. They could see three figures emerge in the black rain. Gavin slammed the gas pedal to the floor. They jerked forward, fell back, then lurched out of the mud back into the center of the dirt road. One of the dark figures behind them raised his arm and, in spite of the rain, they could see he held a gun in his hand pointed at them. Sara threw herself over Aeron, pushing the girl's head down. The night exploded with a single shot.

Aeron heard glass breaking—a window shattering. A hot pain slashed across the skin of her throat as if the blade of a knife were grazing her flesh. A choking scream came from above her. Sara's head fell forward. Blood spurted from a hole in her neck. Aeron was frantic. "Sara's been hit! She's hit! We've got to get to a hospital!"

Gavin pressed his foot against the gas pedal, and they took off down the mountain.

"The junction to Highway 80 is at the bottom of the hill," Lee took charge. "Take it to Reno. We'll go to the hospital there. Hurry!"

Aeron cradled Sara's limp body in her arms as they turned east. "She can't die," Aeron kept saying over and over. "She can't die. It's my fault. That bullet was meant for me."

Aeron held Sara's hand in hers, whispering to her: "You're going to be all right. I know it. Please don't die."

At the same time she said the words, she could see that they were meaningless. Sara's life was already draining away.

At the junction to the highway, the traffic forced them to stop. Just as they were about to make the turn there was something in the road blocking their path. Aeron screamed when she could make out what it was though the rain—the two faces that had haunted her for so long were coming towards the car!

She turned to Gavin to warn him and realized he was actually relieved to see the two identical women. They were flesh and bone, not a vision or a fantasy, and they were coming for her!

The twins opened the back door and reached for her, trying to pull her away from Sara.

"You can't come any further with us." Gavin's voice was so quiet. "It isn't safe."

"Let go of me," Aeron cried.

"Child, listen." Mattie took Aeron's face in her hands and held it tightly. "Stop screaming and feel us. We have been with you since the beginning. Let us in."

Mattie's touch penetrated her skin, her bones, her very soul. She felt herself being pulled into the strange woman's body just as she had always been carried inside the body of the hawk in her dreams. Suddenly she was seeing through the old woman's eyes, but she wasn't looking at this moment in time!

She was seeing herself, a child of three, in the other twin's arms, being grabbed away from a man with a long black coat.

Then she knew. It was they who had saved her the night her mother was killed! It was they who had taken her to the convent.

"Come with us," Mattie insisted.

"I won't leave Sara," Aeron cried, coming back to the present. "She took care of me when I was a baby. I can't let her die."

"Come, there is no time."

Aeron leaned down and kissed Sara on the cheek. "Please live," she said one last time. Then she put her arms around Lee for a moment, and allowed the twins to take her away from the road.

The car disappeared in the rain. They were gone, and she was alone with two strangers that she had known all her life.

They guided her into a wooded park that lay next to the lake. There was a covered structure that gave them some shelter from the storm.

"You are safe here for now. It will take them time to realize that you have left the others."

"You knew that I would be here at this moment," Aeron said. "You saw it all before it happened."

"Yes," Nellie said.

"You knew that bullet would miss me and hit Sara! Why couldn't you do anything to stop it?"

"It is dangerous to interfere with the future once we have seen it. Our very actions can create an alternative to what was meant to be inevitable. Then two realities exist. The difficulty is in knowing which one will cause less harm."

"So you chose to do nothing, and now Sara will die!"

"There is nothing we could have done to change what has happened. If we had come to you instead of Gavin, you would have been killed, and it is our duty to protect you."

Safe from the pouring rain, the twins felt humble as they stood in the presence of the spirit. This was the third time they had been called upon to guard the breath of Juno. The first had been a terrible failure when Paula Campbell had hanged herself in 1972, and they were powerless to stop her. And then they had gone to Wales. For eight years they had guarded the life of Mary Alice Langley. And again they had been unable to prevent the death of the child. Aeron was their last chance to save the spirit.

"Who are you? Why have I been able to see your faces for so many years?"

"We have so little time. You must know who you are if you are to survive," said Mattie. "The dreams you have of the child in the woods and the circle of women dressed in white are a memory of a night long ago when it all began. These women gathered as you see them, to honor the goddess Juno."

"Jean-Marie, the woman in Paris," Aeron remembered. "I can still see her sitting in front of the statue of the Virgin Mary at Notre Dame. She talked to the statue as if it were real. She called it Our Lady Juno. Jean-Marie worshipped this goddess."

Aeron's mind raged with memories. The dreams she'd had all through her life of women gathered in the forest and the baby she'd felt was about to be sacrificed . . . she'd thought it was a fantasy, and here were these twins telling her that it actually happened, almost two thousand years ago.

"The Breath of Juno took mortal life that night. It was destined to grow for one hundred generations until it was strong enough to bend the will of all the world. Now is the moment of its power."

"The Shadows that come to me, they were real lives? They were my life, my spirit!" After all these years, these women had explained both the dreams and the Shadows that had haunted her.

"Does this spirit give me the power to see into the future?"

Even as she asked, she knew the answer. "It comes from you! I see through your eyes. It was you that sent me the dream that brought me here . . . the dream I thought came from my mother. You have given me visions and seen into my thoughts throughout my entire life." The realization frightened her, but strangely, it also comforted her. She had always felt so alone in the world. There had been no constant presence in her life, no one who could share the thread of her life as it unfolded. Now she was discovering that these two identical-looking women had been there all the time. They were an invisible family who had always protected her.

"We can stay with you no longer," Mattie said. "They have already discovered their mistake and are coming back to find you."

"No! You're going to leave me now?"

"You must go on alone." Nellie placed an envelope in Aeron's hand. "Everything you will need . . . documents, tickets, a passport is here." She spoke with greater urgency. "You must go to England. From there you will travel on to Wales. Go to Cardigan Bay and follow the river inland. It will take you home."

"Why can't you come with me?"

"We would only make it more difficult for you. It will be safer for you to be on your own."

"Without you I can't see into the future. I won't be able to protect myself. It was your minds that helped me see all these years."

"You will discover you have powers of your own. We can't guarantee your safety. There isn't much time."

"You're going to leave me here by the highway alone?"

"There's someone coming along this road in a few minutes. A woman with two children. She'll see you standing alone in the rain and think your car broke down. She'll take you down the mountain to Sacramento. From there you'll go by bus to San Francisco and then fly to London."

"What about Sara? Will she live?"

"Child," Mattie said, grasping her hands. "You already know the answer to that. Remember, the spirit picked you because you were strong enough to hold it, to contain it."

Mattie thought of Paula Campbell. The spirit had picked her too and it destroyed her. The truth was that neither she nor Nellie knew if Aeron would survive. Their guardianship of the girl had to end here, or the Sidon would be able to use them to find her. They had agreed before tonight that they would pull a curtain over the future once the girl was on her own.

"The spirit is with you, child. You will never be alone," Mattie said. And with that, the twins walked out into the rain and disappeared.

The future vision was gone. She wouldn't have Lee or Sara, or even her mother by her side. All the years that she had felt alone and abandoned had never been as profound as what she felt at this moment. Sara lay dying, and there was nothing she could do to save her life. She felt no power within her, only emptiness and sorrow. She wanted to rip the spirit out of her body and free herself from the terrible burden she had carried all her life.

She ran back out to the highway. A moment later, a blue station wagon with a woman and two children inside stopped in front of her. The young woman at the wheel got out of her car and asked, "What's the matter? Can I help you?"

The red-headed girl who sat by the road crying looked up. "My car broke down. I need a ride. Are you going down the mountain?"

The Breath of Juno

PART IV

*Shadow of wisdom
Clothe my soul
Find the good road
Take me home*

· 23 ·

From her window seat at the tail of the plane, Aeron looked out to watch the city of San Francisco falling away. Although the sky was cloudless, the pollution that hung over the city wrapped it in a dark blanket so that it became invisible as the aircraft gained altitude.

The pilot took the plane out over the ocean, dipped the wings to the right, and made a wide turn north to take the polar route from San Francisco to London.

The ability to see into the future had come to her sporadically over the years. She had never known when an image would fill her mind, and often she wasn't sure whether she was looking at something that was going to happen in the future or had already happened in the past. But there was always a certainty about the things that she saw, and a sense that she was powerless to change them. And now she knew that the power hadn't come from within her. The twins were the ones who had the ability to see the future. It was their gift, not hers.

Mattie and Nellie had said it was too dangerous, that they couldn't watch or protect her any longer. As the last year of the second millennium closed in, it was more important that they keep a distance from Aeron's life, that they not interfere with her thoughts or give her their vision.

Looking out into the emptiness beyond the window of the plane, she felt alone and vulnerable. The special sight had been a terrifying burden, but she had always believed it was *her* burden. Now without it she would have no idea what the future was to hold. The twins had told her that she would develop her own unique strengths, but she didn't feel powerful at all. She had learned too much too fast.

Exhausted, she pressed her forehead against the cold window pane. I must stay awake, she told herself. I've got to put the pieces together. If the twins were the power that gave me the ability to see into the future, then what else were they able to see? Could they have seen the Shadows as well? Did they put the visions of other people's lives inside my mind? Do the Shadows belong to me or to them?

The questions tormented her. She no longer knew where she began and where she ended.

Nellie had told her, "We're mortal women. We have no power beyond this life."

Aren't I mortal too, Aeron thought. I'm certainly not invulnerable to death. The Sidon wouldn't be trying to kill me if they thought I was immortal. If Sara hadn't pushed my head down, the second before the bullet penetrated the window, I would be dead instead of her.

She thought of Sara lying helplessly in the back seat of Gavin's car, and sadness filled her. What good is all this power if I couldn't save Sara's life? I'm not a healer. I couldn't heal even one dear woman. How can I possibly contain the breath of this mythic goddess, Juno, and be feared as a spirit of darkness? It's insane. I wish Lee was with me. She would be able to explain this in a logical, rational way.

The plane took a heavy bounce, then dropped like an unleashed elevator. It stopped as suddenly as it started. Nausea gripped her body. She felt small, weak, and vulnerable. The plane might lose an engine and crash into the sea. She may have a supernatural power within her; still she could die just as quickly as anyone else.

The flight attendant gave a cookie to the child in the seat across from Aeron, and the aroma of sugar and cinnamon filled the air. She thought of Dora, realizing how much she missed her. If only she could close her eyes, imagine herself in Dora's kitchen, and then open her eyes to find herself in the safety of the Wilkes quiet home. After her summer in Paris, she'd been home only a few days before she and Lee had left for San Francisco and Bodega Bay. Dora knew nothing about the Shadows that had visited her all summer.

The pilot announced that they were at 35,000 feet, well above the clouds. Yet no stars were visible outside the window, only an endless void. She felt herself an insignificant thing, sitting in an aluminum tube, hurling through the air at six hundred miles per hour. How was she ever going to bring the blue back into the sky, if that was her destiny? Is that what the breath was supposed to accomplish in the year 2000? She couldn't fathom how all that power could ever come from her small, mortal body.

When they reached the emptiness of the Arctic Circle, part of her wished that the plane would fall from the sky and disappear, dropping her into the cold northern sea.

Sitting next to her was a plump woman who appeared to be at least ninety years old. She was knitting a scarf and humming softly to herself. Her hands, puffy with age, looked strangely childlike. Swelling had stretched the skin across the wrinkles, making them disappear. The hands reminded her of Jean-Marie, the Shadow that had taken over her body in Paris. She remembered looking at her hands as she stood on the banks of the Seine. Jean-Marie had been only fifty-two years old, yet her hands looked the same as the ninety year-old woman next to her.

This is what progress has given us, Aeron thought. We are living longer. In the Middle Ages, Jean-Marie was old at fifty-two. And this woman knitting next to me so peacefully is over ninety and travelling six hundred miles an hour across the Arctic Circle. Jean-Marie could never have conceived of such a thing. This giant airbus must be consuming thousands of tons of fuel with every flight—fuel that was drilled from beneath the oceans of the world until they were drained dry. If the Prophecy is right, and I live into the third millennium, a flight like this might become impossible. Lee and Dora might never live to be as old as this woman sitting next to me. The twins told me that the Sidon wants to stop me, to kill me because they fear the whole world will be thrown back into the Dark Ages. Maybe they're right.

Aeron remembered that when she had first come to the Wilkes' house she tormented Dora by claiming to be an atheist. The memory of it brought tears to her eyes. She had been so cruel to Dora because she thought her a weak, simple woman who needed an all-knowing God to lean on. She had felt superior to Dora and her beliefs. Now she understood Dora's need to believe in a power greater than herself. Whenever she caught the scent of the damp earth at night, she knew that there had to be something more, a force that existed inside all living things. She searched her mind, not for answers, but for all the questions that haunted her.

If I never believed in Dora's God, why did I let the twins tell me what to believe so easily? Did they crawl inside my mind without my permission and force me to accept their beliefs? Could I actually be inhabited by the Breath of Juno, by a spirit that has lived for almost two thousand years, without believing in the spirit myself? These monks of the Sidon who want me dead—could they all be right? Maybe they weren't murderers at all, just desperate to protect a way of life that makes it possible for this old woman to knit peacefully 35,000 feet above the Arctic Ocean.

She had to push the questions and the fears away, as she had done with the Shadows. There was only this moment, no future, no past. If she didn't learn to concentrate on everything that was happening, they would find her with her guard down, and she would be an easy target.

When their meal arrived, the old woman ate with enthusiasm. Aeron couldn't touch her own food.

She watched the woman eat. She wanted to strike up a conversation with her, to feel connected, to break through the loneliness that made her skin feel like a hard shell surrounding her body.

"What are you knitting?" she asked.

"A scarf . . . just another scarf," the woman said. "I must have knitted a hundred of these in my lifetime. Can't hardly find anyone to give them to anymore. My old hands are just too used to knitting to stop."

She listened to the old woman chat about small things; holidays and grandchildren. There was a comfort in the homey stories and the woman's gentle laughter.

After their trays had been cleared away, Aerons's travelling companion fell asleep, her head gently touching Aeron's shoulder.

Aeron wondered if she fell asleep herself, would her dreams flow into this old woman's mind as they'd done with Lee, Sara, and even Gavin? When she could see that the woman was deeply asleep, a thought came to her. If I can transfer my dreams when I'm asleep, maybe I can transfer my thoughts, projecting them into other people's dreams. If this spirit really exists inside me, can I bring it into my own waking thoughts and send it to this woman sleeping next to me? What image from my dreams can I concentrate on that is precise and clear enough so that she will remember it when she wakes up? I must be careful to pick something that won't frighten or confuse her—a simple soft image.

She remembered the perfect one, something she'd never understood herself. The dream she'd had in Bodega Bay the day that she found Sara again. She began to recreate the dream in her mind, picturing every detail. She was flying over a river that lay between two meadows. On one side there were black sheep grazing peacefully. On the other side there were white.

She watched as one of the black sheep entered the water and swam across. When it came out on the other side it was no longer black but white, and joined the rest of the flock. And then it happened in reverse. A white sheep swam across the river and emerged black.

She thought about the image over and over in her mind. She didn't try to understand it or explain it, she simply saw it happening, again and again.

A half hour later, the pilot's voice came over the intercom. "We are beginning our descent into Heathrow. We should be on the ground in about forty minutes. We are expecting a little turbulence on our approach. Please fasten your seat belts, and bring your seats and tray tables to an upright position."

His voice woke the old woman from her deep sleep. She began to stir slowly, embarrassed that she had found her head resting ever so slightly on Aeron's shoulder. Aeron watched her carefully, afraid to say anything. How can I know if she has received the visions, she wondered?

"Did you have a nice nap?" she asked, trying to sound casual.

"Lovely. It makes the trip go by so much faster when I can sleep for an hour or so. I hope I didn't bother you. I wasn't snoring was I? Sometimes my family tells me that I do."

"No. It looked like you were peacefully dreaming."

"That's true. I was having a wonderful dream."

"Tell me about it. I get so nervous when we're about to land."

"There's nothing to be afraid of. I fly to London to see my son and his family every October."

This wasn't going to work, Aeron thought as the woman began to launch into stories of Octobers past. "I can never remember my dreams," she tried again. "Do you remember yours?"

"Not often, Dear," she paused, as Aeron searched for another tactic. "I do remember the one I just had, though, because it was so unusual. I was sitting on the banks of a beautiful river watching a flock of white sheep grazing."

Aeron felt her hands ball up into fists as she contained her excitement. The woman described the whole scene exactly as Aeron had thought it. When the woman finished, her face was quiet and peaceful.

"What an odd dream. What do you think it means?"

"It doesn't mean anything. It was just a dream," the woman said.

"You looked so happy when you told me about it. What's happy about a bunch of sheep?"

The woman smiled. "That's a good question. You're too young. I think you'd have to be an old woman to understand." She didn't want to say more, but Aeron's curiosity appeared so genuine. "I'm ninety-four years old. It can't be long before I cross that river myself. It's a comfort to see the sheep crossing over, changing their coats and starting again with a new flock. Perhaps that's what is in store for me."

Aeron was astonished. In a few words the old woman had made sense of the vision. The river that had swallowed up the child in her dream wasn't just a place of death, it was a border between lives. If the Shadows that came to her across time were part of her, then she had crossed the river many times.

WHEN THE PLANE landed in London the passengers were shuffled through baggage and customs. Aeron took the old woman's arm and helped her with her luggage. A crowd waited in the main terminal to welcome the travelers. She looked at their eager faces, knowing that there would be no one to meet her.

Children and family greeted the old woman with delighted shouts and hugs. As they swarmed around their mother, grandmother, great grandmother, Aeron moved away from the circle. She envied the old woman, wishing that she had been greeted by a loving family. As she walked through the terminal, she saw couples laughing with the joy of seeing one another again, or crying in farewell embraces. She envied them for showing her how alone and different she was. If this ancient spirit lived within her it, was more of a curse than a power.

There was no one to guide her now—she was completely on her own. She had only the name of a place in Wales, scribbled on a piece of paper by Mattie. Two words: *Cardigan Bay.*

Reluctantly, she walked past the line of taxis to the Underground station that ran the thirty miles into the center of London from the airport. She couldn't afford to be remembered by a cab driver. The tube-shaped subway car burrowed through the earth, vibrating on tracks laid in the 1890's. The shaking of the crowded car had a calming effect.

I can't make any mistakes, she thought, realizing how much she had depended on Lee to help her decide what to do. The Sidon probably knew a great deal about her by now. It would be easy for them to discover that Lee Edwards was a psychiatrist living in San Bernardino, California. Her patient records would provide them with all the information they needed in order to know her identity. They would be looking for an eighteen year-old, a young woman, who had gone by the name Aeron Wilkes for the past five years.

But at this moment she was invisible to everyone. The passport she carried had a poor picture of her with the name Carol Stern stamped on it. The Sidon wouldn't know where to begin looking for her, but it wouldn't take them long to trace everyone she ever knew. They probably already had an army out looking for her.

When she left the poorly-lit station, the bright sunlight hit her, shocking her eyes. It was nine in the morning in London. The streets were full of men and women in suits, dashing to offices that lay inside decaying stone structures built hundreds of years ago. A red double-decker bus stopped in front of the station, letting off a stream of people who rudely shoved one another as they hurried away. Drained, she hugged the brick wall to stay out of their way. She couldn't remember the last time she slept. It felt like days.

Although her body was exhausted her mind was racing. Maps of the city and of the Underground routes were available at a nearby kiosk. She bought one of each and also a detailed map of England and Wales. She followed the wide streets that the map indicated would lead her to Hyde Park. It was a place that sounded familiar.

With each step she become more and more certain that she had been here before, at a time when the streets were more narrow and people rode in carriages. She pushed against the memory that worked to take root in her mind. Nothing could be allowed to distract her now. The slightest confusion could cause her to make a mistake, and just one mistake could cost her her life. Adrenalin coursed through her body, dissolving the invading memory and fixing her thoughts on the problems of the present.

On a small street behind the park, she saw a rundown Tudor house with a sign out front that read *Bed and Breakfast.* She walked to the door and knocked. An East Indian man, bent over with arthritis, greeted her. After grumbling that he usually didn't let guests take a room until three in the afternoon, he showed her to an upstairs bedroom. There was barely enough room for a single bed, a tiny dresser, and a wardrobe closet, but it didn't matter to Aeron. As soon as the man left, she collapsed on the bed and fell asleep.

The next thing she felt was the light of a new dawn breaking through the flimsy curtains. She had slept almost eighteen straight hours, waking without the memory of any dream clouding her consciousness. The bleak sadness and the fear that had flown across the ocean with her were gone.

From a pocket in her jeans she pulled out the child's bracelet with the hawk charm and carefully placed it on the dresser. Then, for the first time since Dora had given her the gold hawk on her eighteenth birthday, she undid the clasp that held the chain around her neck. With a tweezers, she removed the delicate charm from the child's bracelet and attached it to the eyelet that held the hawk around her neck. This way, she thought, she could hold them all close to her heart. She put the chain around her neck once again, then placed the palm of her right hand over the two hawks while she said their names out loud. "Dora, Sara, Mother, stay with me." For a moment she saw Sara's face, still and empty in the back seat of Gavin's car, but she pushed the picture from her mind.

She opened the maps of England and Wales, laying them across the bed, planning her route. The first leg was easy. There was an express train from London to Cardiff in Wales. From there she could change to a local train that would take her to Swansea. She traced the route with her finger. The twins had told her to go to Cardigan Bay. From Swansea she could probably get a bus that would take her over the Cambrian Mountains into Aberystwyth, which appeared to be the largest town on Cardigan Bay. But Cardigan Bay was much larger than San Francisco Bay. There were lots of little dots on the map indicating villages. How would she know where to go once she got to the Bay?

She scanned the names printed above each dot. One name jumped out from all the others—just south of Aberystwyth was a place named

Aberaeron. It lay on Cardigan Bay at the mouth of the Aeron River. She stared at the thin blue line that marked the short river, with its headwaters somewhere in the Cambrian Mountains.

The image of a hawk sitting on the arm of a woman floated up before her eyes. She heard the haunting voice, distant, like wind blowing thought the treetops.

Follow the Aeron, it whispered. *It will take you home.*

· 24 ·

When she arrived in the seaside village of Aberaeron, she asked a fisherman if he would take her up the Aeron River. He refused, saying that the summer rains had swollen the once placid river, making it dangerous for small boats. She offered him twice the original sum of money but it didn't make him anymore willing to be her private boatman. The generous offer only served to increase his curiosity. He was uncomfortable with prying into the affairs of others, but this redheaded girl's request was strange. He wanted to know where she was going and why.

"There's nothing up river but pasture lands and mountains. What's a pretty young thing like you doing traveling up there all alone?" When she didn't give him an answer, he said, "You're American, aren't you? Never been to these parts before, have you?"

His questions made her nervous. She had gotten this far without making a mistake. It would be foolish to make one now that she was so close to her destination. "Never mind," she told him. "I just thought it would be lovely to take a ride up the river, but if it's dangerous, I don't want to go."

The sign in front of the pub on the dock read *The Black Swan*. She went inside and ordered fish and chips. When the food came, she ate the greasy cod without tasting it, trying to decide who she might approach next. An old man sat down at her table without asking permission to join her. Rotting teeth dominated his face, making it difficult to see his other more pleasant features.

"Terrible hot for October, isn't it?" he said. "Been getting hotter every year."

She nodded, not wanting to encourage him, but he kept on talking, mostly about the weather. When she finished her meal, she told the old man it had been nice talking with him and got up to go. He reached out and grabbed her arm, pulling her back down to her chair. She was frightened by his sudden move—this was a public place. What did he intend to do?

"You wouldn't be wanting a boatman, would you," he asked quietly. "I've got a sturdy craft that can take you right up the river to have a bit of a look-see if you like."

There was a conspiratorial look in the man's eye as he grinned at her, displaying a full mouth of decaying teeth. How could he have guessed what she was looking for? It was a tiny village; maybe the first fisherman she had spoken to had wandered into this pub earlier, talking about the strange girl he had met on the dock looking for a ride up the river. She had to be careful what she said and who she said it to. A stranger in the area would be instant gossip. Everything she did would be the subject of talk in the local pub. But if this man was willing to take her up the river, she better accept. She may not find anyone else who would take her without asking questions. She offered him the same amount of money as the first fisherman. He seemed disinterested in the figure, as if anything she said would be fine with him.

"When can we go?" she asked.

"What's the matter with right now?"

"It will be dark in less than an hour. Shouldn't we wait until morning?"

"Nah, the view will be prettier at night. You can see the Pleiades and the Great Bear. It will be a brilliant night for a ride up the river."

He finished his pint of lager, then walked her over to the river's mouth where his boat was moored. The thought of going off alone with this scruffy man worried her, but she followed him obediently. When she saw his weathered old row boat tied to a post in the muddy shallows, she thought perhaps the first fisherman was right. But spending a night in this little town, Aberaeron, with her name embedded in its title, seemed even more dangerous.

Gingerly she got into the boat. He pushed them away from the shore, and they glided out into the black water. He lifted the rotting wooden oars, locked them in place and began rowing upstream against a heavy current. With every few feet that they advanced, they seemed to go half that distance back again. At this rate it would be morning before they cleared sight of the town. With his spindly little arms pushing against the bulky oars, she wondered why he had been willing to take this journey with her. The river currents made their own waves. The back eddies that splashed up against the side of the boat threatened to dump water into the weak little vessel. They were making so little progress she felt they would do better if she took the oars herself. Certainly she was stronger than he was.

After thirty minutes of painfully slow progress, the town was beginning to recede from their vision. Her boatman began to hum an odd tune. She looked into his eyes—they were staring at her knowingly. Her skin grew cool. Who was this man? Maybe it wasn't an accident that she had run into him at *The Black Swan*. Could he have been sent by the priest she had seen in her vision? Could he be from the Sidon?

Moments after the fear came to her, he pulled the oars inside the boat. From under a thin canvas cover he revealed an outboard motor that had been carefully hidden from view. Once they rounded the bend in the river and were completely out of sight from the village, he allowed the boat to be pushed towards the shore by the current. When they were in shallow water, he got out of the boat and went about the work of attaching the motor.

The two of them were silent. She watched him, trying to decide what to do. Should she jump out of the boat and escape? He might attempt to stop her. If it came to that, she felt sure she could overpower him. Or should she confront him? What if she was wrong? It could be a fatal mistake.

Then she looked more closely at the boat. The flimsy boards that held the outsides together were only a facade. Underneath was a new aluminum structure that looked worthy enough to handle the Irish Sea. Once the motor was attached, he pushed the craft back out into the middle of the churning river, and they took off at such a high speed that they were unaffected by the waves. The rushing river crashed against the boat's sides, but there was no threat of capsizing.

The boatman continued to stare at her, but there seemed to be no harm in his gaze, rather a sense of awe and reverence. And suddenly she understood. It was true. He knew who she was! He *had* been sent! But not by the Sidon.

The old man finally spoke, and when he did it was not the voice of the man she met in the pub. There was no pretense at homily or insecurity. He spoke with strength, confidence, and a clear sense of purpose.

"Kayla," he said over the roar of the motor. "Welcome home." Coming from his mouth, the name frightened her. Kayla. It belonged to a child who had been lost for so long in her memory—a child who was once innocent and loved. Kayla had disappeared on the night her mother was killed. The name could never belong to her again.

Without the ability to look into the future, now that the twins could no longer influence her thoughts, she didn't know what to say to the man. He knew more than she did of what lay up the river.

She leaned closer to him. "Where are you taking me?"

"The top of the river, the headwaters. There's a wee channel we'll take off into the Cambrian Mountains. From there it's about a two-hour trek to the Mother Home. I'll be leaving you at the headwaters. You'll be met there and guided safely."

"Won't they think it's odd in the village when you return without your passenger?"

"I won't be returning until the middle of the night. I'll tell them you just wanted to see the stars, that I took you up a bit and you left on the morning bus. A tourist, nothing more. They'll ask questions. You'll be the gossip of the pub for a bit; then they'll forget you. You see, you don't look all that foreign to them with your red hair and green eyes. But for your accent, you could be from these parts. Don't worry. Nobody will know you were here. I'll take care of it."

His voice comforted her. She knew instinctively that he could be trusted. The twins had told her they had to leave her on her own, that they could no longer interfere with her life. But they must have gotten word to the Mother Home that she was on her way. This man had been sent as her guide and boatman. Mattie had promised that though she would no longer have the power of future vision, it would be replaced with new powers that would get stronger each day as she moved towards the year 2000.

Looking closely at the boatman, who no longer looked as old as she first thought, she began to understand what Mattie had meant. She couldn't read his mind, but she was aware of the sensation that emanated from his body, a simple benign feeling that he meant her no harm. Perhaps she could also tell when she was near someone who did mean her harm. Maybe it was a radar she would develop, a sixth sense that would help her instantly identify anyone who was a danger.

They continued up the river in silence. At one point the river bent to the left and there were two wide meadows, one on each bank. It was exactly as she had seen it in her dream!

Although the night was warm, a cold chill ran through her body, and she knew that it was exactly at this wide bend in the Aeron River that she had seen a child struggling to keep her rowboat afloat. It had tipped over in a sudden wind that churned the river and tossed her young body into the dark waters. As they passed over the spot, she felt a strong temptation to jump into the blackness herself.

In the dream she had been sucked down into the body of the young girl and pulled beneath the water. She had struggled to bring herself back to the surface, to turn the small girl's arms into the heavy wings of the hawk, and to fly away from the threatening river.

The same blond-haired child had appeared to her in that dank-smelling bedroom at Sara's cabin. Had there really been such a person who drowned in the Aeron River? If she had lived, why had Aeron seen her in her dream and again in the cabin? She would never forget the words that came from the mouth of the soaking wet child. *I am of you.* But the child wasn't like the Shadows who took over her body.

Could that child have been a vision, sent by the twins, to guide her? The thin voice had also whispered *Father will come to you.* Had the Welshman been the child's father?

Aeron remembered how the old woman on the plane had helped her understand the meaning of the black and white sheep crossing from one bank to another, changing their color—the reincarnation that they represented in her own life. The dream and the vision of the drowning girl, she thought, must also have a deeper significance.

The half moon was just cresting over the mountain range when they reached the headwaters. The river came to an end in a canyon. The old man pulled the boat over to the side and reached his hand down to help her out. When she touched it, he looked startled—as if her touch held a magic over which she had no control.

"I'll remember this moment for the rest of my days," he said. Guiding her to the shore, he took her small duffle bag from the seat of the boat and handed it to her. "I leave you here. Walk down this path about half a mile; they'll be someone waiting for you. May all the grace of God go with you and protect you. Good fortune, my child." And with that final farewell, he climbed back into his boat and pushed it out into the center of the river.

She stood on the bank watching him go. When she could no longer see his boat in the dull moonlight, she turned away from the river. She was alone once again. Slowly she began making her way through the thick underbrush, wondering if there were snakes in Wales. In spite of the awe the old boatman had shown at her touch, she knew that she was still mortal and could die from the bite of a poisonous snake like anyone else. The howl of a lone wolf broke the silence of the black night. She wanted to run, but then she heard the familiar shrill cry of a hawk. Her hand went quickly to her throat as she grasped the two charms that hung so close to her heart. Above her in the darkness it hovered, watching her, protecting her.

The path led up, away from the river, until it became difficult to follow. Just when she thought she might lose the trail, she came to a clearing where she saw three people appear as if from nowhere— two men and a woman, dressed in dark blue jackets. They bowed their heads and respectfully approached her. The woman spoke first.

"We are sent to take you home, to guide you through the woods." She kept her eyes down as if she was afraid to look directly at Aeron's face. The four of them passed over unmarked ground in silence as the moon moved across the sky. Aeron wanted to speak with them, but she took their silence as a warning that it might be dangerous to break the stillness of the night.

The way became steeper as they wound up the side of the mountain range. When they finally reached the crest, clouds covered the moon, making it impossible to see the valley on the other side. For a moment her guides stopped, looking into the darkness. Then the taller of the two men released a handmade torch from the strap that held it to his side and lit the end with a match. He allowed it to burn brightly for only a moment, then he thrust the flames into the dirt and stamped them out.

"They are watching for us," he whispered to Aeron. "It is too rocky to descend on foot in the dark." He saw her shiver with the wind that came up the east side of the mountains from the valley below, and offered her his fleece-lined coat. In a few moments two men on horseback came over the ridge, each of them leading another horse. The

The Breath of Juno

woman and the shorter man quickly mounted one of the horses. The man who had given her the coat jumped on the back of the other and reached down for her arm. He pulled her up behind him, and the four horses moved in single file across the narrow ridge of the mountain.

The midnight ride made her feel as if she was in a magnificent fairy tale. It reminded her of the wonderful English stories she had read as a child, the tales of princesses and dragons, of King Arthur's court, magical swords and wondrous powers. She had never seen the image of the four horses on the narrow crest of the mountain, moving through the night, in any of her dreams. It didn't belong to any of the Shadows. It was hers and hers alone, and it was thrilling.

They rode in silence, into the night. The man she rode behind pulled the reins to the right, turning their horse down a steep trail into the valley. The sure-footed animals held the path. The moon broke free from the dark cloud that had masked its light. In another hour Aeron was able to see what looked like a prehistoric ruin, a stone structure built by an ancient civilization, long abandoned. As they came closer she realized that there was something hidden behind the crumbling stone walls.

They dismounted, and Aeron was taken through a passageway in the stone. It lead to the door of a wooden house that had been crudely constructed behind the walls of the ruins. Her guides opened the door to reveal a single cavernous room with a high-beamed ceiling. A few women and men dressed in identical blue pants and gray tunics were scattered throughout the room, reading and working at long tables by the light of oil lamps. All activity stopped the moment she walked through the door. Eyes looked upon her in the same way that the old boatman had when he touched her hand.

At first, no one spoke. Then a middle-aged woman, her black hair pulled tightly back from her delicate face, came to her and broke the silence. "Kayla," she said. "Welcome home."

"Where am I?" Aeron asked. "Is this . . . ?"

"Yes." The woman spoke with an Italian accent but her English was perfect. "This is the Mother Home of the Juno Society. My name is Tamara. Come in, dear child. We have been waiting here for you all of your life."

• 25 •

When Aeron woke the following morning, nothing looked familiar. She couldn't remember where she was. Soft light filtered in from a thin window that had been cut just below the ceiling, giving her the feeling of daylight. The room was comfortable enough, larger and more luxurious than the Bed and Breakfast where she had stayed during her first night in London. A pair of dark blue pants and a gray tunic were laid out at the foot of her bed. The men and women she had seen last night on her arrival were wearing these uniforms, but she didn't feel comfortable putting them on. It made her feel more like she was in an alien place, a retreat from normal life. She wanted to be part of the world, not separate from it.

She found her jeans neatly folded in a corner, along with the sweatshirt she was wearing the night before. She dressed herself in her own clothes, opened the door of the bedchamber, and went back to the central cavity of the building.

"Good morning, Kayla, I hope you slept well." Tamara was sitting motionless, meditating, when Aeron entered.

"Please don't call me Kayla. It sounds so foreign to me. My name is Aeron."

"Yes, that's right. The Aeron." Tamara rose to greet her. "We were surprised when we learned that you had begun to call yourself Aeron. Mattie and Nellie were forbidden to give you a vision of the Mother Home, so you couldn't have known it lay in the mountains above the Aeron River. How did you come to know of the river?"

"Until yesterday I never knew this river existed. I didn't name myself after the river. The name was given to me by a vision in a dream. It was the first time she appeared to me." Aeron still felt excited when she remembered that fantastic moment when the hawk woman spoke to her. "She called me Aeron."

The Breath of Juno

"What exactly did she say to you?"

"Follow the Aeron, it will take you home." She whispered the words as she had heard them, and the stone walls of the room amplified the whispers, giving them a magical resonance. "Maybe she wasn't giving me a name, but calling me to this river, telling me to follow it. I was only thirteen when I first saw her. I didn't understand what any of it meant." Yet, she thought, that dream had provided her first true identity. From that time on she didn't belong to any temporary family. She belonged only to herself.

"If it will make you more comfortable," Tamara said, "I'll be happy to call you Aeron. It is, after all, the gateway to this hidden place, and most appropriate." She opened her arms to welcome the girl. Aeron backed away.

"Now please, let me get you something to eat. Then we can talk more." When she left the room, Aeron suddenly felt terribly alone. There was still so much she didn't understand about this strange power within her.

After a few minutes, Tamara returned with a plate of warm bread, figs, and a peach. Aeron hadn't realized how hungry she was until she saw the food in front of her. The aroma of freshly baked bread filled the damp stone room, reminding Aeron of Dora's kitchen. How she longed to be there now instead of in this remote dwelling filled with strangers.

"Doesn't anyone know this place is here?" she asked, taking a bite of a biscuit. "How've you kept it secret for so long?"

Tamara was glad to see her eating. "The Juno Society stretches all over the world. There are thousands of people who gather each month under the full moon to worship the spirit of the goddess Juno and the essence of her power on earth. But only a very few of them know where we are now."

"Do you ever go out into the world?"

"For the small family here at the Mother Home, this is our world. We do not give up contact with the outside world without regret. When the millennium arrives, we will all be free to leave this place. If you've been successful, the world will be full of promise for all of us."

"And if not?" Aeron said.

"I'm afraid we cannot be sure of anything. As I told you, I cannot see into the future."

"Am I safe here?"

"I think you are for now."

"You're not sure?"

"No, I wish I could say that I was. I can't lie to you, Aeron. They will look for you all over the world. They have so little time before your strength and power make it impossible for them to take your life."

"Are you the head of this order . . . the Juno Society?"

"No. We have no head. We all have different responsibilities. The twins, Mattie and Nellie, are guardians. It is their duty to protect you from anyone who would harm you."

"They told me they were able to know my thoughts, even put visions in my mind. They've been with me throughout my whole life. How is that possible?"

"Guardians are chosen very carefully. Their birth is always marked by some unusual sign so the Society is able to find them. Mattie and Nellie were Siamese twins, born with the power to see into each other and into the future. Their mother was a devoted member of the Juno Society. It was from her that we learned of their special telepathic powers. You must understand that their power is in no way supernatural, but rather an extended sensitivity of their sixth sense.

"If the spirit lives, one day we may all be able to see as they see. The power gives them the ability to look into your mind so that they will know how to protect you."

"They were born with the power to protect me?"

"You, and those who have come before you within the twins' lifetime."

"They've protected others?" All her life she had felt so unique. It came as a great relief to realize that there had been others before her who experienced the same strange things that she had.

"You will learn all about them here. If you are done with your meal, I'll show you where all the records are kept."

Tamara guided her through the main hall into a room that was lit by four oil lamps. It appeared to be a library. Tall shelves ran the length of the walls, and all of them were carefully stacked with manuscripts. Aeron paced the long narrow room, looking at the rows of loosely bound papers.

"Please read," Tamara said, as Aeron pulled a manuscript from the pile above her. It was written in longhand and the pages were yellowed with age.

"It's not written in English. I can't read it."

"Most of the older records were first written in Latin and then Italian. But they are also here in English. They have been translated for you. As I told you last night, we have been preparing for you since the day you were born. In time you will be able to read the originals." Tamara reached for a manuscript and handed it to Aeron. "Try this one."

Aeron read a few lines describing a village in China, and immediately the place seemed familiar to her. An intense thirst came to her dry mouth. She looked up at Tamara.

"You know about my dreams and the people that visit me from other times, don't you?"

"We don't know it all." Tamara was cautious, afraid of overwhelming the girl. She sat down at a desk that had been created from an oak door. "Your guardians have told us much over the years, but in many ways you know more than us. As to the history, that's our task. That's what these archives are for. We've kept it all here." She indicated the rows of papers. "All the records for the past two thousand years. We want you to stay here with us for as long as it takes you to blend together what we know with what you remember, until you are ready."

"Ready for what?"

"Ready to allow the spirit to come forth from you. To awaken the sleeping unconscious of people all over the world. It is important that your stay here be as short as possible."

"What am I supposed to learn here?"

"There is much for you to know. You must recall everything you have forgotten."

Tamara showed Aeron how the small library was organized. "These books are the antiquities." She indicated twelve thick volumes. "They are all the records that were kept before the printing press. It is all hand-scribed with some of it using original Roman letters, so it will be difficult for you to make out. It is essential that you read every word yourself."

"I am to read everything in this room?"

"I know the task seems overwhelming to you, Aeron. Once you get started it will feel very different. You see, you are not reading history books. You are reading about *your own life*. Everything in this room is about you. These books contain pieces of your history. I know that you have seen parts . . . you call them *Shadows*. Here you will be able to read it all. From before the time of Juno, Apollo, and all the gods of the Roman Pantheon."

"None of those gods were real," Aeron said, suddenly feeling she was surrounded by madness. "They are just ancient mythologies. What do they have to do with the power within me?"

"What is real, Aeron? Is the wind real? Is fire real? Is the power of the earth to regenerate herself real? What makes these ancient myths seem so unreal to us is that the Greeks and the Romans, and so many other civilizations, named their gods and gave them human personalities, until they appeared silly and irrelevant in our eyes. Yet what they represented . . . the powers of nature . . . those things were always real.

"You see, Juno was simply the name they gave to a spirit that lives buried deep inside all of us. She is our instinct to survive, to nurture ourselves and the earth we live upon. It is an entity that we worship, not a name.

"The spirit within you was a simple and uneducated thing when it was breathed into that first child two thousand years ago. It was an insignificant spirit with little power. It grew with the experience of each lifetime as it was infused with intelligence and learning. The wisdom gained through living blended together with our deepest memories, the species memory that we all share . . . our collective unconscious. That is the essence of the power that creates and spreads the dreams.

"This is not a magical power, Aeron. You are full of ancient wisdom. You have watched our mistakes, our failures, and our successes for two thousand years . . . and all of that knowledge you will now be ready to give to us. Once you have read everything that exists in this room, all the memories will come back to you whole, and they will be welded together with your instincts."

Aeron felt tears break free from her eyes. "How can all this be possible? I never believed in any god, and now you're telling me that I've lived on this earth for over two thousand years in the lives of others. It's too much for me to believe."

"I know it must seem a burden to you and I can't ask you to

believe everything I'm telling you. It really isn't important whether you believe what I say. Your intelligence may not allow you to believe in so ancient a prophecy. The power does not ask you to accept and believe. It is beyond that need.

"Your destiny is already written. When you leave here, you will be a force powerful enough to change the course of human evolution.

"Aeron, you don't need faith to believe my words. You can see yourself that the human species has been climbing towards the door of extinction. We have fouled our air and our water. We have desecrated the body of the whole earth. If we are to endure, we must learn to survive as a species. You are the power that will give us the ability to survive. You are the final step in our evolution."

"One hundred lifetimes!" Aeron felt the wonder of Tamara's words. "And for all that time the Juno Society has watched it, traced it, recorded it, in all these books and papers?"

"The records are not unbroken. That's why it is important that you read every word. A name, a sentence, a place may bring back a whole lifetime to you, a lifetime that we missed completely."

Aeron saw the face of Father DeCarlo before her eyes. He would destroy all of the memories, the lives, in these archives as easily as he had killed her mother. If she was to be the one to fight him and the Sidon, she would have to be as determined and as strong as they were.

"I was born in 1980. Who held the breath before me?"

"She died very young. She was only eight years old when she drowned right here in the Aeron River," Tamara said.

"Drowned! So that's who she was. She pulled me down into the water with her. I thought I would drown as well. Then she appeared to me in Lake Tahoe."

"Her name was Mary Alice Langley. She was born right here on the banks of the Aeron in a little village called Llangeitho. Her mother died giving birth. She came so suddenly, there wasn't time to take them to a hospital, and the baby was born breach. But Mary Alice thrived, and her father, Gavin, took care of her, and loved her."

Gavin, the Welshman! It was true—he was Mary Alice's father! Had he saved her because he thought she was the reincarnation of his own child?

"What was she doing out on a boat by herself in the dark when she was only eight years old?" The minute she asked the question, she could feel the answer. "She was called, wasn't she? She was called by the full moon and by the hawk woman. I saw the wind churn up the river and capsize the boat. She was called to her death by the spirit."

"I can't know that," Tamara said. "It is believed that if the spirit feels it is housed in a body that is not strong enough to hold it, it may choose to leave, and it can only leave with the death of the child. You see, it had so little time left. You are its last chance."

"You believe that I am the last lifetime?"

"Yes."

"If I die, the spirit will be born again."

"No," Tamara said softly. "We are at the threshold of the next millennium, the year 2000. You are the hundredth life to carry the spirit. Your death releases the Breath of Juno from this mortal world. If the spirit comes again to protect the earth, it will be long after we have made it uninhabitable for human life to exist. If the Sidon succeeds in taking your life, the prophecy will be denied.

"Perhaps it's best if I leave you alone now."

When Tamara had gone, Aeron walked the length of the narrow, windowless room. The dreams and the Shadows would never let her rest. Her destiny was woven together with the destiny of the spirit.

The shelves were arranged by location and date. She knew where she wanted to begin—France, seven hundred years ago. Was it possible that she would find the life of Jean-Marie Gallisone in this strange library? She pulled several thick manuscripts from the shelves and carried them back to the table. Hours passed without her awareness as she turned the pages, looking for Jean-Marie. Nothing. The woman she had found so vividly in Paris was not here. Then a different name startled her.

Born, 1412 in Lorraine . . . a shepherd girl who began hearing voices calling to her when she was thirteen years old. Her visions were spoken of all over France. As Aeron read, the wooden walls of the room turned to stone—the walls of a tower prison. Her vision blurred until the name on the yellowing paper in front of her was all she could see. *Jeanne d'Arc*. Then the prison disappeared and she was in a court yard—hundreds of faces all around her, screaming and praying as flames began to lick her naked legs. Pain shot through her

The Breath of Juno

body. The skin on her arms blackened and curled. Hot air seared the inside of her lungs as she rose up, out of the burning young body. She flew above the smell of smoke and burnt flesh, wings carrying her away from the horror below.

In an instant she was back, sitting at the long table. She touched the name written on the page before her with the tips of her fingers. Hot tears ran down her cheeks. *Joan of Arc, Died 1431.* She was nineteen! The same as me, Aeron realized.

She forced herself to read on.

· 26 ·

Dawn broke on the second of October, three weeks since the terrible night at Lake Tahoe. Lee switched on the coffee pot as she watched the first light of morning turn the San Bernardino Mountains a hazy shade of red. Looking out at these mountains had once given her a feeling of security and peace. Whatever happened in her life, they stood before her each morning, promising the beauty of a new day. Now she wondered if she would ever feel peaceful again.

For the first few days after Sara's death and Aeron's disappearance, she and Gavin had been asked to remain in the area while the police investigated Sara's murder.

Lee and Gavin had been cautious, saying little. They were both afraid that a full-scale search would lead to Father DeCarlo and the Sidon, and that might put Aeron in even greater danger. Finally, the police had allowed them to leave the area.

Lee had been eager to return to San Bernardino. Aeron might try to contact her there. She would also have to explain to the Wilkes what had happened as best she could.

Gavin had no idea where he should go. He wanted to find the girl who held the spirit of his daughter, to touch her face, to feel Mary Alice within her, but he didn't know where to begin. When Lee asked him if he would go back to San Bernardino with her, he went without hesitation.

HE HAD BEEN AT her home ever since, sleeping on the sofa in the living room. As shattered as Lee had been by the events of that night, she thought Gavin seemed even more destroyed. Usually a quiet, soft-spoken man, he could not stop talking about the past. She had listened patiently as he told her things that had taken place almost two decades ago. She found herself staring at him when his hand cupped his beard and he spoke of his daughter, Mary Alice. The pain in his voice had not been dulled by time. Lee felt compassion for Gavin and wanted to comfort him, but she also wished that his thoughts would stop wandering back so many years.

When he told her that he had always believed that there had been something unnatural about his daughter's death, Lee pleaded with him to let go of the things that had happened so long ago. She had implored him to focus on their immediate concerns. They needed to talk about Aeron, how they could find her, what they could do to help her. For a few moments he would listen and agree, then his mind would travel back and he would see the faces of the twins watching his daughter.

Lee worried that he was losing control of his thoughts—becoming unable to deal with what had happened.

Now, just as she was about to go out to the patio, she heard him stirring. The coffee was ready, so Lee poured it into two cups, took a sip of her own, and then carried the other into the living room.

"Are you awake?" she asked quietly, looking over the couch.

His eyes were open, puffy, and red from worry and lack of sleep. He smiled at her.

"How is it that you can look so fresh and lovely at this hour of the morning?" He rubbed his beard self-consciously. "I must look like a mountain man who hasn't washed in weeks."

She didn't know what to say when he complimented her. It made her feel uncomfortable. Circumstance had thrown them together awkwardly. She didn't know how to behave with this man who had been a total stranger just three weeks ago and now was sleeping on her sofa, without any apparent plans to leave. Not that she wanted him to leave.

"One morning you're going to wake up before me and then you'll find out what I really look like in the morning," she laughed. "I've been up for over an hour already. I can't sleep," she admitted.

It was memories of that night, of Sara Morgan's death, and of Aeron's disappearance, that kept her from sleeping. But there was more to it than that. When she woke during the night, the horror of that moment would come back to her, and she replayed it in her mind over and over, wishing that there was something she could do to change the outcome. Then, as she lay there watching the clock, her thoughts turned to the man lying on the sofa in the next room—his sleeping body so close to hers. She would hear the sound of his voice, and see the gentle way he moved his hands when he spoke.

She thought of his strong graceful hands, wondering how they would feel, touching her body, caressing her cheek, stroking her back. She wanted to feel his arms around her. She had never known any man so tender.

It had been so long since she'd been with a man that she'd forgotten how delicious it could feel to lie quietly, her head resting on a man's chest, his arm behind her back, his hand against her shoulder.

So many times in the past few weeks she'd wanted to get up out of bed, go to the living room, remove the thin blanket that covered his body, and lie down next to him. And now, as he looked up at her, she searched for words to hide her thoughts. He would think her terribly insensitive to be thinking about such things after all they had been through.

"I brought you some coffee," was all she could say.

He took the coffee and sat up, so that she could join him on the sofa. They had grown close in a short period of time, finding solace in one another.

"I don't think your sleeping pills are working," he said, patting her knee with his hand. "I'm afraid you look as tired as I do."

"A moment ago, you told me I looked fresh and lovely. Or is that just what you're used to saying first thing in the morning?"

He laughed so easily that she felt as if she'd known him for years. Their lives had come together so quickly. There had been no period where they could get to know one another. Instead, their personalities were burned into each other's souls instantly. They felt like old friends before they really knew one another.

Lee thought they must look like an old married couple, sitting on the sofa, drinking coffee in the early morning hours. They talked of little things for as long as they could.

"It's about time for a bath, don't you think," he said, getting up and smiling down at her. For a moment, she thought it was an invitation. But he put down his cup of coffee and walked off to the bathroom. She liked that he took baths instead of showers. She liked thinking about him, lying in a tub of warm water, scrubbing his body with soap. She'd never known a man who took baths; they never had time for it. A quick shower, and then they were off.

When he emerged from the bathroom a half hour later, his beard was trimmed and he smelled clean. She had breakfast waiting for him.

"Now I could get used to this," he said. "Do you always wait on your men?"

"I've had very few to wait on."

"I find that hard to believe."

She looked at him, her face stern. With a touch of anger in her voice she said, "Why do you find that hard to believe? Is it because you think I'm attractive, intelligent? That no man could resist me?"

"Well, yes, if you put it that way, I guess that's exactly what I think."

"Just because you had a wonderful marriage, Gavin, doesn't mean that's what everybody wants. There are lots of women like me who aren't married. There are other things in life, you know. Getting married isn't the most important thing in the world."

He reached across the table and took her hand. "If I've said something to offend you, I'm sorry . . . terribly sorry. You've been so kind, keeping me here like this. Maybe it's time I returned home to Wales." He didn't let go of her hand but held it even more firmly.

"I don't know how to begin looking for her . . . for Kayla . . . Aeron . . . Mary Alice . . . but staying here may not be of any help," he said.

Lee could hardly hear his words. She was so pleased at the touch of his hand. She was embarrassed at her sharp words. He broke the awkward moment by releasing her hand and eating the breakfast she had prepared.

"I'm not much of a cook," she said, trying to change the subject. "This is called 'Eggs in Holes.' You just tear the center out of a piece of bread, throw it in a pan, crack an egg in the middle. That's the extent of my skills in the kitchen."

"Angels on Horseback," he said. "That's what we used to call them when I was a little one. Wonder where they got that name from. Sounds a bit unappetizing doesn't it?"

"Stay here with me," Lee said without thinking. "I don't know how to begin looking either. She knows where I am. Maybe she'll find a way to get in touch. And if she does, I'll need you with me."

"Good," he said. "I'm pleased you feel that way because I don't want to be leaving here. When those twins appeared before me on the beach that night, I thought it was a vision from long ago. I almost expected to be able to gaze out over that lake and see my Mary Alice still alive, clinging to the side of her small boat. It's like a moment frozen in time, a moment that never took place in front of my eyes, but I see it still.

"Oh Lee, I wish you could believe the tale that the twins told me that night. I wish you could understand and see it the way I do now. I know it all sounds insane to you, but the moment they began telling me of this spirit, I knew that it had lived inside my daughter."

Gavin got up from the table and looked out the window.

"Maybe it's not a magical spirit," he said almost to himself, "not a mystical power like they spoke of it, but there was a force within her, and it was too strong for her tiny body."

"Gavin, I can't begin to give you a rational explanation for what has happened." Lee wanted to go to him, to put her arms around his back, to hold him, but she forced herself to stay at the table. "I can't explain Aeron's dreams, or the strange experiences she had when she felt she was living someone else's life. Maybe these things did happen to your daughter as well. There must be some explanation for it."

Then to her surprise, he walked behind her chair and put his hands on her head and let his fingers run down through her long brown hair. "Is it really that different," he said, "from Christian beliefs? You could just as easily call that a mythology. God breathing life into Adam, or an intangible God fathering a human son. Millions of people accept this supernatural event as absolute truth, so why, tell me, is it so difficult to believe that a spirit that they call Juno breathed its essence into a human child, my child, and then Aeron?"

"I'm sorry," she said, feeling his hands rest on her shoulders, "that line of reasoning doesn't work on me. I can't buy the Christian myth either. There's just too much of the practical scientist in me. I only believe in things I experience myself."

"Then," he said, turning her face to his, "how do you explain the dream that we all shared? She sent it to you, and to me as well. Wasn't that the spirit of Juno, communicating to us through Aeron's mind?"

"It's too mystical. I can't believe it."

"Then you will think me terrible if I tell you that many things we take for granted are mystical. When I first saw my wife, she was just eighteen years old, a girl fresh from school. She was walking along a river, the river Aeron where our daughter drowned. I knew, the minute I saw her, that I would make her my wife. Is that too mystical for you to believe?"

His face was so close to hers, she had to break away. "Love at first sight? It's the stuff of all the great romances," she tried to laugh, but the sound never came from her throat.

"How could I love a woman I didn't know? Was it just the way she looked? I don't think so. I saw inside her. There was something of me in her, and I knew that we belonged to each other before we even spoke. That's not a very American way to think, is it?"

Lee felt tears welling up in her eyes. He was speaking of his wife as he touched her hair.

"It's a wonderful feeling I never thought I would have again," he said. "The magic of knowing, of being so sure, that your soul belongs with the soul of another, that you were meant to be together, and that somehow you would find each other.

"Lee, it may be a terrible time to say it to you, but it's a feeling I am having again. When I first saw you in that market in Sherwin Creek, I felt the same as I did so many years ago. I know you think it sounds impossible, that you won't be able to believe it, but it's there nonetheless. I don't expect you to return these feelings. We've only known each other for a few weeks. Every night, as I lie on your sofa, I ache for you, and I haven't known a feeling like that for so many years. Are you going to tell me that there is nothing magical in that?"

Her arms went around his neck. "No," she whispered. "I'm not."

Beverly Olevin

The Breath of Juno

PART V

*River of women
Flow through time
Touch me with courage
Bring us the dawn*

• 27 •

1999: Africa

THE HEAT HELD HER IN A VICE, PRESSING down on her back even as it rose up from the wet pavement through her feet, into the bones of her legs laboring her walk, shortening her breath. She moved through the streets that sat above the middle of the earth, on the shores of Lake Victoria. The bright colors of the native dress worn by the women in the marketplace of the old city danced before her eyes as the heat diffused the light, blurring her vision. She had come to Kampala, the capital of Uganda, to the headwaters of the Nile, to the cradle of humankind.

She thought it would be a safe place to begin. Kampala was now a teeming modern city with over a million people, but everything she remembered about it still existed. She recognized the smell of the fetid soil, the gray light that filtered through the constant rain, the enormous lake and the earthbound clouds that always clung to the Mountains of the Moon—the Ruwenzores—to the west.

She had been here in another time, long before the British had called this land theirs, when the native tribes gathered around campfires singing to their children, telling stories into the night. She had been a child here, squatting at one of those campfires on the equator, tasting the deliciousness of bananas mashed together with sweet potatoes. A life she felt was not in the vast records of the Juno Society. It had come to her just before she left the Mother Home. She believed it came to guide her to Africa, to this place. It was here that she was to begin.

For five months she had stayed at the fortress in the Cambrian Mountains in Wales, and one by one they came back to her, all those who had traveled across the centuries with her. Each day her memory had grown as the Shadows that lived in the crevices of her brain spread, until she thought she could no longer contain so many lives. And still they kept coming back to her with such clarity and precision, it was as if she had lived them all in a single unbroken lifetime. She remembered them not just with her mind but with her body. She could smell the light scent of lemon that blew in from the sea and across the groves in Alexandria. She could feel the rough sackcloth against her skin when Jean-Marie lived in her memory. And she could see the seven hills of Rome from the banks of the Tiber River.

What she had first felt as a burden became a joy. She grew with the memories, welcoming them to a single home in her mind. Hidden in the mountains of Wales she became an ocean of memories, and as they came each brought precious gifts. They brought her their pain and their suffering—their sadness as they left their mortal lives. But they also brought her their joys, triumphs and their secrets. She cried for those who died young with so many of their dreams unfulfilled. And through them all she grew as their strength became her power.

Amy Talbot, who had died when she was only twenty-nine, had kept a diary of her daily life in Bodie, the frontier town where greed and violence ruled. And Aeron wrote it again, with her, seeing it all as it lay upon the page. Amy's spirit burned bright, and yet the diary was lost to a fire three years after she died, unread and unknown. At first Aeron had grieved for Amy and so many of the Shadows that lived their lives in obscurity, girls and women who left no footprints upon the earth. Then, as more lives came into her, she realized they had formed a chain and linked gracefully into one another until they were a river, a ribbon of women just as she had seen it in her dreams, snaking through the woods of time. Mary Alice Langley, Paula Campbell, Jean-Marie Gallisone. None of their lives were lost. They flowed into one another, coming up through the generations, coming to her. She was the vessel waiting to contain them all, for through her, all of their voices would be remembered. None of their sorrows would be in vain, for they still walked with her as she carried their spirit across the bridge into the new millennium.

As she walked through the ancient part of Kampala, the streets narrowed and the high rises were replaced by one-story wood houses with dirt yards full of nervous chickens and sickly cats licking themselves. At the marketplace the dusty road filled with men and women pressing against one another as they bartered with vendors for fruits and colorful fabrics. Few of the people here wore western dress as they did in the modern part of the city, but even if she hadn't worn jeans and a sleeveless white shirt, they would have stared at her. Her red hair, pale skin, and her eyes, the green of the forest, made her stand out from the crowd.

No one here could possibly know who she was. Still, at any moment, she feared someone from the Sidon would discover her. As she walked through the marketplace she imagined someone creeping up behind her, looking for her in the cross hairs of a rifle, squeezing a finger against a trigger, sending a bullet flying towards its target, smashing through her skull, ending all that had traveled for two thousand years. The image of Sara never left her mind; life was so very fragile. And in spite of everything she had seen, she was mortal. Her own wits, her memory, and the power of the spirit were the only weapons she had to protect her from a sudden death. It was strange, she thought, that though she remembered all of the lives that had come before her, she still feared for her single mortal existence.

Tomorrow morning her journey would truly begin. She had arranged to have a local guide take her into the bush, three hours west of Kampala, where she would stay with a native tribe. There she would allow the spirit to fly on the wings of the hawk and spread its message to the villages below. The experiment on the plane with the old woman had convinced her that she did not need to be asleep in order for her dream to spread into the subconscious minds of others. She could call it up and send it to others at will.

What she didn't yet know was whether she could enter the minds of others only through their dreams, or if she could send the spirit to them when they were awake. Lee and Sara had her dream in the cabin in Lake Tahoe before she even knew how to consciously send it to them, and then Gavin had said he had experienced it as well. Had that been the twins' doing? Had they pulled the dream from her and given it to him? Could she do it alone? How close did she have to be in order for people to hear her calling them?

She had picked the heart of Africa because she knew she could go deep into the bush where primitive peoples still feel the power of their unconscious. Here they had always believed that the birds and beasts that visited them in their dreams were gods coming to bring them messages, words from their gods that could only be seen in the dream world. Here it was not uncommon for whole tribes to report having experienced the same dream. The phenomenon would not cause a stir. It would not be news in London, Paris, or Rome where the Sidon was sure to see it and learn where she was.

That night in her hotel room she practiced a sweet smile to give to her native guide the next day. It mimicked an innocence she no longer felt. It lit her face with eager youth and belied the ancient spirit that lay just beneath the surface. When the smile looked back at her from the mirror, she was amazed to see that she was still so young.

The next morning in the pouring rain, Aeron went with her guide, Ngudu, into the bush to begin her journey. He was an elegant black man, tall and lean with rich polished skin. His high cheekbones and broad forehead looked like they had been chiseled from granite. They traveled all day by jeep across lands once covered with herds of wildebeest, now empty and still. She kept her eyes and hair covered, wearing dark glasses and a black scarf. A camera hung around her neck and a pair of binoculars at her side. She wanted to look like a tourist, a visitor and not an intruder.

Ngudu took her to his own tribal home where she was greeted by the tribe's elders, a man and a woman. The old man, perhaps once the height of her guide, had now shrunk, causing his sun-baked skin to hang in loose folds around his bare chest and stomach. Aeron was disturbed to see how fragile he looked. His legs were bone and skin, no thicker around than her own arms. But when he spoke in his native tongue, his voice was strong and clear.

"Butunge welcomes you to our home," Ngudu translated.

The old man smiled at her, his gray eyes shining. Then he touched her red hair and spoke excitedly.

"He says you are the fire that burns within the earth."

The old woman laughed, holding her hands in front of her open mouth. Thick bands scarred into her flesh adorned her wrists and ankles like onyx bracelets. When Ngudu introduced her as their holy medicine woman, she spit on both her hands, rubbed her palms together in small circular motions, then placed them on Aeron's cheeks. Her laughter became a rhythmic song as she swayed the girl back and forth with her hands.

"She says you have come to bless us with your fire."

"She's right," Aeron smiled.

When the women of the small tribe began to prepare the evening meal, Aeron offered to help them. This is a good place to begin, she thought. For these people, life has changed little over the centuries. They live much as their ancestors had for thousands of years.

That night as she broke bread with them and listened to their stories, told in Swahili and translated by her guide, she felt strange knowing she was about to fall into an incredibly intimate relationship with them as she penetrated their minds and touched the deepest part of their dreams.

She dipped her soft brown bread into a thick soup made from manioc root, and looked at the faces of the men, women, and children who ate with her. There was a peaceful feeling in knowing that this simple act of gathering around a fire at night and sharing a meal had taken place among family tribes since the beginning of human time.

She thought about the people who formed the circle and all who had gone before them. Each of us, she thought, must have buried within us a whole reservoir of knowledge that we've accumulated as a species through the long march of our evolution. She thought of the remaining animal herds that still roamed the plains of Africa. They live by collective thought patterns. They know how to behave because each of their brains contain ancient instincts. If all animals have these instincts, why should humans be the only species devoid of all traces of their evolution?

The journey she would begin tonight with this tribe of people was a journey of hope. A journey that had to begin inside the deepest psyche of the human mind. She had to learn to allow the message of her dreams to soar with the hawk, so that the spirit could awake the lost soul within.

Even Tamara couldn't tell her what would happen to people once the spirit had touched them. Would they change all at once or would it be a gradual evolution?

After her many months at the Mother Home she had come to see the spirit within her as the gift of complete memory—memory that did not end with a single lifetime. But now as she sat alone on a canvas bed under a thatched roof in the shadow of the Mountains of the Moon, a fear stilled her breath.

How could she know if all these tribespeople would accept the dream she pushed into their sleep? The old woman on the plane had been comforted by the vision of the sheep crossing the river, but now everything was different. She wasn't willing them to see a simple dream. She was forcing them to open an entire part of their mind to her. What if some of them resisted the spirit? Could the struggle tear them apart, leaving them frightened and insane until they were driven to take their own lives?

For an instant she felt herself in the thirteen year-old body of Paula Campbell, her hands placing the rope around her neck. She pushed away the vision, but the fear of the moment remained. If this power within her brought death to Paula, would it not do the same to others? The Sidon tried to kill Aeron because they believed her power to be an evil thing. Could they be right?

The people of the village had welcomed her, shared their meal with her, and now they slept, innocent of her true purpose, unaware of her power. She looked up at the dark sky, the moon hidden by clouds. Tonight, she hoped, would not be dangerous for these people who live close to the earth. They would be able to accept the spirit.

She closed her eyes, raised her head to the sky and spoke to the night.

"It begins now! Give me the strength to fulfill your dream."

She breathed deeply and filled the hawk with power, sending it with broad wings to fly over the valley.

The spirit soared with such power and strength from her body she was afraid it would tear her to pieces. It was so hungry to fly.

THE MEDICINE WOMAN slept on a grass mat, her head tucked into her chest, her neck curved. Her eyelids twitched slightly as a dream began to unfold.

Light as a feather, her thin body was floating up towards the clouds. Above her a magnificent bird called to her, though no sound came from its silver beak. Higher and higher she rose until she was beneath its powerful wings.

When the great bird lowered its head, she saw the slanted black eyes slowly close. When they opened again they had become emerald green. The crowning feathers were a brilliant red. The sharp pointed beak began to shrink until the features of a young woman replaced those of the hawk. It was a face she recognized.

No longer outside, but within!

The old woman was within the bird. It's wings were her own. It's eyes gave her vision.

My death, she thought. She felt no fear, only the wonder of the idea.

This is the moment of my death.

The broad wings sliced through the thin air.

She looked down through the hawk's eyes, expecting to see her own human body lying lifeless on the ground below.

The whole village was now barely visible as the hawk carried her further into the sky. So high that she could see the curve of the earth—the horizon bending—a never ending circle.

She felt her old heart beating faster. The rapid beating of a bird's heart.

If my heart beats, she wondered, do I still live? Do I still breathe?

A warm wind chanted all around her. Breathing in and out. Breathing just as the earth was breathing below her. Not a solid mass of rock and soil, but a single organism, a life, breathing as all living things breathe.

The earth was breathing its life into her. They were a single animal breathing as one. Breathing in unison.

Each breath filled her memory as it filled her lungs. And the memory was as vast as the sky. It reached back through her ancestral tree—through the whole tree of human existence. It reached forward to memories yet to be.

The immortal breath of the earth.

As the power of the spirit breathed into the medicine woman and the others of the tribe, it was pulled deep inside the earth itself. It pulsated with such vigor that the ground moved for hundreds of miles around the village. It was not a sudden violent shaking, but a gentle rocking as if the earth itself was slowly waking up.

The motion of the earth didn't frighten Aeron like the many violent earthquakes in Southern California had over the years. Instead, she thrilled with the sensation. The ground seemed to move with her own heart beat.

The Breath of Juno

Excited voices were shouting all around her. She jumped from her matted bed and searched for Ngudu. She found him dancing and shouting happily with the others.

"What is it?" she asked, grabbing his arm to get his attention. At first he ignored her, not wanting to still his exuberance. When she spoke to him again, he turned suddenly to her.

"It is you," he said softly, and as if by an unspoken command, the whole tribe fell silent and moved in a circle around her. One by one they came forward to touch her. She felt no fear as they pressed to be near her. It was the spirit they wanted to touch, not her. They understood that she had brought it to them, but they also knew it didn't belong to her. Once they touched her, they moved away, talking excitedly to one another. She needed no translator to understand their words, for she found she could see within their minds.

They were full of joy as they spoke of their ancestors, as if they still walked among them today. She was amazed that she could feel their emotions and know their thoughts. Through their minds she could see a vision of a small boy growing into a young man—a mother holding a baby turning into a child herself. The past and the future became one!

Before tonight the ability to see into the lives of others had been given to her by the twins. They were not with her now! The magic of the spirit's power had begun. Once the Breath of Juno had entered their sleeping minds, they were able to send their thoughts freely to her. She no longer needed the telepathy of the twins. It was a power that would belong to everyone who felt the spirit.

WHEN SHE LEFT THE next day at noon, all the villagers wished her a good journey. The medicine woman gave her a small leather bag of herbs to keep her and the spirit within her strong and well.

Ngudu was silent for over an hour as they travelled back to Kampala. Finally he spoke.

"It is a long time, many generations, since the earth goddess has flown into our hearts. This is a great day."

He said these words not to her, but to the vast plains around them, and as he spoke she understood that the spirit had been known to these people long before it was called to live in human form by the women of Juno. It was not the power of a goddess brought to them by a woman of white skin from the west, but a spirit they had known from the beginning—a spirit that belonged to the living earth mother. In this life it passed through her, but it had always lived with them.

• 28 •

FATHER DECARLO LOOKED OUT OVER THE SEA. She was out there waiting for him. His frockcoat hung loosely on his fragile decaying frame.

"Come to me," he whispered to the blue waters beneath him. "Do not hide from me any longer. I found you in the mountains. I will find you again. You reached back into the past, saw into my eyes, and guided me to you by showing me your vision. You know who I am and why I must hunt you. My cause is righteous. Let me free you from the evil that lives within your soul."

Every night since she had slipped away from him, he looked for her in his dreams. Her anger had flown to him when she was in Sherwin Creek, revealing where he would find her. It would happen again. Once she was on the move, breathing her power into sleeping minds, he was certain that he would be able to feel her again. Now that she had seen him as the instrument of her mother's death, her rage would not let her hide. She would allow him to see her. He would go to her himself, and his power would be stronger than hers.

BROTHER MARTIN NO longer trusted Father DeCarlo's ability to find the girl. He was afraid that the man had become obsessed with his own private hunt. There was pleasure in DeCarlo's thin smile when he spoke of facing the spirit himself, sucking away its power. He was an old man who wanted a final battle against the cruel force of nature that bent his bones, twisted his fingers, bowed his legs, and curved his spine. But the priest would only get in the way. The girl had to be found. Time was running out.

In December, Brother Martin had left the island sanctuary and gone to Rome, taking many of the monks with him. He had his own way of searching for the girl. Father DeCarlo was a man of the past;

he was a man of the future. It was impossible for her to hide from the International Information System. Events all over the world could be monitored on a computer information highway. He put Brother Anthony in charge of searching the system daily for any news that would lead them to the girl.

It wasn't until February of the following year that Brother Anthony discovered the first piece of significant information. A small article in Uganda's leading newspaper reported that tribes across the country were speaking of the return of the moon goddess. They told how she flew into their dreams with the wings of a hawk and the face of a woman. It was a common dream shared by thousands of people. When Brother Martin learned of Anthony's discovery, the old monk was not impressed.

"These are primitive people. They probably have such common visions all the time. I cannot believe she is in Africa. These stories you found don't have anything to do with the spirit of Juno. It's an isolated incident from mere natives."

But Anthony kept watching the area as more reports came in. At first it was only rural tribes who experienced the dream. Then it moved north and was being experienced by larger groups of people. The image was always the same: the hawk woman.

A week later Brother Anthony called the monks of the order together. He placed a map of Africa on the table before them. He started with the small tribe outside of Kampala where the first report had made the newspapers. He stuck a pin on the map at that spot.

"This is where the first news story came from. The members of the tribe all said they saw the hawk woman in their dreams, but they also claimed to have experienced a dozen other dreams together. After a few days there were no more news stories, but I found rumors circulating from the surrounding countries of Zaire, Tanzania, and Rwanda."

As he named each country, he placed pins on the map.

"Earthquakes have been reported in all these areas. They are strange . . . low in intensity but they seem to last for a long time, even hours.

"In April another shared dream story was reported in Khartoum in the Sudan." He placed another pin. "Two days ago I learned of a story from Aswan in Egypt."

The pins moved up the banks of the Nile.

"You've found her!" Brother Martin jumped to his feet.

"She's traveling mostly by ground." Brother Anthony was enjoying his success. "I think she started in more primitive areas where it was easier for her to use her powers. Slowly she's moved on as she's become more confident and seen the results. These points show where she has been. If she continues along this line, it can also tell us where she's going. It seems that she has to physically be near people in order for them to receive her powers. She is communicating with them telepathically, but there is a geographical limit to how far the dreams can travel."

"Have the earthquakes followed her path?" Brother Martin could not believe that the power of the spirit was already penetrating the earth itself. It is much too soon, he worried.

"Yes. The report's are all the same."

"She's going to Cairo!," Brother Martin concluded delightedly. "We will stop her there before she has touched too many people. You will select ten monks and go to Cairo tonight. It must be her next destination."

"How do we avoid being affected by the dream?" one of the monks asked, expecting a straightforward answer. He was taken back by the silence in the room.

Brother Martin broke the silence. "It is the Sidon that first spoke the prophecy. It is our destiny to deny it."

He clutched the pendant that hung around his neck, a pyramid with a single eye in the center. It represented the all-seeing eye of prophecy.

"She may be hypnotic to others," he said, "but not to the monks of the Sidon. We shall prepare ourselves carefully so that our minds cannot be invaded by the power of this spirit."

He spoke with a confidence he did not feel. In truth, he feared what would happen when the appointed monks were face to face with the power within the woman.

"Brother Anthony, select who will go with you, and we shall purify them now."

Ten men where chosen. Obediently they pulled their linen tunics over their heads, then removed undergarments. Their naked flesh was dry and pasty from frequent cleansing. One by one their bodies were washed and shaved by the other monks.

It was a sin for any hair to remain protruding from their skin. The head was shaved first, then the face. Their chests, arms and legs were then scraped clean. Pubic hair was the last to be removed. On the island Father DeCarlo had insisted that any remaining hairs be plucked from the body but there was no time for that now.

Thick olive oil scented with cloves and limes was rubbed into their scalp, then down their backs, their buttocks, their smooth legs.

Brother Martin examined the naked bodies of the ten men and was satisfied. They were made of God, not of animal. He fell to his knees in front of the chosen monks and prayed that they would not be touched by this heathen earthly spirit. That they were above her pagan powers. That the Breath of Juno never enter their consecrated bodies.

AERON BEGAN HER journey up the Nile, moving from village to village, sometimes traveling by foot, sometimes on horseback, and then by train up through Uganda into the Sudan and Egypt. Cairo was to be her first large city. When she let the hawk fly there, the spirit would soar into the minds of tens of thousands of people. The entire population would speak of nothing else the following day. The ground would roll beneath their feet and the power of the breathing earth would begin to transform their lives.

Then the Sidon could easily find her. She had to be quicker than they. She had to be able to match their power with her own. Her mind raged with questions still unanswered. Could she send the spirit's power to those who hunted her? Would it destroy their desire to kill her? Just how strong are they, and how strong is she?

When she reached Aswan in southern Egypt, she boarded a midnight train that would take her to Cairo. She preferred to travel late at night. In spite of the hour, the cars were crowded with people pushing to find a seat. The women were covered in black from head to toe, with only their hands and faces visible. The men wore the traditional galabia, the long cotton shirts that hung to the ground, allowing air to move freely around their bodies, giving them relief from the heat. Children in dirty corduroy pants scrambled for seats.

She covered her nose and mouth to protect herself form the smell of old cheese, rotting fruit, and urine that permeated the stifling air in the cars. There was a single seat next to a young woman carrying a baby in a basket. She slid into it. The cracked green vinyl stuck to her back; still she was grateful for a moment to rest. The train shuddered as if protesting the sheer human mass it carried, then reluctantly pulled out of the station.

It was impossible to find comfort in the straight-back seat, but as the hour advanced, passengers were rocked to sleep by the swaying of the car on the narrow tracks. Only the baby in the basket was still awake—its eyes wide open, staring at her as if it knew who she was and what she was about to do. She smiled at the infant, and the corners of the tiny mouth turned upward in response. "Sleep," she whispered. "Sleep and I will bring you a splendid dream."

She closed her own eyes and allowed the spirit to seep into the people who surrounded her. In their dream world they were not hostile to the wondrous visions that filled their imaginations. When they gave her access to their senses, a marvelous bird appeared in their sleeping vision—a giant hawk, its wings beating to the rhythm of their own hearts. All awareness of their physical boundaries was lost as they were carried above the earth within the body of the hawk—seeing with its eyes—seeing as they had never seen before.

She watched them sleep, envious of their peaceful faces, as the train took her closer to Cairo. Just before dawn broke she felt an odd tightening sensation in her throat—then the sense that someone was watching her. The sensation increased. It was fear, specific and tangible, lodging against her lungs, her throat. She remembered the calm feeling she had when she realized that the boatman who took her up the Aeron River knew who she was; she could sense that he was sent to guide and protect her. She had felt the same when Gavin had come to the cabin in Lake Tahoe. But this feeling in her throat meant just the opposite. Someone was looking for her, coming to her! They were there, in Cairo, waiting for her! If the Sidon had found her, what defense did she have? How could she use her powers against them?

WHEN THE TRAIN pulled into the last station outside of the city, Aeron felt them step on the first platform and board the train several cars in front of her. How could they know where she was so soon? Had they been waiting for her in Cairo, watching the train and bus stations and the airports?

The train jerked forward, slowly pulling out of the station. She could feel them coming towards her. They would go through the railway cars looking for her. In a moment they would find her. She had to get off the train before it picked up speed. She pushed past the woman with the baby and ran down the aisle, causing a commotion. She shoved open the door at the back of the car, and stepped onto the outside platform.

She could see the tracks through the wood planks. The ground moved more quickly beneath her feet. The impulse to jump was overwhelming. It was the only possible way to escape, but the rocks and gravel that would greet her thin body would tear her to shreds. She pushed opened the door to the next car.

They were closing in on her. She moved through the remaining three cars until she was at the open platform at the back of the train. Her breath came in short gasps as she felt her throat closing, as if someone's hands were circling her thin neck. All the strength drained from her body as panic took over.

Desperately she looked around for someplace to hide. There was nothing on the small platform. She bent over the railing that ran around the sides and looked down for a ladder, for anything she could cling to. Nothing! She turned around to face the door, expecting it to fly open at any moment.

At least she would make them look at her before they tried to take her life. But then she saw, just to the left of the door, four wooden barrels—maybe large enough for her small body. She rushed to them and pushed the heavy lid slightly off the nearest one. It was full of water. Of course, she thought, this was the desert. She might be able to fit inside, but water would spill all over the platform, giving her away.

She slid the lid across the next barrel. Only half-full! Quickly she squeezed inside the narrow space, causing the water to rise. A fraction of an inch remained to give her air. She raised her hands and pulled the lid back in place. In the same instant she heard the door open.

With most of her head underwater she couldn't hear them, but she could see inside their minds. They were arguing with one another, each blaming the other for not finding her. Beneath their anger she could feel both fear and reverence. Her head pounded. She could sense they had spotted the water barrels. She took a breath, grabbed the sides of the barrel, and pulled herself to the bottom.

They removed the lid of the first barrel and were looking inside. She was knocked against the wood as one of them kicked her hiding place. She held her breath, her lungs burning. Then, frustrated, they retreated back inside the rail car.

The air exploded from her lungs as she pulled herself from the barrel. The morning air was warm on her wet body, but still she shivered.

They would try again. They would be everywhere looking for her, watching all the airports and train stations. She had to get out of Cairo. Where could she go?

She realized that she had one advantage over them. She had been here before, in a different time. She knew routes out of Cairo that they could never know. She would go overland without taking any modern transportation.

She would go to the Red Sea. There she would cross over to the Sinai, move up through Israel, Syria, across Turkey, to Greece. She would use the old routes, the old ways, spreading the spirit in all these ancient lands.

THE WORD TRAVELED across the land of the hawk spirit who came in the night and of the hypnotizing earthquakes. But even as her power grew, Aeron looked over her shoulder, watching for those who hunted her and wanted her dead. She could no longer hide from them.

Changes were already beginning to take place. Modern cities were becoming like large villages as people came out of their homes and gathered in the streets, feeling connected to one another in a way they had never known before. Once they had seen with the hawk's eyes and breathed with the pulse of the earth, they understood without thinking.

They knew instinctively that they all shared the same needs, that they were part of one another. Their own life, their essence, was much more than what was held together by the skin surrounding their bodies. Deep fears of death and their own mortality began to disappear. They were no longer isolated in their brief lives.

They were a part of something greater than themselves.

• 29 •

AERON WALKED THROUGH THE RUINS OF the Acropolis, looking at the remains of statues built to honor the gods of the Greek Pantheon. There was an entire temple built to Athena, goddess of wisdom. Where, she thought, was the goddess Hera, wife of Zeus? The Romans later gave the same goddess the name Juno.

She had come here to feel the strength of the Shadows who had lived in this ancient city. Smells of freshly baked bread, sweet feta cheese and the licorice scent of ouzo filled the air. Vendors lined the streets that led down from the Acropolis. Aeron stopped at the stall of an old woman who sold small cast iron statues of the Greek gods.

"Do you have a statue of Hera?" Aeron asked the woman whose face was barely visible under a black scarf.

"You want Hera," the woman said in a surprisingly loud voice. "She was the queen of the heavens."

Aeron was about to walk away from the stall before she attracted attention, but the old woman handed her a heavy statue of a woman with a baby to her breast.

"The original stood in Crete facing the sea," the woman said. "Buy her. She will bring you good fortune."

Aeron took the sculpted figure and clutched it to her breast. It was the exact statue of the Virgin Mary that Jean-Marie had knelt before in Notre Dame. She had called her Juno.

The ancient beliefs were all parts of the one great legend. Whatever their name, whoever worshiped them, they all spoke of the same eternal spirit.

Aeron quickly bought the statue, then went to the Plaka where Greek men danced on the tables and the tourists laughed. She laughed and danced with them to the rhythm of the passionate music. Their energy bubbled up into the streets. Aeron sang with them and for a

The Breath of Juno

night she was an ordinary young woman dancing in the streets.

She returned to her small hotel room just outside the Plaka at two in the morning, exhausted. She fell into bed, hoping that she would be able to get at least a few hours of rest. Sleep had become so elusive since she'd begun the journey. The spirit was hungry to spread, to use her body all her waking hours. It denied her sleep and forced her to stay on the move. Yet her mortal body hungered for peace.

Just as she was closing her eyes, a familiar sensation came to her. It began in her throat, a thickening as if her throat would close, cutting off her breath. It spread up to her face, leaving her tongue and lips numb. It was happening again.

They had found her!

If they had felt the spirit in their dreams, could they deny it and still succeed in killing her?

How could she defend herself against them?

She no longer felt like a powerful entity, traveling the world, spreading an intangible force. She was only a young woman, mortal, frightened, and alone. She began to softly chant, the chant she had heard so many times in her dreams. The chant of the ritual on the night of the full moon. The chant to the goddess Juno to protect her.

With the chanting, her throat tightened even more. She ignored it, giving the low tones more power, allowing the sounds to vibrate the bones of her body, to thunder against her skull and her chest. She forced the chant out into the air, pushing it towards the threat coming at her. Her head pounded with pain, still she continued chanting throughout the night.

Even as the haunting chant filled the air, she felt the fear coming closer. She sent them her visions, and still they came. She wanted to run out into the streets, to beg for help, to hide in a narrow alleyway, but there was no place where she could hide from them. They had been watching for her. Now they had seen her.

They had found her.

She huddled in her small bed, pushing her body against the gray wall, pulling her knees to her chest, chanting as loudly as she could with her now throbbing throat. Her heart pounded violently, threatening to explode within her chest.

They were close, so close!

Footsteps on the roof. Movement behind the curtains. A sickening sweet scent of cloves and lime. Glass breaking!

The window flew open and two men burst into the room. They wore hoods and black coats.

This was to be the moment, she realized, looking at the men who stood before her. She continued to chant and to force the power of the spirit into the intruders.

"Don't listen to her," she heard one of them whisper. "We must do it quickly."

The two stood closely together before the helpless girl, unable to move. They had heard her throughout the night, heard her calling to them, and yet they had kept coming. And now that they were in the room with her, the sound of her low voice was overwhelming. It held them rooted to the floor. Their heads pulsated with her unending chant. Their breathing slowed, falling in sync with her deep breathing.

"Go on," the man nearest the window pushed his elbow into the other man's side. "We have to do it quickly," he urged.

She heard the reluctance in the voice. Was he afraid of her? The taller man moved towards her, his lips pressed tightly together, his eyes narrow and determined. His left hand disappeared beneath his coat, then reappeared holding a steel blade.

He bent down and grabbed her by the arm, yanking her from the bed. Her knees buckled as he turned her around so that her back was against his chest.

Holding her with his left arm, he put the knife to her neck. The chanting stopped. She fell silent. His hand trembled as he pushed the blade against her throat.

Aeron reached up and gently touched the hand that held the knife with her own.

Her skin was against his gloved hand, and yet he could feel her touch through the leather.

He could not will his hand to pull the blade across her thin neck.

"Do it!" the other man screamed. "Do it now!"

The man dropped the blade from her neck and pushed himself away from Aeron, crying out, "I cannot!"

He raced from the room. The other one followed him, retreating in fear.

Aeron's hands slowly went to her throat. There was the smallest trickle of blood across her neck where the blade had rested.

IT WAS BROTHER Anthony who called Father DeCarlo to tell him of the failure.

"They couldn't do it," the monk told him. "They were in her room. They saw her, touched her. She pushed them away. That's how they described it. She pushed them away with her words and her voice."

"So soon," Father DeCarlo whispered, almost to himself. He was not surprised that Brother Martin's way had not succeeded in destroying the spirit. Rather than frustrating or disappointing him, Brother Anthony's news was exhilarating. The prophecy that had obsessed him all his life was coming to pass. The spirit was growing. Still, it was not too late. He had always known it would come to this moment. He alone had the power to deny the spirit. It was his destiny to bring her to him, and with his own hands, smother the Breath of Juno.

He walked out on his balcony where he had been standing for many hours, watching the sea, calling her to him, waiting for her to hear him, to see him. She would come, he knew it. She would come.

AFTER THE ATTACK IN Athens, Aeron began to feel confident that no one would be able to get close enough to kill her, that the spirit within her was now too powerful. She was no longer vulnerable. She moved west through the villages and towns of Greece to the Ionian Sea. It was there that she planned to cross to the town of Brindisi in southern Italy. Then she would go straight to the gates of Rome.

She boarded the Greek transport ferry late at night, knowing that she would see the sun rise from the Italian shore. That night she felt nauseous and broke out into a cold sweat. The sickness spread throughout her body.

A vision burned before her eyes. She saw it perfectly clearly, all at once. An old man in a red robe with a black cape, standing on a balcony, looking over a blue sea. She knew him instantly, for she had seen him through her three year-old eyes that terrible night in her mother's home.

He flashed before her again, his arm flung out to one side as he pushed her mother against the wall, her body falling to the floor, her head hitting the steel radiator. He stood before Aeron, calling her to him. The rage grew in her body as the sickness spread. She would send this illness to him, to invade his aging body with a mortal disease, to rob him from within.

Then she remembered. She remembered the tragic mistake she had made in Lake Tahoe the night after she had seen her mother's death. She had allowed her anger to soar, mingled with the spirit within her, and it had found a target in this priest of the Sidon.

Because of that rash unguarded moment the Sidon had been able to find her in the mountain cabin, and because of her, Sara Morgan was dead. She would not allow him to find her again. She masked her thoughts, held back her anger. She would wait until the moment was hers. She would not allow him to come to her and find her alone and unprotected. She would choose her moment. She would go to him.

FATHER DECARLO WOKE, his body feverish. He could remember nothing. She had been there! She had visited him in the night, showed him where she was. But he could not see her.

He got out of bed quickly and dressed. He was alone in the monastery. All the monks had gone to Rome to help Brother Martin and Brother Anthony find the girl. He knew their search would be in vain. It would end here. She would come to him on the island and he would be the one to take her life.

All day he sensed her moving towards him. He didn't feel fear, only exhilaration. He had waited for this moment all his life. He wanted to look into her eyes, to see the entity that lived within her, the ancient spirit his own brotherhood predicted would live until this moment. And he would end it all here. Two thousand years it had traveled to die in this moment, by his hand.

His heart pounded in his chest with excitement. He had waited for this moment. He wanted it.

THE BOAT DOCKED early the next morning in Brindisi. Aeron went south to Sicily. She traveled all day by slow local buses, and everywhere she went, she let the spirit fly. People felt her coming and gathered in the streets to greet her.

By night fall she was in Mazara on the west coast of Sicily. There she found a fisherman who promised to take her to Isola di Pantella the next day. She knew that by tomorrow everyone one on the small island would know that she was coming to them. But he would know first!

They were so close—only a few dozen miles of sea lie between them now. She wanted to penetrate his mind, to own his soul, to destroy his desire to resist her.

Aeron closed her eyes and summoned the power within her. She transformed herself once again into a hawk, but this time her talons grew sharp as knives. They curled inward under her heavy body. She flew out over the Mediterranean Sea, and from high in the sky she looked down through her piercing eyes at the small island beneath her. She circled three times, each time moving closer, until she could see the white sanctuary on the north end of the island—the home of the Sidon.

Her brilliant green eyes blazed with fury as she saw the home of the man who had taken her mother's life and tried to take her own.

I'm coming, she thought, you needn't call me any more.

WHEN THE FULL MOON reached its zenith it shone brilliantly, washing away the light of the stars. Father DeCarlo went out onto his balcony where he had spent hours calling to her. It was December, yet it felt like the middle of August. The heat baked into his skin. He felt as if it would ignite his very body. He pulled off his heavy red robe and then his linen cloak, and finally the silk undergarment that he always wore next to his skin. He stood naked on the balcony, waiting for her.

The closer she came, the harder it was for him to breathe. The air grew thinner, his chest tighter, his lungs burned. The pain in his body was the exquisite pleasure of wanting her.

He looked up into the warm light of the moon and it appeared to come down from the heavens, falling towards him. His head fell softly to his chest, his eyes closed, and then she was there! She was a giant hawk in the sky above him. The creature covered the heavens and eclipsed the moon, swallowing the bright night with eternal darkness.

And as he saw it, he called out to the spirit he had hunted all his life. Suddenly he no longer wanted to destroy it. He wanted to possess it himself.

"Yes!" he cried out passionately. "Come to me. Give me your power. Live within me!"

The hawk began to descend as if answering his call. He fell to his knees and clasped his hands together in prayer.

"Abandon this useless girl," he pleaded. "She is nothing. She spreads your power like seeds blown in the wind. She will turn you to dust. Enter my body and become immortal in my flesh."

He longed to feel the glory of her power inside his body, pushing her breath into him.

Then the creature transformed before his eyes. A woman's face, her face, with searing green eyes, a silver beak jutting from her forehead and skin the color of copper.

She swooped down towards him, her talons reaching for him. He resisted with every ounce of his remaining strength.

"You shall not have me," he thundered, shielding his face with his arms.

The hawk's talons sunk into his flesh. Its sharp beak penetrated his forehead. For a brief second he looked into its cold green eyes. They seemed to stare at him, with pity but without remorse.

As the claws lifted him into the air and carried him over the ocean, he knew that his time was at an end. In his last terrifying moments he understood that the prophecy was to be fulfilled, and it didn't matter to him. All he cared about was his own ancient life. He didn't want to die.

"Release me!" he screamed with his last breath. He felt the hawk's talons free him, and he was falling, slowly falling through the air. He saw the blue sea below, welcoming him. He would slide into it, and the waters would receive him, holding him afloat. They would not dare to shatter his body—rather they would cradle him, carrying him in their gentle waves back to the shore.

AERON ARRIVED ON THE south side of the island the next morning. The people of the small village had all felt her coming, and they knew that her presence had much to do with the white sanctuary in the far north of the island. They gathered around her to take her to the monastery. A long ribbon of people followed her across the valleys and hills. The entire population of the island came to see the young woman with startling red hair go to the priest that they had feared all their lives.

The crowd of islanders smashed the locks and pulled open the gigantic wooden doors that had been shut for so long. Inside they found nothing.

Aeron climbed the stairs to Father DeCarlo's quarters. She walked through his bedchamber and saw the robes lying on the linens. Then she moved out to the balcony. A crowd had gathered on the stone terrace beneath her. They parted when they saw her above them, and formed a circle around the mangled body that lay at its center.

Father DeCarlo's naked body lay broken on the ground.

"He must have fallen or jumped from the balcony," she heard them saying below.

Instead of feeling relieved that the man who had hunted her and who had killed her mother now lay dead beneath her, she felt a terrible sense of guilt and confusion. I have done this, she realized. I have murdered this man as surely as if I had done it with my own hands.

She had defeated the Sidon. Her enemies were dead. They could no longer touch her. She would go on.

The prophecy would come to pass.

But instead of triumph she felt only fear.

The spirit within her was awakening the people and the long abused earth. But it was now clear to her that the spirit was the power of nature, and nature could be brutal.

· 30 ·

AFTER THE DEATH OF FATHER DECARLO, Aeron had gone north to the cities of Florence and Venice. She crossed the Alps and traveled up through Germany, first to Munich and now Berlin. Soon all of Europe would know the wonder and the power of the spirit within her. Then she would go to the East—to India and China.

Nothing mattered now but the burning need of the power inside her. She would do its bidding.

Memories of the old priest, his shriveled lifeless body, haunted her with each step. She had hoped that his death would expunge the pain in her heart, the longing she had always felt for her mother's love. Instead it had made her feel even more alone. She and the power of the spirit had taken a life. She was no better than the priest himself. How could she ever go back home to the people she loved?

Aeron walked boldly through the streets of Berlin. Let them see me, she thought. Let them know they cannot touch me. Let them aim their guns at me and feel their fingers go soft on the triggers. Let them know I am invulnerable to their attacks, that I can walk right through them, that it is too late. I have touched them all with the power, and none of them has the strength or desire to kill me.

As these words formed themselves in her mind, she realized she was saying them out loud. There was no one close enough to hear her. Even if there had been, it didn't matter anymore. Everywhere, she knew, they watched her still—the monks of the dead priest—the remains of the Sidon. There was danger in none of them.

The simple directness of purpose and the courage she felt during the day melted away at night, when loneliness crept into her heart. Despite all the miraculous things happening to her, she was still mortal, with human needs, nourishment, sleep, and love. She pulled sleep towards her, holding it close, begging it to stay with her as long as possible. Her last thought before she drifted into sleep was of her mother, sitting at the side of the bed, her soft voice telling a story.

IT BEGAN EARLY THE next morning—the same sensation as before, a thickening in her throat. Then the tingling and numbness in her mouth, on her tongue. It became more intense as the hour advanced. Aeron felt a presence coming towards her again. Yet this time the feeling was different—it was feminine, and it carried no danger. Her first thought was of the twins, Mattie and Nellie. Maybe they'd waited until her power grew, and now that she was strong enough, they could come to her, travel with her, and stay by her side until the end.

The sensation grew stronger, but she was without fear. She wondered if the twins could still see within her mind. The thought that they were with her filled her with hope. She'd been alone for so long. She needed them. That morning, feeling their presence seemed the most important thing in the world.

Like a weight pressing against the air around her body, she felt a single figure moving towards her room. She rose from her bed with excitement and went to the door. There was someone standing silently on the other side.

Her excitement turned suddenly to terror. She couldn't move. Then a faint knock broke the silence. She unlocked the latch but left the safety chain on so the door opened only a few inches. Through the narrow opening she saw a red scarf and an abundance of gray hair hanging waist-length against a black dress.

A bony hand slid into the crack of the door. An angry red rash was visible on the palm.

"Open the door, child," a soft voice commanded her.

Unthinking, she responded like an obedient girl would to a parent, and released the chain. She stepped back as the door opened. Facing her was an older woman, tall, with steel gray hair billowing wildly around her face.

"Kayla," Helga Hydinger said kindly, a smile forcing its way across the sharp angles of her face, "you're exactly as they described you."

"Who are you?" Aeron regretted the arrogance she had felt the day before. She had allowed herself to believe that she was no longer vulnerable to anyone, so she had let down her guard. But this woman, appearing from nowhere at her door, calling her Kayla, terrified her.

Helga walked into the room as if she were a welcome guest and sat calmly on the only chair, facing the bed, indicating that Aeron should join her.

Aeron didn't move. They stared at one another, each looking behind the other's eyes.

"Please Kayla, sit down." The woman had a heavy German accent. Her voice was soft, disarmingly so. It was as if she'd come for a casual visit. "You don't know who I am, but I have known you since you were born."

In spite of her fear, Aeron was pulled in by the stranger. How could this woman have known her all her life!

"Who are you? Why are you here?"

"My name is Helga Hydinger. I was a Sensor for the women of Juno for much of my life. Did you not wonder how they were able to gather all that you read? I can feel the breath when it moves from one life to another. That's why they were always able to locate the child who would carry the breath forward. Without the Sensors, the women of Juno would be lost."

A chill ran through Aeron's body. She couldn't penetrate this woman's mind. It was as if the old woman had carefully sealed herself off from the spirit's power.

"I felt the breath as it moved over the ocean from Wales, crossed the continent to the Americas and slid inside your tiny body. I have known you since the beginning. It is through me alone that the Sidon knew how to find the children."

Aeron was sickened by the old woman's words. "You betrayed your own people!"

"I left the Juno Society many years ago because I no longer believed."

Aeron willed the fear to leave her body. She wouldn't let this woman feel her weakness. She forced herself to walk towards her, to sit calmly on the bed next to the woman.

"You didn't believe in the Prophecy . . . in the power within me?"

"Oh, yes." Helga leaned so close to Aeron they could feel each others' breath. "I do believe in that. I wouldn't be here if I didn't believe in the power."

Then Aeron understood the purpose of the strange woman's visit.

"You have come here to stop me! Why?"

"I left the Juno Society in the forties when I saw the world torn to pieces with war." Helga's gaze fixed on an invisible vision before her eyes. Aeron watched the years melt from Helga's face until she was a young woman in her twenties. But the face was already twisted by anguish and fear. They sat in silence for a few moments. When Helga spoke again her voice was filled with the pain of loss.

"I saw the evil that the human race was capable of inflicting." She turned to Aeron. "It was so long before you were born, you can't begin to understand the terror we lived through. So many of us believed that it was wrong.

"You see, Kayla, that is why it must end here. If we are pushing ourselves to the edge of extinction, then perhaps that is where we ought to go. Are we such a marvelous species? Are we worthy to inherit this earth? Did the spirit intend for an animal capable of war and murder as we are to inherit her precious earth? I don't think so," she said sadly.

Aeron was touched by Helga's words. She felt compassion and tenderness for the woman.

"Child, the Sidon believes you will throw us back into darkness. Centuries of enlightenment and human progress will vanish. They're right, you know. That is just what will happen if you live into the next millennium. Slowly we will all change, and out of that change there will be healing."

"Then I don't understand," Aeron said. "If you see that healing, why don't you want it to take place?"

"Because I don't believe in us anymore. My dear child, you're so young. You think you're old because you have so many lives within you. But you still sit there on that bed a young woman, and there is so much you don't understand. You haven't seen the horrors with the eyes of my body. You haven't lived through a war. You haven't seen bodies burned, people tortured. You haven't seen the cruelty that man has done to man.

"That's why the breath cannot live into the next millennium. We are at the door of extinction. And I am, for one, happy to open that door, to allow some more worthy species to become the stewards of this sacred world."

Aeron was genuinely moved by Helga's passion. "But by killing me, you are killing hope."

"Yes. When I take your life, I take the last hope of our survival. It is a killing of mercy."

Helga raised her arm, putting her thin hand against Aeron's cheek. "The doing of it is something I cannot even bring myself to imagine. You're so young, you have so many years upon this earth . . . taking your life will be the hardest thing I have ever had to do."

"Others have tried to kill me and failed."

Helga smiled apologetically. "There is no way that you can stop me. I am impervious to the breath. It is the spirit of evolution, and I am a spirit of extinction. It cannot touch me. You see, Kayla, I am even older than you are. All those months in the archives reading about the lives that we recorded over the centuries—you think you've been alive for one hundred generations, but I've been alive even longer."

She placed her bony hands in her lap with the palms facing upward. In the center of her left hand, just below the index finger, Aeron saw an angry red birth mark shaped like a crescent moon. Helga lifted the hand in front of Aeron's face.

"The mark of the Sensors. You see, we are a direct blood line. We come from the womb of our mothers from one generation to another in an unbroken line.

"The ability to see the breath began even before it was drawn into the first child. It was the Sensors who called to Juno, beckoning her to take human form and walk upon this earth, to gain the knowledge of our ways, and to build the strength to save our species. We were here before you."

Aeron bent her head, overcome by the magnitude of what she was hearing.

Helga stood, walking to the window that overlooked the skyline of Berlin. "There is one way that your life can be saved." She waited a moment for the idea to sink into Aeron's mind.

"You see," she continued, turning to Aeron. "You think of yourself and the breath as one thing. You're not. The breath has lived in one hundred different lives. You've read about these lives and you've remembered them. I know they have visited you many times over the years. You think about them as your own, as reincarnations of yourself. Yet they are not incarnations of you.

"It is the breath that has inhabited all these lives. When it came into you, it came complete with all the memories. It is a thing that lives *within* you but is not *of* you. It is not the essence of your soul, your being. You can expel it from your body and live on."

"How is that possible? The spirit can only leave my body when I die. How can I live without it?"

"I can call it from you."

Aeron was startled. "How is that possible?"

"I don't only have the power to feel the breath when it moves from one life to another, I can pull it from a life and send it off on a journey to find another girl-child born at that same moment."

Aeron's mind raced wildly. She thought of Paula Campbell who had hung herself at thirteen when the dreams began to invade her life.

"Have you done this before?" Aeron jumped to her feet, accusing Helga. "Did you pull the breath from Paula Campbell, leaving her insane so that she killed herself?"

"No. That was not of my doing."

"What about Mary Alice?" Aeron demanded.

Helga lowered her eyes from Aeron's sharp accusation. "Yes, I thought she was to be the last one. And so, you are right. I took the breath from her when she was eight years old."

"She died! You told me that you could take the breath from me and I would still live!"

"As I felt I could with her," Helga said sadly. "As it escaped from her body, the power of the spirit churned up the river and capsized her boat. The drowning was an accident."

"An accident? You killed her!" Aeron wanted to strike the woman, but her arms suddenly felt heavy at her sides and could not be willed to move.

"I didn't intend to," Helga admitted. "I didn't know that the child was on a rowboat in the middle of the river. I was in Aberaeron that night at St. Mary's Cathedral. I pulled it slowly away from her, but it happened so fast. She was such a tiny little thing. I scooped it right out of her body. When I learned that she drowned, I felt responsible for her death."

"You were responsible," Aeron said, "and you will be responsible for my death."

"You cannot tell me that you will take death over life if I give you the choice."

"You think you can separate me and the spirit . . . that we're two different things, but you're wrong. All those lives . . . they do belong to me. They're as much a part of me as any of my own memories. They're woven together. There's no way you can kill part of me and not kill all of me."

"So be it, my child," said Helga. She moved towards Aeron slowly, backing the girl up to the bed. "I'm truly sorry it has to be this way."

Helga threw back her head and opened her mouth as if in a silent scream. Then she breathed so deeply that the air seemed to be sucked from the room.

She reached out with her left hand. The red mark on her palm grew a deeper red as she pressed it against Aeron's forehead.

Aeron felt herself falling, collapsing on the bed. Her throat was swelling, closing. She was choking!

The breath was being pulled from her lungs as Helga stood above her, mutely calling the spirit from Aeron's body.

She was paralyzed—unable to stop Helga.

Aeron's vision blurred. The power within her was dying.

Just before darkness overcame her, Aeron saw two disembodied faces floating above her—the twins!

Their mouths moved in unison.

"Aeron," they whispered. "Take her life. She holds the spirit in her power, but *you* still live."

Their words gave Aeron strength. She reached out and found the iron statue of Hera at the side of the bed.

"Child," they cried. "Take her life!"

With one swing Aeron smashed the statue into Helga's skull.

As the breath went out of Helga's body, Aeron felt her own power return.

· 31 ·

2000: Wales

Alone, Aeron went on.

As the year—the millennium—was nearing an end, an amazing thing happened to her. The weight of the spirit's power began to diminish within her. She was no longer the only conduit for the spirit and the Breath of Juno. People shared it with one another, unconsciously.

She felt the burden of carrying it alone fall away from her. It was no longer her sole responsibility to take the breath over the bridge into the new millennium. There were now millions of people carrying it with her.

Though crowds of people greeted her wherever she went, she knew that she was becoming less unique every day. It would be only a short time before the spirit that lived within her was the same as the energy she had transmitted to people all over the world.

A cold winter wind blew across the water, penetrating her wool coat, chilling her thin tired body. Held aloft by the wind, her red hair trailed after her. She walked along the banks of the Aeron River waiting for the dawn. The ground breathed peacefully beneath her feet. She sat on the rocky bank at the bend in the river where Mary Alice had drowned. This was where she wanted to be when the morning sun broke over the mountains.

For months she had watched, along with everyone else, as changes began to take place around the world. With each breath the earth sucked in the foulness that poisoned the air, and purified it—a living thing healing itself. The oceans filled with new plankton and coral.

Seas, long dead, welcomed back teeming schools of fish.

The first rays of the sun slid through a valley above, touching Aeron's hair with light. Silently, she watched as the vast sky turned an intense blue, reflecting the blue of the cleansed oceans around the world.

This morning, Aeron thought, is the dawn of time. This must be what the world looked like when people first came from caves and walked upon the earth.

This is the beginning.

• 32 •

2000: San Bernardino

Lee and Gavin sat on the back porch of their San Bernardino home. They had married after the first of the year, on January eleventh, in the year 2000.

Lee rested her legs on the railing of the porch and watched the last rays of the sun disappear behind the San Bernardino Mountains. The slightest touch of snow capped their peaks. She gently placed her hand on her stomach.

"In spite of all this beauty, I'm frightened," she said. "What kind of world will our child grow up in? The twins told you that the Sidon believed the spirit would throw us back, back to the Dark Ages. Is that where we're going, backwards? Of course, I want the clean air and unpolluted water for my daughter, but all the things we've taken for granted . . . will they disappear?"

"The future is uncharted territory," Gavin said. "But isn't it better to live in a place with unknown landmarks than to be on a road leading to oblivion and extinction?"

"Well," Lee said, "It's no longer in our hands. Aeron has won."

"It was never a contest," Gavin said, sitting on the porch steps next to her. "And I think you're wrong. It is in our hands. That's the very point. It's in all of our hands now. She's brought the power back to us. We will be able to make decisions differently."

"Perhaps we'll make the same mistakes again," Lee said. "What if the spirit that has infected us only exists within us, this generation?" She patted her stomach. "What if it doesn't pass on to our children? Maybe they'll just rebel against everything that we have come to understand and believe.

"Progress will start all over again and drive us down the same narrow path. In another hundred years we could be exactly where we were. I don't know whether it's a terrible time to be having a child, or a wonderful time. I'm forty years old. I'm bringing a new life into this world and I have no idea what kind of world it will be. It seems a terrible risk."

Gavin reached up and put his hand on her stomach. "Perhaps expectant mothers have said just that since the beginning of time. Has there ever been a good time to bring a child into this life? Good or bad, we keep bringing them.

"So many species have gone extinct on the earth," he said sadly. "We've come to accept it as a common occurrence. The very thought that dinosaurs once lived and then suddenly disappeared is devastating. And there are millions of other species, much smaller and less dramatic who have become extinct.

"It's such a final thing, don't you think, extinction. It's like trying to imagine infinity. I think it's beyond our ability to understand.

"Before the spirit came it was impossible for us to truly believe that we could become extinct as a species, and now that reality is part of our conscious thoughts, influencing all of our actions.

"Lee, my love, whatever kind of world our child grows up in will be one where people work together and fight for the survival of the species. Whatever else may happen, I find that a comforting thought."

"Aeron doesn't know about the baby," Lee said. I want her to be here when our child is born. Do you think she would like it if we named her Kayla?"

Gavin laughed. "I don't know why you're so certain that it's a girl. You keep talking about *her*. We won't have the results of the tests until next week. We could be having a son, you know."

"Women can feel these things. Call it intuition."

"We all have intuition now," Gavin smiled. "But no ability to see into the future. I suggest we wait until the tests are in."

"How I ache for a sip of your wine. I know . . . I promised. Nothing until after the baby's born.

"Aeron will be twenty in June. I can hardly believe she's so young. After all she's been through, she's still just a child."

DORA AND BUD WERE waiting at Los Angeles International Airport when Aeron returned to California. Dora knew that Aeron was the center of a phenomenon that was larger than anything she could comprehend. All that mattered to her was that in a few moments Aeron would walk through the door, and she would be able to hold her in her arms once again.

It had been almost a year and a half since Aeron had driven away with Lee Edwards. Whatever she was in everyone else's eyes, Aeron was still her daughter, and she wanted her to come home.

The minute Aeron saw Dora's rotund silhouette moving towards her in the terminal, she knew that it was over. When Dora's arms went around her thin body, Aeron felt she was truly home for the first time in her life.

During the drive back to the Wilkes' home, Dora chatted about things that had happened. Bud rode silently, but Aeron knew he was content.

That terrible night in Berlin, when Helga had tried to pull the breath from her body, seemed a distant memory. She listened to Dora talk about the azaleas that were in bloom in the backyard, and how she wanted to put in tomatoes, and maybe even grow sweet peas up the back trellis for the summer.

Lee and Gavin were waiting for Aeron at the Wilkes' home when the car arrived. They'd been too eager to wait for an official invitation. Aeron was astounded by Lee's appearance.

"You didn't tell me you were pregnant," she said, hugging Lee.

"I wanted it to be a surprise."

"It's wonderful," Aeron said. "I'm so happy for both of you."

Then she saw the tears forming in Gavin's eyes and knew that he was searching for a hint of Mary Alice in her face. She put her arms around his neck and kissed his moist cheek.

"Don't grieve for her any longer," Aeron whispered in his ear. "She lives within me."

He held her close for a moment, then reluctantly let her go.

They went inside the small living room, and Dora hurried to the kitchen to prepare food for her guests. For a year and half Aeron had remembered the smells in that kitchen. Whenever the loneliness overcame her, it comforted her to know that across the ocean was a woman who could bake her soul into her bread, and that she was waiting for Aeron to return home.

The five of them talked late into the night. It wasn't until they were about to leave that Aeron asked the question Lee had expected much earlier.

"Do you know if you're going to have a boy or a girl?"

"Don't you know that?" Lee teased her.

"I don't know anything any more. Nothing. I don't know anything more than you do. It's wonderful. I can't see into the future. I'm not haunted by the past. There's only now."

"She wanted a girl," Gavin said, "so that she could call her Kayla, after you. But now, we're going to have to change that plan."

"You're going to have a son?" Aeron asked.

"Not exactly," Lee replied.

"Well, what other possibilities are there?" Dora was confused.

"The ultrasound was pretty definitive," Lee said. "I'm going to have twins, both boys. Two sons, just as you predicted, Aeron."

"My God," Aeron said. She looked at Gavin and smiled. "I hope they're not identical."

Just as Lee and Gavin were leaving, he took Aeron aside.

"I thought you might like to have this," he said, handing her a small white envelope. "It was in the Lake Tahoe Police files."

IN THE MIDDLE OF the night Aeron went to the garden behind the house. Bud had hung a hammock between two young oak trees that grew near the back fence. She lay down and swung gently in the light breeze. The full moon filled the sky with light. She took the white envelope, carefully broke the seal, and slipped out the contents—a single picture of a beautiful young woman with long red hair holding a baby in her arms. Aeron pressed the photograph to her lips. "Mother," she whispered. "You will always be with me." Her eyes closed as sleep came to her.

A fog gathered around her, caressing her cheek, stroking her hair. An image formed itself from the mist. A low whisper hung in the night air, calling to her.

"Eve, Eve . . . ."

The sound was so familiar. Sara's loving voice.

"Eve, I christen you Eve, and from you a new world is born."